READERS' REVIEWS OF ANN LIVESAY'S

The Isis Command

"*Isis Command* is fantastic! Your characters are well done and the magic of Egypt delightfully portrayed."
Betty Bartlett, Flagstaff, Arizona

"What an exciting plot! I enjoyed and learned a lot from the vignettes on natural history, history and anthropology scattered throughout."
Elizabeth Hambleton, Williamsburg, Virginia

"The setting was unusual, and very intriguing. Characters were well drawn and their conversation so convincing. It is an all around good mystery."
Mary Louise Pride, Medford, Oregon

"The story and plot proceed with pace and conviction, and it is one of those books you cannot put down until the final dénoûment."
Norman LeFort, Middleton-on-Sea, England

"I kept hoping no one would interrupt me as I read it."
Jane O'Sullivan, Medford, Oregon

"An intriguing story on the fast track."
Mary Allshouse, Albuquerque, New Mexico

"I like the short chapters. Scenes change at a good pace. Keeps the reader wondering, what's next?"
Peg Wilson, Medford, Oregon

"I want all the rest of the series."
Mrs. James G. Snyder, San Carlos, California

"A diabolically clever murder, taking place among the spellbinding artifacts of Egypt. Wonderful reading and travel."
Happy Blue, Medford, Oregon

DEATH IN THE AMAZON

A Barry Ross International Mystery

by Ann Livesay

Silver River Books
Medford ○ Boise ○ London

This Silver River Book contains
the complete text of the original novel.

DEATH IN THE AMAZON

A Barry Ross International Mystery

First Edition AUGUST 1998
All Rights Reserved.

For information address:
Silver River, Inc., 1619 Meadowview Drive, Medford, OR 97504, USA.
The Silver River web site address is http://www.silverriver.com

Library of Congress Catalog Card Number: 98-90555

ISBN 0-9662817-1-3

PRINTED IN THE UNITED STATES OF AMERICA
10 9 8 7 6 5 4 3 2 1

BOOKS BY ANN and MYRON SUTTON

Eastern Forests: An Audubon Society Nature Guide
The Audubon Society Book of Trees
Wildlife of the Forests
The Wild Shores of North America
The Pacific Crest Trail: Escape to the Wilderness
Wilderness Areas of North America
The Wild Places: A Photographic Celebration of Unspoiled America
Yellowstone: A Century of the Wilderness Idea
The Secret Places: Wonders of Scenic America
The Wilderness World of the Grand Canyon
New Worlds for Wildlife
The American West: A Natural History
The Appalachian Trail: Wilderness on the Doorstep
Among the Maya Ruins: The Story of John Lloyd Stephens and
 Frederick Catherwood
The Life of the Desert
Animals on the Move
Journey Into Ice: Sir John Franklin and the Northwest Passage
Guarding the Treasured Lands
Exploring with the Bartrams
Nature on the Rampage
Steller of the North

INTERNATIONAL EDITIONS

The Audubon Society Book of Trees (Japanese)
Le Monde des Arbes
Walder
Bomen uit de Gehele Wereld
Wildlife of the Forests (Japanese)
Knaurs Tierleben im Wald
Animaux des Forêts
Dierenleven in de Bossen
I Maya
Tiere Unterwegs
Hur Flyttar Djuren?
The Endless Quest
Irrfahrt im Beringmeer

Also in this Series

FOREWORD

So unkind has human history been to the Amazon basin and its native peoples, that some of the events in this story such as the episodes recounted by Monty Adams may seem beyond belief. Likewise, the situation involving the owl and the ocelot, which I found on the main street in Florencia myself, may not seem possible to a civilized person. The warehouses for parakeets and white-lipped marmosets, which were shown to me in Leticia, on the Amazon River, defy logic in the modern world. They are not fiction. Nor have they been embellished. It is difficult to exaggerate in the Amazon.

You might also think that the cruelty of the miners to Palkuh Mamha-uh and his people is overblown. According to the Associated Press, two thousand Indians in Brazil, in a region east of the locale of this story, died during recent years in armed clashes with miners, and from diseases brought by the miners. In July, 1993, miners slaughtered 16 Yanomami Indians, mostly women and children, in two ambushes.

I also met a curmudgeonly but very sincere woman who was adamantly opposed to zoos. You will recognize her in this story. Nevertheless, this book is a work of fiction, even though some of the events are based on actual happenings and take place in actual locales: Florencia, Puerto Lara, the Orteguaza, Pinilla, Micalla, and Caquetá Rivers, a settler's hut, two Correguaje Indian villages, Tres Esquinas Air Force Base on the Caquetá River, and Leticia on the Amazon, all in Colombia.

I am grateful to many Colombians—government civilian and military officials, professors, priests, students, guides, and Correguaje Indians—for assistance in getting to know their Amazon.

I am especially indebted to Eduardo Arango, Regional Director of INDERENA, in Barranquilla, for his remarkable and pioneering philosophy of conservation, and to Padre Antonio Olivares, in Florencia, for his vast knowledge in the field of wildlife biology, especially birds of the Amazon ecosystems. Robert Neely provided a great deal of assistance in traveling the Rio Orteguaza and its tributaries by dugout canoe. He also helped in taping the list of Correguaje words, which I place in the hands of the British linguist, Carol Lynn Arden-Jones.

For a splendid introduction to Huitoto chants, and to folk songs and patriotic music of Colombia, I can never forget the help of Uldarico and Saúl Guzmán, Luis Angel Nieto and Nubia V. de Tovar and the evenings we spent with Latin music. In northern Colombia, Arturo Delgado Flores first sang *La Negra Celina* for me at Santa Marta, and I am grateful for his insights into Afro-Cuban and Colombian folk music. Joe Muck loved that music. All the members of Barry's embattled little group did. If you ever hear it, you'll know why.

At the U.S. Embassy in Bogotá I also got splendid counsel from the Chief of Mission that widened my perspective on the Amazon region. Yet who can know it all? Living there for a while, as I did, in both the Ecuadorian and Colombian Amazon, I developed a deep appreciation for it.

Well, at least for that small part of the great vastness I came to know...

Ann Livesay

A NOTE TO THE READER FROM BARRY ROSS

Ever since the appearance of *The Isis Command*, I have been repeatedly asked how on earth I met Joe Muck and whatever prompted me to hire such a zany, good-natured oddball for my team. This puts pressure on me to recount the harrowing events down on the Orteguaza River and the Amazon, which will satisfy that curiosity. And that will lead to an account of Joe's remarkable bravery in the Himalayas of Nepal: *The Madman of Mount Everest*. All in due course.

Others have asked about Julie, and I shall get to *The Chala Project: Murder in the Grand Canyon* as soon as I can. That's where Joe and I met Julie, a truly remarkable person.

On the other hand, as I am told, readers are also anxious to hear the story of the deaths on Dinkum Island, on the Great Barrier Reef of Australia. That's where Julie, Joe and I were heading when we left Cairo on that fateful night when the Isis matter was solved. To interrupt that would do disservice to the continuity of my tales, but I think the Amazon pressure is the greater. Please forgive me and be patient.

With your indulgence, I shall press on with the Amazon events. I promise that The Dinkum Deaths will come forward as soon as I get rested from the harrowing trip to the Orinoco Basin. If you're confused, that puts us on an even keel...

Barry

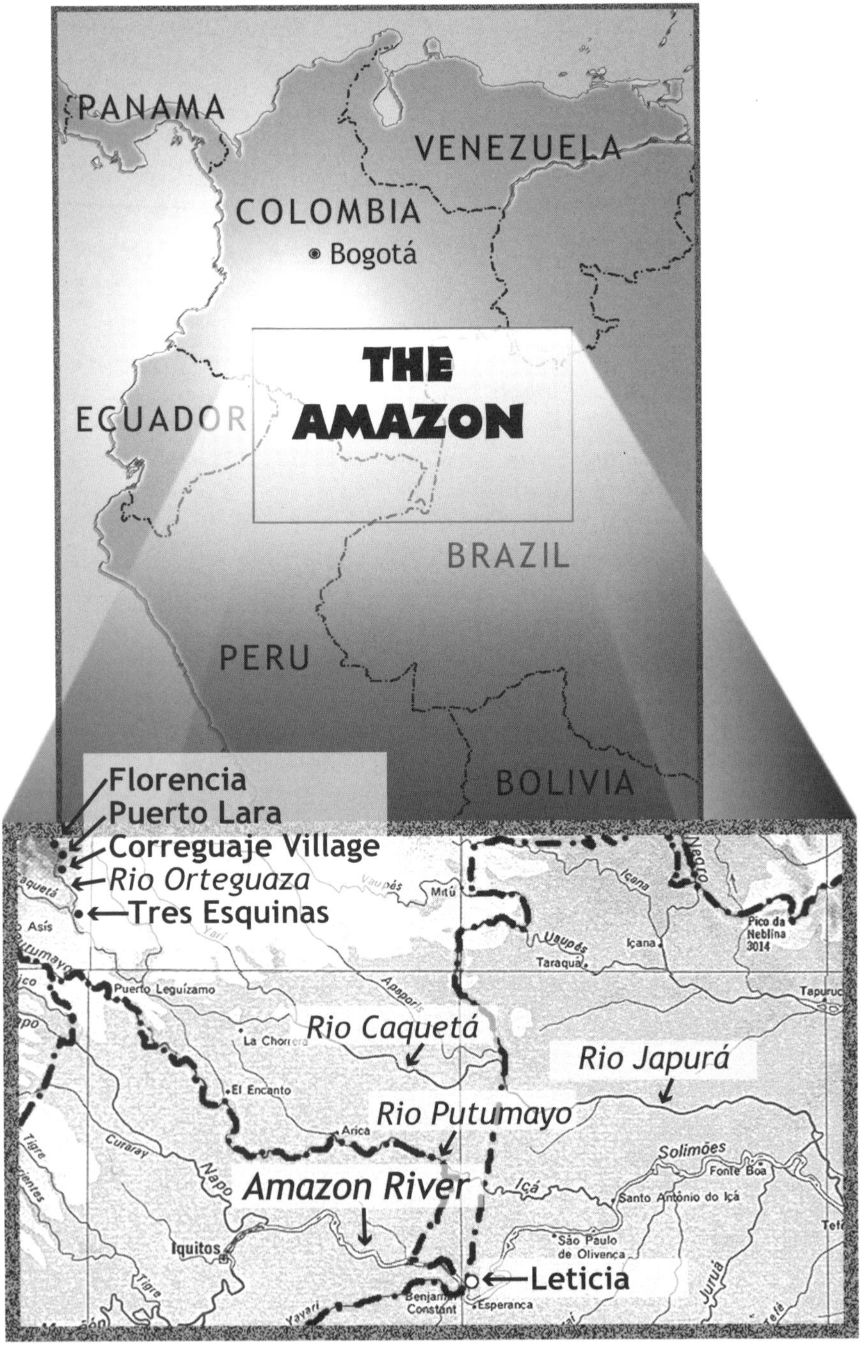

PANAMA
VENEZUELA
COLOMBIA
Bogotá
THE AMAZON
ECUADOR
BRAZIL
PERU
BOLIVIA
Florencia
Puerto Lara
Correguaje Village
Rio Orteguaza
Tres Esquinas
Vaupés
Mitú
Içana
Negro
Uaupés
Içana
Taraquá
Pico da Neblina 3014
Puerto Leguízamo
Apaporis
Rio Caquetá
La Chorrera
Rio Japurá
El Encanto
Rio Putumayo
Arica
Curaray
Napo
Tigre
Solimões
Fonte Boa
Amazon River
Içá
Santo Antônio do Içá
São Paulo de Olivença
Iquitos
Leticia
Benjamin Constant
Esperança
Yavari
Juruá

A corpse has never been
retrieved from the Amazon.

Henri Michaux, 1929

CHAPTER 1

Trouble began before we could even board the dug-out canoes at Puerto Lara.

Beryl Fisher's condition worsened. After what she had seen yesterday on the street in Florencia, I didn't wonder. She was young, tender and trusting, which made her vulnerable to the world's realities. She became so weak I almost expected her to lapse into a coma. Greg Fisher stayed beside her and did what he could. But he was gentle, too, and had little power to bring her out of it.

Then the Dana bombshell.

In a few minutes we would board the canoes and take off in piranha-infested waters down the Orteguaza River. A treacherous brown river, full of mud banks, sand bars, and gravel deposits that could pitch us headlong into the water without a moment's notice. So now we discover that Dana Briggle can't swim.

Not a lick. I couldn't believe it.

Dana, young, dark-haired, handsomely featured like, say, Demi Moore, was a real enigma: she was afraid of the water and scared to death, but she wanted to go, and had come to Colombia in spite of it all.

I had a hard time believing that, too.

Mo Briggle, also dark-haired and medium height, a computer wiz from Silicon Valley, had already come to me and suggested they back out.

Joe Muck, the lanky blonde cowboy from the University of Wyoming, would absolutely not hear of it.

"No way, guys! You're smack in the midst of the most wonderful tropical forest on earth. You're about to spend a week with an Indian tribe you never met. Or even heard of. And you want to turn back! Get it right out of your system or I'll lasso you both and tie you to the canoe."

Mo Briggle, dressed in a white shirt, even down here in the tropical forest, seemed bewildered. "Joe, I appreciate your concern. I really do. But..."

"No buts about it. Mo, you gotta stay with us. Both of you. If we go into the water, I'll ferry Dana to the river bank. Promise."

Dana gave Joe a *fuerte abrazo*, hugging him like an old friend. "Joe, I *love* you for that."

She was game. All go. She'd *learn* to swim. She promised.

But I could tell she was still scared.

We had arrived at 6:30, just as rays of the rising sun broke through the clouds, struck the water, and sent up dancing swirls of mist. Puerto Lara was scarcely a port at all, just a place where the road from Florencia ended at some steps down the bank to the sand bar. That is where people waited for the little ferry to come putt-putting into view. Climbing down from the truck, day pack in hand, we'd surveyed the scene from the embankment. The river stretched nearly two hundred yards to the opposite shore. The sprawling gray-brown mass flowed powerfully, its currents changing direction, surging against the river bank and moving out again to the center.

Joe Muck came up. "Whew! This is the Orteguaza?"

"I assume so. It's big enough for canoes."

"Man alive! It's big enough for steamboats!"

"Not quite, Joe."

Tall clumps of bamboo, their flexible trunks rising and curving like trees bending in the wind, lined the far bank. Unbroken dark green tropical forest stretched as far as could be seen up and down the river.

In places, portions of the bank had given way and slumped, obedient to under-cutting by restless currents. A dozen feet below the edge, two passenger launches lay tied to a makeshift wooden dock. The dock itself appeared to have seen years of service as an old barge plying the river.

Upstream, four dugout canoes, each fitted with a 30-horsepower motor, lay nudged against a sand bar, chained to a high post stabbed into the sand. All held little more than rough-hewn wooden chairs disarranged from bow to stern. One held an oil barrel. Some had piles of canvas tarp to be pulled over cargo in case of rain.

Our own expedition had two canoes, one for passengers, one for equipment. The boatmen in charge of transferring luggage from the dock to the supply canoe sat talking with Monty Adams, our guide.

"Why aren't they loading?" Joe asked. "Aren't we about to take off?"

"Joe," I responded, "you are in Colombia now. Things don't go as smoothly here as in Wyoming."

"Who said things go smoothly in Wyoming?"

I laughed, but he was right. There should have been a beehive of activity over there, not a casual morning chat. Why they weren't working, I didn't know. I just hoped this wasn't something I'd have to fix.

Somebody must have put a curse on me at birth. Every time I try to relax, do something peaceful, go on vacation, get some rest, I get embroiled. I acknowledge the prevailing opinion that criminal investigators attract trouble. I don't believe it, but the evidence is mounting.

For once, I wasn't looking for anybody. No one to fight. No one to chase or apprehend. I liked that. All I wanted was a quiet trip down the river with other participants. We'd just had a demanding Conference on Amazon Ecology, and were ready for a little down time. I'd promoted this post-conference tour. Monty Adams was in charge, but I felt half way responsible.

I just wanted to relax in the canoe and watch the passing river, trees, herons, crocodiles... Was that too much to ask?

We'd stay a week with the Correguaje Indians. Study their ways. Look for wildlife. Maybe even fish a little.

I don't know all the reasons why, but I feel at peace in the tropics. In fact, I feel more at peace in South America than anywhere else on earth. (Well, maybe on par with Australia and New Zealand and French Polynesia. But let's not get into comparisons.)

Especially do I feel biologically at home in such a rich and primeval forest as the Amazon. I can't explain it. That's just the way I feel. And I have a sense of being at home among the gentle human beings who live in these shadowy glades. Not that I'm sympathetic with these people because I was born poor. I wasn't. Aunt Kelly took me over after my parents disappeared in southern China when I was twelve. She taught me to believe that we ought to take this planet and its inhabitants seriously. Save it and clean it up. That's what she's been paying and pushing—and I do mean pushing—for me to do ever since. Sent me to the Sorbonne for training in language and international law, funded trips around the world, saw that I got FBI training, a United Nations internship, and introductions to top officials...

Sure I loved it. How exciting can life get? But there comes a time when you want to get away from all that. Maybe—perish the thought—do absolutely nothing for a day. At such times, I always remember the Ozark farmer who went down in history by saying: "Sometimes I sets and thinks. And sometimes I jes' sets."

This time, Kelly wanted me to come to the Amazon Basin and clean it up in a week. That's the way she is.

So I rebelled. And why not? Why shouldn't I be entitled to a peaceful trip down this river?

Goodbye, logic.

Along came Boris Kolinski, and I have ever since wondered why in the name of billy hell we had to be saddled with a guy like that in such a peaceful place. He came out of nowhere and petitioned Monty to occupy the one extra seat. Monty resisted, but a fistful of pesos had persuasive value.

CHAPTER 2

This trip was ill-fated from the moment we'd left Florencia. I didn't see it in advance. Or else I didn't want to see it. How could I have predicted it?

We'd had a good conference. I told the Colombians, Ecuadorians, Peruvians and Brazilians in attendance that if they didn't protect their Amazon, disaster could follow like a plague.

I was blunt. I didn't sugar-coat my words. That's not my way. They could have branded me an Ugly American and walked out. They didn't. And for one special reason dear to my heart. I gave the whole peroration in Spanish.

They flocked up afterwards and almost hugged me to death.

"Bravo!" they kept saying. *"Palabras muy, muy importante!"*

Of course they were very, very important words. It's just that coming from an outsider, somebody who knew the whole world like I did, knew about man-made disasters happening elsewhere, those words carried special weight.

"Bravo Barry-O! *Tu eres amigo de toda la America Latina."*

Sure I was. I'd always been a friend of Latin America. God, I loved these people. I've galloped with gauchos, sung folk songs with the *estudiantil*, supped with Presidents, and climbed among rare araucaria pines to some of the world's most powerful vistas.

So I was glowing. Maybe that's how I missed the evil omens. Or maybe I'd just become too callous to the ways a lot of Latins treat their animal life. Their forests. Their future.

Beryl Fisher brought me back to reality. So did Spider Webb, who would have fought the devil himself in defense of a mouse.

And there was Joe Muck, irreverent young grad student, heart of gold, eager, fun, combative. And I didn't see the seeds of trouble?

I, Barry Ross, echo of Bogey and Marlowe, see it all, know it all, famous investigator into environmental crimes worldwide? If you ask how that can be, I can only respond with a lame reply.

I was tired.

I wanted a week's rest. Go down the Orteguaza and stay with the Correguajes. Eat with them. Laugh with them. That would calm anyone. A post-conference trip in a dugout canoe, led by Monty Adams, a Floridian who runs tours down here under some of the most trying conditions on earth.

Get away from it all.

Away from Aunt Kelly wanting me to solve six other problems somewhere else. Away from Sam Petrie at the United Nations, wondering when I was going to leave for Kathmandu. Away from Della, my assistant in Washington, calling me constantly on the military digital satellite network to convey all the pleas for help.

So the only way to get peace, quiet, and tranquillity would be to go so far down into the Amazon Basin that no one could find me.

Vain hope! It didn't happen. Not from the moment we left Florencia in that big, dilapidated $2^1/_2$-ton truck and drove scarcely two miles down the road toward Puerto Lara.

At five o'clock, the sun hadn't even started to rise. Hadn't even brought a hint of light to the *madrugada*, the black dawn of the tropics. The truck had only one head-light, and a dim one at that. The driver couldn't see ten feet down the black, muddy road.

And because of that, he almost ran into the landslide.

Not a big *derrumbe*, only the collapse of a high em-bankment at the edge of a road cut. But the soil was wet from rains and black as the ace of spades. It blocked the road and spilled into an adjacent ditch.

The driver got out, surveyed the situation with a flash-light, opened the tailgate and ordered us all to disembark, backpacks, camera bags and all.

That done, we stood and watched as the truck went forward. Its front tires almost disappeared into the soft soil that filled the ditch. The vehicle listed to the left, sank further into the loose soil, and came to a halt.

Joe started forward, but I caught his arm.

"He's already embarrassed," I said. "Don't make it worse."

"Huh?" he asked. "Whaddaya mean by that? I just wanta help."

"He asked the passengers to stay back and he'll re-peat it if you take another step forward."

The others heard me. Mo Briggle, the computer en-gineer, said: "We have to push. All of us. We'll be late get-ting to Puerto Lara."

I said: "Mo, you're in Latin America now. Things are different here. This is the driver's show. He got into it. He'll get out of it."

Cowboy Joe Muck couldn't quite accept that. "Aw, Barry, in Wyoming, anybody pitches in to help somebody in trouble..."

"That's in Wyoming," I answered. "This is Colombia. We'll help if we have to. They know that. They'll ask. But I can tell you from my experience that Latins are competent. They know how to handle things like this. They just do it in their own way."

Joe shook his head dizzily. "So we just wait here, shivering in the dark and freezing our asses off? Not me..."

I restrained him again. "Okay. I'll go talk to him, but I want the rest of you to stay here."

They accepted my assertion of authority—I was the only one, except Boris Kolinski, who had been to Latin America before—and waited until my return a few minutes later.

"He's digging out," I informed the rest of the passengers. "He says it won't be but a few minutes and we'll be around this."

"Bullshit!" said the heavy-set, Kolinski, clad in a dark poncho. "They'll get us into more of a mess. I know these pissant Latinos. You can take it from me. If they can screw us up, they will."

CHAPTER 3

That made my ears burn. I was tempted to haul off and give Boris a stinging double-fist across the side of the head.

As it was, I had to hold cowboy Joe back again.

"Let me get this straight to you, buster," Joe snarled. "I happen to think these guys are some of the salt of the earth. I like Latins. They have been my buddies in class and on the football field. I don't have any friends more faithful than they are. If I hear you once more..."

I had to stop this. "Joe," I said, trying to keep a calm voice. "Take it easy. You know as well as any of us here that Boris is entitled to his opinion. I disagree with him, too. But if you try to hit him because of what he believes in, you're worse than he is."

That rocked Joe back on his heels. He retired up the road, muttering to himself, out of hearing.

I couldn't categorize Boris. He'd just arrived. He hadn't been at dinner last night when we all introduced ourselves. We tried to be friendly to him. After all, he would be a fellow passenger. I gave him a hearty handshake, welcomed him, told him we were glad to have him along.

But he had irritated nearly everybody from the moment we boarded the truck. He'd come across as a crude, inconsiderate, know-it-all, ready to bash the natives any chance he got.

I have tolerance. Most people do. I can find a lot of interest in almost any human being. But sometimes there are those who try our souls.

None more than Elsie Webb, the crusty anti-zoo crusader from Texas. We called her "Spider." She categorized Boris right off the bat.

She'd tried to be nice, telling Boris how much she was looking forward to seeing wild animals in their natural habitat.

"What for?" he'd barked. "What good are they? The sooner we get rid of them, the better."

Nothing could have been more calculated to throw Spider off balance. She fumed silently and walked away from him. This surprised me. I think it was a sign that she thought him such an insect that she wasn't going to dignify his remark with a response.

As we were loading onto the truck, Spider whispered to me: "I'm not going down the river with that son-of-a-bitch. It's either him or me."

The driver interrupted to say that the truck had gotten through. We reboarded and bounced in the back of the truck all the way to Puerto Lara.

CHAPTER 4

Now we waited. None as impatiently as Spider.

Talk about a strong personality! I pride myself on being able to handle any kind of human being, any where, any time. But Spider Webb is a challenge if there ever was one.

As we stood there in the early morning light beside the Orteguaza River at Puerto Lara, waiting for the canoes to load, I said: "Spider, you've been looking forward to this trip for years. You told us last night that the only way you want to see wild animals is alive in their natural habitat. Now you've got your wish. You're starting on a trip into the biggest tropical forest on the planet."

"With the biggest asshole on the planet," she added promptly.

I shook my head. "Come now, Spider. Are you going to let Boris screw you out of a trip like this?"

That made her even madder. "Don't you bet your pigeon squabble on it. Damn right, I'm going. Nobody's going to stop me. But let me tell you right now, Mister Criminal Investigator. I have a right to kick the shit out of that bastard if I want do."

"Take it easy, Spider."

"Why? One more statement about turning the jungle into housing developments, and I'm going to give him a Texas whopper, right smack across the kisser."

I answered that statement in as authoritative a tone as I could muster. "Did you hear what I told Joe?"

"Yes."

I gave it to her straight. "Boris has a legal right to his opinion. Don't let me see you hitting anyone. Violence is my business. If anyone is going to hit somebody on this trip, it's going to be me. Do I make myself clear?"

Spider reeled back slightly. "You take your honorary commission with the Colombian government seriously, don't you?"

"I sure do. And so do they."

She relented and smiled. She'd heard my talk yesterday in Florencia, and told me I was a hero in her book from then on. "Okay," she said. "But I ain't lettin' nobody else boss me around. Especially not that fathead."

I looked her straight in the eye. "Just take it *easy!*"

She lowered her eyes in disgust. "Yes, sir."

"We have to accept that Boris's *business* is dealing with people, not animals. My guess is that he's here on some kind of study."

"Then why doesn't he use a company boat instead of wrecking our trip?"

I couldn't answer that one. "All I can say, Spider, is that I'm going to try to get along with him. I'm going to try to enjoy this trip, come what may."

She sighed and gave up. "I'll do it for your sake, Barry. But I don't have to like it. And I don't have to like him."

She walked away, fuming. I didn't blame her. I felt the same way.

I followed Spider over to see how Beryl Fisher was doing. Greg and Joe sat beside her in the sand, Greg stroking her brown hair. Beryl, a very attractive young woman, had more supersensitivity to animal welfare than anyone I knew. Anyone. I've never met an animal-lover who wore her heart so openly on her sleeve.

She and Greg ran a nature center in Wisconsin. She came by it naturally, I had to say that.

"Greg," Spider asked, "how's she doing?"

Beryl herself answered, opening her blue eyes and forcing a smile. "I'm all right, Spider. Thank you."

Spider snapped: "No you're not, or you wouldn't be lying flat on your back in the sand."

Greg, an amiable, sandy-haired biologist, turned his worried brown eyes up toward Spider. "I've been talking with her. This has happened before. She'll come out of it."

"Come out of what?" Spider rubbed her hand through dark hair streaked with white. "What do you mean? What on earth happened back there?"

Greg spoke slowly and softly. The event pained him, too.

"We went out of the hotel with Barry yesterday afternoon to look around Florencia."

He stopped and frowned, not wanting to go on. I took over and told the story.

It was their first trip to the tropics. I wanted to help introduce them to the city. For a while, we just walked around, looking.

Florencia differs little from other towns between Bogotá and the Tropic of Capricorn. Stucco houses with wrought iron windows—no glass, no screens. Blue tiled floors. Dim doorways with dark children who chewed their thumbs and watched the traffic pass. Emaciated dogs that limped among old boxes. Piles of soda bottles, battered dolls, broken bricks. In the yard—a tree in tatters. At the side or in back, sagging ropes strung with rags, gray tee shirts and faded red dresses. Behind, up on the hills, nicer homes with glassed-in verandas. At the end of the street, the cathedral spire with a cross on top and a broken clock in the tower. The kind of generic settlement you see around the Equator from Mombasa to Surabaya.

Somewhere up the street a loudspeaker blared the latest lilting, almost celestial, song by Puma. *Voy a conquistarte... un día cualquiera...* Electronic booms ricocheted from one side of the street to the other and died away in the distance.

Old men gathered, smoked and grumbled. Young men curled around on bicycles, going nowhere. Young women by twos and threes wandered in and out of stores marked with foot-high red scrawls:

EN VENTA - PRECIOS INCREÍBLES

looking for "sales at unbelievable prices."

Greg continued: "We came to a place where vendors sold live animals in the street. One guy had an owl chained to the top of a cage, its feathers plucked out so it couldn't fly."

Spider recoiled. "God, no..."

"Then we saw the ocelot."

"Lucky!" Spider interrupted. "That's one of the most beautiful wild cats in the Amazon. I wish I could have seen it."

"No, you don't," Greg replied, shaking his head and lowering his eyes.

Spider frowned. "Huh?"

"This ocelot was curled up into a ball and wrapped in chicken wire...lying in the gutter...for sale."

He could hardly get the words out himself. Beryl closed her eyes again, burying her chin in her jacket.

Spider choked and let out a string of blue expletives. When she calmed a little, she said: "I cannot believe it."

Greg answered: "This is Colombia. It's possible."

Spider shook her shoulders and stamped her foot. "It's goddamned illegal, too."

"This far from Bogotá?"

"What does that matter?"

Greg managed half a smile. "We looked at Barry, wondering if there wasn't something he could do. Like maybe, go get the police."

"Did he?"

Greg shook his head and took on a look I assumed to mean disbelief. "You don't know Barry very well. He walked up to the owl, unhooked it from its chain and handed it to me. Then he took the ocelot wrapped in wire and went over and hired a taxi."

Spider snapped her head toward me. "You did?"

She had an aghast look on her face. I'd not seen her quite so astonished.

I answered in a soft voice. "I knew it was illegal. The owner came up to get payment, and I talked to him for a while..."

Joe interrupted: "What did you say?"

"*Creo que estos animales se vende ilegalmente, no? Qué le quieres? Llamo a los oficiales? O, dada que estoy enforzando la ley como huésped oficial del gobierno nacional, sacar pistol?*"

Joe slumped: "Thanks. You're a lot of help."

"You asked what I said."

"All right, now I'm asking for it in English."

I laughed. "Well, I put it to him bluntly. I told him that, considering these animals were on sale illegally, he had two choices. I could call the authorities, or since I was an official guest of the Colombian government in the field of law enforcement, I could pull out a pistol right now."

Joe beamed. "Yeah, man! Wow! What'd he do?"

"Disappeared very fast into the shadows."

Spider hugged me. "Barry, I love you for that. What happened then?"

Greg answered. "He rented the taxi, put the animals in the back seat, and drove us out of Florencia until we could find a place in the forest where we could let them go."

Spider turned to me again. "How come? You know they can't survive out there, wounded like that."

I responded: "What would you have done?"

Surprised by the question, she turned silent.

I went on. "I thought of taking them to Dr. Garcia's house, only he's gone. Left right after the conference yesterday."

Greg commented: "It was a helluva lot better fate than being sold and eaten."

Spider screwed her eyes closed and said: "I would have killed the goddamned vendor. Go on."

"Well," Greg said, "Barry let the owl go, and it hopped into the trees. Then he unwrapped the ocelot. At first it couldn't walk. It uncurled itself; it was a little one, a young one and lay on the ground for a while. It tried to rise, but couldn't. Looked up at us with the most pitiful eyes... Finally made it, and staggered around for a while. Then it wandered kind of dizzy-like off into the woods."

Spider closed her eyes and shook her head. "No wonder Beryl is sick. Honey, I'm sick to my heart right this minute."

Beryl opened her eyes again, and said, weakly: "It was the most awful thing I've ever seen. I can't imagine any human being so cruel."

"I can, honey. We've got some Texas zoos where they ...Oh, well, never mind. This forest is full of wildlife, and by God, I'm not going to miss any of it..."

She stopped. Beryl had closed her eyes again. Greg looked up and shook his head almost imperceptibly.

We turned and walked away.

CHAPTER 5

Impatient as ever, Joe started toward the upriver end of the sand bar where Monty conversed with the boatmen.

I called to him. "Not too close. Those are delicate discussions."

"Doesn't look like it to me," Joe whispered. "They're just chatting, wasting time, when we're supposed to be loading."

I could understand his impatience. He'd come all the way from the University of Wyoming to work on his Master's thesis in tropical ecology. We were supposed to be off by seven a.m. and here it was eight.

Monty Adams rose and came to meet us. From Monty's face, brown in color and the consistency of leather, you could tell he'd spent a lot of time in the open down here. He was short, brown-haired, and wore a weather-beaten leather vest over an orange tee shirt. The floppy hat, anointed with grime and grease from who knows how many expeditions like this, gave him a real charisma. Yet from what we'd seen of him, he kept in the background, quiet and unassuming, managing the details with simple efficiency and very hard work.

"Why don't y'all load into the canoe," he said in his Florida drawl.

I asked if he was having any problem or needed any help.

"Nuthin' I cain't handle. I'll be right along."

He turned and left. No explanation. No details.

Joe asked: "What is that supposed to mean?"

I turned and started toward the canoe. My judgment was that Monty would be longer than he thought. There were a lot of details to attend to in getting a group like this off on a trip into the interior. Still, he was the boss, so maybe we should do as he said.

I said: "Let's board up."

I went down to the canoe, not without some trepidation. Spider was going to get into the canoe with Boris Kolinski, and I steeled myself for fireworks.

With good reason. Spider felt, with every ounce of her vehement soul, that nobody on earth had the right to tell any animal where it should go or what it should do. Much less tie it up, neuter it, or otherwise abuse it. If anyone tried to talk her out of those ideas she would state flatly that most people on earth felt the same way. She would cite the Jains, Hindus, Sherpas, Coyote Clans—a seemingly endless list—and go on as long as she could hold attention.

On the day she pulled up to the Texas Institute of Biomedical Research, as she related the story in the lounge last night, she had a grim look in her eye. She parked and turned off the ignition of her aging Ford Bronco.

Grabbing her briefcase, she got out and went inside.

"I'm Elsie Webb. I have an appointment with Dr. Swinden."

"Oh, yes, Miss Webb. He's expecting you. This way, please."

Young Doctor Swinden—so delicate and pink, fresh from med school—came forward with hands extended. "Miss Webb! Your letter caused a great deal of excitement around here."

She said as they sat: "My husband died many years ago. He was so young, went through such an ordeal. I vowed if I ever got rich..."

The doctor leaned back and touched together his fingertips. "What you propose is very generous. With such a grant we could equip an entire lab."

"It isn't much."

"Oh, but it is. We pride ourselves on innovation here. We try to head off diseases before they take hold. And, of course, try new methods..."

"That's one thing that drew me back. I like that, Doctor. You must find it difficult."

"With gifts from people like you, we're able to explore new fields. Some of them a bit bizarre," he added with a coy grin.

Spider squirmed. "For example?"

"Well, disease interchange. We think one abnormality might have the capacity to react against another. Just a possibility, of course. If we can infect animals, we can find out."

"Oh, that's fascinating. Any breakthroughs?"

He smiled as though harboring a dark secret. "Victory is achieved in bits and pieces. Wouldn't you agree?"

"Of course, I would. What do you mean?"

"Well, some hospitals these days are trying to find in animals the antidotes to human ailments."

She brightened. "My husband was always interested in that."

"We think, for example, that electrical mechanisms might have a role in the treatment of schizophrenia..."

"Shock treatments? That's not new, is it?"

"No, no. Not shock treatments. We want to try a different approach. We'd like to look into the electric apparatus of certain bioluminescent organisms. We want to examine the properties of electric motor systems of other animals as a cure for dysfunctions in human neurological and motor systems."

"Other animals?"

"Eels, principally. Don't you find that intriguing?"

"I certainly do. Perhaps I could participate in the funding of that. My husband had a very difficult... If only there had been a cure then..."

"I sympathize deeply, Miss Webb. I really believe that we can make a go of this. Our computer models suggest that the electric eel might be of service to humankind."

"Yes, I saw a note to that effect in the Health Journal. I confess that's drawn me here. How far are you along?"

"We've worked out the theoretical possibilities. We are now confident enough to begin specimen acquisition..."

"Eels?"

"Yes."

"From the sea?"

"We need fresh water eels for this work, we think."

"From rivers?"

"Yes. Some can produce very powerful electrical discharges. We're about to place an order for four hundred from the Amazon."

"Bully for you."

"Thank you."

"Will they be easy to obtain?"

"I don't know. We leave that to the suppliers. Since we only need the mechanism, I think they will merely cut out the electrical apparatus and send that to us."

I can imagine this statement burning Spider's brain like a branding iron. She scowled. Her voice suddenly sharpened. "What happens to the rest of the eel?"

He looked at her with a suddenly surprised expression. "I beg your pardon?"

She persisted. "You don't know, do you?"

No response.

"You don't give a shit, either, do you?"

Silence.

"You don't give a good goddamn how many wild animals you sacrifice for your research. Why don't you use humans? We have an oversupply of them. Cut out their brains."

Swinden sat stunned, lowering his eyes in disgust, ending the conversation.

She rose. "I'm leaving for the Amazon tomorrow. I will damn well find out who's doing your dirty work for you. When I get all the details, I'll give 'em to *The New York Times*, the *Herald* in Dallas, the *Telegram* in Fort Worth, the *Statesman* in Austin... Then we'll see what happens to your specimen acquisition. And, may I add, don't expect a red cent from me! Not a goddammed farthing... you... murderers!" She put her card on the desk and left, slamming the door on the way out.

He watched her stomp out to her car, get in and drive away. Then he picked up her card.

Elsie "Spider" Webb
*Texas Association
for the Elimination
of Zoological Parks*

1 Whitworth Way, Lubbock

I believed every word of it. We all gave her a round of applause.

But now, this curmudgeon was about to get into the same canoe with Boris Kolinski, someone far more callous than the young Texas doctor she'd upbraided.

CHAPTER 6

When we got to the canoes, Boris was pulling out a bottle of zubrovka.

I jumped on him without a moment's hesitation. "I don't think you got a copy of Monty's memo to all of us, Boris, about liquor."

Boris, squat and overweight, wore a black poncho with greasy white pants. His black eyes turned on me.

"Now don't get riled up. I was just trying to warm up the little lady. Emergency medical purposes, don't you think?" He smirked and turned to Carol Lynn Arden-Jones. "Here, Sweetie, a nip of this and you'll forget the cold nights in the Amazon."

She turned away. Carol-Lynn and Chris, linguists on the faculty at Oxford University in England, seemed embarrassed by Boris's effrontery. They had traveled little, which may explain her costume. She stood out in this crowd because of her sand-colored travel dress and string of pearls. Had she intended to observe a fox hunt this morning and later take tea, her dress would have fit the occasion. It did not match a canoe stained with oil, fish blood, and river mud. Moreover, the lightweight fabric had been designed for tropical heat which did not exist at dawn. She shivered helplessly. Monty had warned us all to wear practical light-weight tropical clothing that we could layer as needed.

"He didn't tell us how cold it got in the Amazon," she said, defensively. "I came dressed too lightly."

I looked at my lapel thermometer. "Sixty five degrees Fahrenheit," I said. "You could get hypothermia. But it will warm up fast."

Joe Muck took off his denim jacket and put it around Carol Lynn's shoulders.

She protested. "Oh, Joe, you're frightfully generous, but I can't take this from you. You'll catch..."

He interrupted by pointing to the family waiting on the far end of the sand bar. "I'm going over there to see if she wants to sell me her poncho."

"Okay, Joe," I cautioned. "But call it a ruana."

Joe wore a tattered, compressed straw cowboy hat, which brought out laughter in every crowd he met. Before long he had become locked in animated negotiations with the Colombian woman for her shoulder cape.

I steered the rest toward the canoe. "Beryl and Greg first. Then the Arden-Joneses. After them the Briggles. Then Boris and Joe. And finally Spider and me. But let's wait till Monty gets here before we board up."

You'd have thought I was pulling a fast one on Joe, assigning him to sit with Boris while he couldn't be here to register a complaint. You're right. It was a neat solution to the whole problem unless he sat in the rear beside Monty.

The Briggles came to me. Mo spoke softly. "Barry, we'll have to cancel our trip."

He'd told us about the day two weeks ago when he'd said the same thing to Dana. "Why?" she asked, incredulous. "You need the rest. You can't go back on it. You need a complete change. You've been working so hard on the bio-imaging project. That's why they want you to give a paper at the meeting in Florencia."

He waited before answering. "That's just it. It's all over. We've lost. Forward Imaging beat us to it. We knew they'd been working on it, but we didn't know they were so far ahead. They're even starting to ship. It's killed us. Killed me, anyway."

She put her arm around his shoulder, her temple to his. "Oh, honey, it doesn't deny your brilliance."

"It sure plays hell with my sense of timing. I didn't work fast enough. Spent evenings with my wife instead of at the computers, at the lab."

She whispered, "I love you."

He lifted his head and sipped his drink. "I don't care what happens. Not one damned bit. But I can't go to the Amazon."

"Why? Why not?"

"I'm vulnerable. I lost this race. I could get fired. That could affect you. They may want me to load onto a new project right away. I'd have to run with it."

"Oh, Mo, they've already okayed your time off. You need a rest before starting on something else. You'll burn out. Kill yourself."

"Well, it's a little late to ask, but why the hell did we decide on the Amazon?"

"We answered that, honey. We wanted to do something completely different. Something we've never done before."

"Has a hollow ring now, doesn't it?"

She put her hand on his shoulder. "No. It's more important than ever."

He sat in thought, mulling his wife's loyalty. Contemplating the enthusiasm in her voice. She'd planned this trip to the last detail, pared every item of luggage to the last ounce. On a dugout canoe you don't take suitcases. She had gotten everything into their two small backpacks. Then he said, almost as though addressing his briefcase, "We'll be among lots of wild plants and animals..."

"Millions of kinds," she said quickly. "I've been reading. There just isn't a richer forest anywhere."

"If I could find something down there to run tests on, compare charts—no, it won't work."

"Why?"

"For one thing, there won't be any scientists along to help, nobody who knows the forest the way I'd have to know it. I wouldn't even know what equipment to take."

"Don Radcliffe said you ought to look at some sector down there for possible imaging. If the boss says it, you should do it."

"I can't carry that heavy stuff. I'd need porters myself."

"Maybe..."

"Nah, they've billed this whole trip as an introduction to the ecology and Indians of rain forests. My work is too specialized."

Dana spread her hands. "Well, then, we'll just go along for the ride."

He turned to her. "I could reconnoiter. See what's down there. Make some contacts." She saw some of the load falling from his shoulders. For a moment his gaze drifted from one of her deep brown eyes to the other. "You want to go."

She smiled. "Of course, I want to go. I've been looking forward to it. Especially now."

He repeated. "You do want to go."

"Yes," she said. "And so do you."

Now, here on the river bank, decision time again. Last chance to decide whether to get into the canoe and sit down and decide to go with the crowd.

"I can't take her down there," Mo told me, sweeping his hand down river. "What if something happened to her? What if she got chewed up by piranhas? I just couldn't take it. I'd never be able to..."

I took his arm, mustering as much of a fatherly tone as I could. "Mo, human life does not succeed on a what-if basis. You never do anything if you live in fear. You know that as well as I do. It's the unknown ahead of us that worries you. I understand. But you just can't be afraid of it and let it stop you. You'd never forgive yourself for depriving her of this trip. You know that, too."

He lowered his head and nodded. I went on. "You'll be surrounded by friends. We're all alert to the fact that she can't swim. We'll teach her. We'll help you take care of her. The fact is that she wants to go."

He looked at me with eyes that seemed about to melt.

"Dead set on it," I added.

After a long moment, he shrugged.

Without another word, he took Dana's arm and they returned to the dock.

CHAPTER 7

The port hummed with human activity. Coming back with his newly purchased ruana under his arm, Joe looked off to one side, where a talus slope of rocks led from the top of the embankment to the river's edge.

"Now that is energy efficiency!"

A dark-skinned heavy-set woman in a threadbare sleeveless dress sat washing clothes. She had placed a narrow wooden plank across two rocks nearest the water. She sat astraddle this, both feet in the water. Within reach she had placed on the rocks pans and baskets overflowing with laundry. Her practiced hands, gripping a chunk of soap as large as her fist, moved at a leisurely pace. Rubbing the soap in circular motions on the board, she saturated each garment, folded it, pushed it, and soaped it again. Then raised it, dipped it in the river, rinsed it, squeezed it, dipped it again. Still not satisfied, she placed it on the board for another round of scrubbing, rinsing, and wringing. When done, she laid the scoured garment in a basket cradled among the rocks.

"Why can't American wives do that?"

"They did, Joe," I answered. "Your grandmother used a washboard, didn't she?"

"Why doesn't she just buy a washing machine?"

I laughed. "It takes money."

"We could take up a collection."

I grinned. "Joe, you've got the golden heart of a cow-boy."

Nearby, on a sandy strip connected to shore, a family of ten Colombians stood among piles of cardboard boxes. Tethered to an aging leather satchel perched a drowsing parrot. Brown chickens pecked in the sand. One woman held a rope attached to the neck and torso of a black and white pig. Another circulated among people on shore and dock, offering for sale a red and green macaw perched on her arm. Greg Fisher started toward her, only to be restrained by his wife. They scowled and turned away.

As we made our way toward the canoe, Colombians turned to stare at Joe, the tall, lanky, blond cowboy in dilapidated denim shorts, black sandals, and white tee. On his shirt a huge distorted piranha, deadly fish of the Amazon, had been imprinted. The artist had reduced the body to nearly nothing, then enlarged the huge open mouth, full of bloodstained razor-sharp teeth, to reach from side to side. Imprinted at the bottom was one word: "Megabite."

No one could suppress a grin. Joe smiled back, saluted, and said: "Howdy!"

He displayed his newly purchased ruana. They saluted and responded: *"Buenos días, Señor."*

I couldn't suppress a grin. "That shirt is going to get you places."

Joe turned. "Where's our canoe?"

"Joe, you can answer that yourself. Find Adams."

Joe searched for Monty Adams, the trip leader. "I see him. And Eduardo. The other guy must be José." Then he saw the canoe and gulped. "We're going down the river in that?"

"Looks like it. What did you expect?"

Joe's voice had a tinge of disgust. "It's got a roof on it!"

By roof he meant a canopy of heavy brown canvas held up by hoops. Like the old Conestoga covered wagons that used to be pulled along the Oregon Trail past Fort Laramie.

Joe felt betrayed. "I thought we were going in a canoe."

"That's the genuine item, Joe. A real dugout."

"We don't need a roof! How we gonna see up? How we gonna see out? Who wants to go down the river in a tunnel?"

I tried to calm him. "You see those little ropes along the edge of the canvas?"

"Okay, so the top rolls up. I still don't..."

"Relax, Joe. If my guess is right, you'll be glad to have a roof overhead when the storms arrive."

Clouds had already coalesced and blotted out the sunrise. A cool breeze laved us as we made our way to the sand bank.

The canoe had been gouged from a tree trunk measuring thrice the length of Joe. Just back from the pointed prow had been mounted a single seat for the lookout. The passenger seats, Joe noted with relief, could be relocated or moved around, a blessing for long-legged cowboys. On the outside, he saw pits, scrapes, scratches and holes from encounters, he guessed, with debris in the river. A heavy plank across the cutoff stern held the motor.

Joe snarled in disgust. "Do we have to have a motor? I'd rather paddle."

"Not on this river," I responded. "See those currents?"

For the first time, Joe examined the river in detail. Surges of water from deep within rose and sank again. Thus roiled by powerful forces, the surface broke into shifting eddies and spinning whirlpools. Bubbles rose, whirled in vortices, and vanished. Patches of foam (or soap suds) broke into stringy segments swiftly swept away. Logs floated past like low-slung barges, their glistening trunks barely showing above the water. Patches of grass went by, attached to floating chunks of soil ripped away from banks upstream.

And the usual debris: discarded boxes, plastic bottles, scraps of cloth.

Joe hung his head. "You win. I'd still rather paddle."

"So would I. But from the look of the river, we might need those motors now and then to get us out of a bad fix."

Joe looked up. "Bad fix?"

"Case we run aground. Or capsize."

His eyes widened, but he said no more.

CHAPTER 8

When we got to the canoe, everybody stood waiting. Monty came over, saying shyly: "Camera bags only on board. Everything else on the supply canoe over there."

The supply canoe, not yet loaded, had no canopy, only an inchoate mass of canvas bundled in the back. On the dock adjacent we could see our personal baggage, heaped alongside paraphernalia of the trip: cardboard boxes, sacks of food, canvas bags, crates, cages, barrels, oil cans, netting, hammocks, and rope. Plus case after case of Coca Cola in bottles.

Greg Fisher, relaxed in denim shorts, expedition shirt and photo vest, with binoculars ever present around his neck, wondered aloud: "Why all the Coke?"

Adams answered simply: "Only pure water we'll have."

"What are those animals in cages? Chickens?"

Beryl Fisher answered that one. "Only fresh meat we'll have."

The clatter and bustle grew in intensity as the passengers milled around the canoe waiting to load.

Boris made his way among the waiting passengers, shaking hands occasionally to cinch a formal acquaintance. He wore a straw planter's hat and carried a leather briefcase so old, scuffed and stuffed that it seemed on the verge of splitting. The tail of his gray shirt hung loosely, camouflaging his paunch.

"I'm Boris Kolinski. Glad to meetcha. Sorry I wasn't with you at dinner last night. My driver got delayed out of Neiva. This is going to be some trip, huh? Look at all that Coke! We'll need a barrel of rum!" Joe held up his hand. "Boris, that Coke is a replacement for drinking water."

Kolinski emitted a deep hollow guffaw. "Hah! Water? What's that? Well! So. They must have oranges in this jungle. I know how to make a real rum screwdriver. You wait and see! And look at all those palm trees. Yes, sir! We'll have rum coconut and gin coco. Only, Monty—hey, Monty! Where we gonna get enough ice for a crowd this size?"

Adams ignored Kolinski's flagrant violation of his rule. He had already thought of Colombia's number one beverage. A dented coffee pot sat on a bed of coals in the sand. Some passengers held tin cups full of coffee to help ward off the chill and sipped the steaming liquid slowly for internal warmth.

Boris came up, as though to Carol Lynn's rescue. "Here, Miss, let me slip a little zubrovka in your coffee. That will warm you up!"

She drew back. "No thank you, sir. I shall be quite right, I think."

"Call me Boris, please."

Kolinski went off to circulate among the others. "I got some bottles of bourbon and golden gin. What did you bring along? Maybe we can get together. Gotta do something to counteract all that Coke!"

One by one the passengers ducked under the canopy and went on board. By some mixup I still can't quite understand, Spider got seated alongside Boris. I couldn't believe she'd relented. She seemed not to notice. Spider, who hated hats, had yielded to Adams's admonition: "Whatever you do, bring something to guard against the tropical sun. It can burn you in minutes if you don't watch out."

Her sun hat's four-inch brim, to hear Kolinski's complaint in a crowded canoe, made her head as wide as a Texas longhorn's.

To which she responded acidly: "And if your rump wasn't as wide as a longhorn's, we'd both be better off."

He growled a muted epithet.

She took off the hat and, searching for a place to put it, draped it over the pack in her lap, which merely placed the problem in another location. Boris glanced to the heavens and turned away.

To her credit, Spider's frayed twill trousers and ragged tee shirt fitted Amazon river fashion better than floral skirts and pearl necklaces, with one exception. The front of her tee shirt bore a silk-screened portrait of a northern timber wolf rather than the likeness of a jaguar. No one, at least, could mistake her depth of feeling for animals.

I found myself in the last chair, alongside Joe Muck. Monty Adams would perch on a pile of canvas at the rear, Eduardo at the motor. Absence of any canopy that far back gave them views of the river to starboard, port and aft. They looked ahead through the canopy tunnel, above the heads of passengers. Not a wide view, to be sure. As became apparent moments later, it didn't have to be.

An Indian scout, whom the passengers had not seen before, waded through the shallow water beside the canoe and swung up to a perch on the prow. His would evidently be the vessel's eyes to the front. From him would come any signal of impending disaster.

Joe frowned. "Ow, these seats are hard. Why didn't I bring a pillow?" He looked under his seat. "Where are the life preservers, Monty?"

Spider answered: "Any other jokes?"

Kolinski leaned forward. "You on a Caribbean cruise, kid? What I want to know is how the hell long we have to sit crammed in like this?"

Greg Fisher called back. "I'd like to know if the supply boat will get there before or after we do."

Mo Briggle added: "What if it doesn't get there at all?"

Carol Lynn: "My goodness, Mo. Perish the thought. Don't even think of it! Of course, you don't suppose such a thing could actually happen, do you? I can't imagine these log canoes sinking. Aren't they designed to float? Doesn't wood float? I always thought it did."

Joe added. "The supply boat could sink. When our bags and all the supplies get aboard it'll be down to the gunwales. Especially with all those Cokes and Boris's supply of gin."

Carol Lynn recoiled. "What a monstrous thought! What would we do?"

Boris spoke up from the back. "Paint our faces and wear grass skirts."

Carol Lynn: "Is that what they wear down here?"

Boris went on. "Then we start drinking coconut juice. Ugh! Without gin or rum that's no drink at all!"

Spider sniffed. "Are you ever sober? Don't you think of anything but spirits?"

"Yeah, Spider girl. Not very often, though. Anyway, after a while we'll go out and dig for roots, and we can go catfishing. Any catfish in here?"

Greg Fisher went back to his original question.

"I'd still like to know if the supply boat will be behind us or ahead of us all day. Monty?"

No answer. Spider turned to look behind her.

"He's gone. So's the boatman."

CHAPTER 9

Their eyes all turned toward the dock, and the supply canoe. Monty Adams huddled with his assistants in muffled conversation.

Boris Kolinski bellowed: "Good! They're going back to get more rum to go with the Cokes."

The breeze abated. Clouds still cloaked the sun but the air grew warmer.

I said: "Boris, we all introduced ourselves at dinner last night. While we're waiting, why don't you tell us who you are, where you came from, and why you're here in the Amazon."

"Glad to. Glad to. I wasn't there so I don't know anything about you folks, either. You'll all have to fill me in as we go along. Well, I'm down here to meet the people."

Spider, sitting beside him, interrupted. "What people?"

"Indians, settlers, everybody. I'm an anthropologist. I like to study people. How they behave, you know? I'm from New Jersey, so I know something about people."

Carol Lynn Arden-Jones asked: "Are you working on a thesis or research project, Mr. Kolinski?"

"Boris, my dear. All of you, call me Boris. Let's just say I'm interested in the natives and how they live down here. I like what I've seen so far. I might even stay down here."

Carol Lynn shuddered. "*Live* here? How could you?"

"Maybe for a while. Might not be so bad. I'd like to get to know these people better. Yeah, maybe some day write a paper on them. You got to gather a lot of stuff to do that."

Beryl asked: "Do you teach at a university?"

Boris passed off the question quickly. "Nah. I work for a company you never heard of."

The questions flowed freely.

"You live in Bogotá?"

"Near there."

"Been in Colombia long?"

"Quite a while."

"You travel a lot?"

"Yes."

I could see that he was telling us nothing. I didn't care. I could have gotten into a sparring match with him. But to what purpose? At least this conversation was a way of passing time.

"You've been to the Amazon before?"

"No. First time."

"What people are you looking for?"

"Everybody. Indians. Settlers. Miners."

This began to wear thin. The passengers became as restless as the river flowing beside them. Greg Fisher looked behind him.

"What's the hold up? Hasn't Monty come back?"

They looked again over toward the supply boat, where nothing whatever had happened. No baggage moved. Supply canoe still empty. Adams, Eduardo, José and the baggage handlers conversing in tones so low, the passengers could not overhear them.

Mo Briggle frowned. "They should have loaded the canoe hours ago. We've already been delayed by the landslide. And it's getting hotter. We've got a long way to go."

Joe squirmed on his seat. "I'm getting cramped."

The passengers began to wipe their brows. Few breezes stirred the air. As the morning sun bore down, even through the clouds, and the air grew hotter, I knew that human temperatures would grow hotter, too. I couldn't blame them. We had arrived all keyed up to get into the canoe and go. All set to relax and float along the river watching the trees drift by...

They had been grumbling since we left Florencia. I had no idea of how to defuse their irritations, but I could try. I rose and stepped out on to the sand bank.

"I'll go see if I can find out anything. I think I know what's wrong."

It didn't take two minutes of conversation with Monty Adams. When I got back to the canoe, I gave it to the passengers straight. "The crewmen have chosen this moment to talk about their remuneration for the trip."

Joe Muck's face turned blank. "Talk about their what?"

Spider Webb asked: "Now? Right now? You mean these arrangements weren't settled ages ago?"

I answered. "Yes, I imagine they were."

Greg Fisher shook his head. "They're striking for higher pay."

Spider let out an expletive of disgust. "They wait till we're all aboard. Then they strike."

Dana Briggle, bewildered, said: "I can't believe this."

I smiled wanly. "No better time to strike."

Boris blared forth in a guttural voice. "Ah, hell! They only want some extra pesos. Everybody in this goddamned country's got their hands out for extra pesos." He started to rise. "If that's it, I'll go give the bastards some extra pesos."

I laid a hand on his shoulder and said: "I believe we'd better not."

"Ah, don't worry, Barry. I don't mind. I got extra pesos. Won't cost the rest of you nothing. Be my guest."

I repeated. "I believe we'd better not."

Boris scowled. "Why not? What's with you? We paid good money for this trip. Now we're hours late. I want to get going. Hell, we all do."

I answered: "This is Monty's show."

"Well, some show! He's botching it up. If you ask me, he's looking for us to help. You know how these guys are. This is a tricky little way to get extra money. Charge us more for the trip. Get what I mean?"

I couldn't quite stomach that. "I don't think so, Boris. If we go over there and throw money into that situation, it will ruin Monty's operation."

"Ruin it?"

"Monty would get a reputation as gutless. They'd say he passes problems to his passengers. Puts a fix on them for more money at the last minute. The baggage-handlers would hold up every one of Monty's future passengers from then on."

"Screw Monty! Screw business. All we care about is getting the hell out of here. Get a little air out on the river. I'm suffocating. I say let's give in to the bastards and get going."

I remained adamant. "Do that, and what would keep them from striking when we get to the Indian village? We'd *really* be marooned, then. They wouldn't stop until all our money disappeared. Monty won't give in to that kind of robbery. I'd say he's shrewd."

Boris started out of the canoe again. "I'll show 'em who's shrewd."

I stopped him with a hand on the shoulder and a voice as icy as frosted steel. *"I said no."*

Boris: "Get your hands off me!"

I responded: "Sit *down*."

Boris began to sputter. "Who the hell do you think you are? You ain't in charge here."

Joe spoke up. "You better believe it, Boris. He has an honorary commission from the Colombian government. He works with the FBI, Scotland Yard, everybody. When he says 'Git,' you git. When he says 'Sit,' you *sit*."

Boris: "Who's gonna make me?"

Joe went on: "You'd better get your ass back down on the seat before you get thrown on it."

Boris laughed. "You?"

Joe said slowly: "I've thrown bulls a lot bigger'n you in the rodeo arena."

Suddenly a piercing shriek filled the air. Dana Briggle reached down and pulled up her pant leg. A centipede, five inches long and an inch wide clung to the inner side of her leg. Joe looked down, saw the animal, grabbed it with his hand, pulled it off and flung it out on the river bank.

Monty came rushing over. "Somethin' wrong?"

Dana let down her pant leg and regained as much composure as she could. "I'm awfully sorry. It was so sudden..."

"Only a centipede," Joe said. "It wasn't poisonous ."

Monty Adams went back into a huddle with his assistants.

Mo Briggle began to get impatient. "What's Monty trying to do? We should be on our way by now."

I placed my foot on the edge of the canoe. "He's trying to be very patient. These people may be poor, but they are smart negotiators."

"Smart?" Boris grumbled. "What makes you think so?"

"If Monty fires them and hires other people, he's a strikebreaker. That won't go over well with people in town. He's a Yankee trying to run a business here. If he doesn't stay on good terms with people in town he's finished. It's a damned delicate position to be in."

"So?"

"These guys need money and Monty knows it. He's just facing them down. Holding firm, or maybe giving in a little. It's a ritual. Comes with the business."

Boris: "What the hell are they talking about? I know what *I'd* say to them!"

"Unless I miss my guess, they are not talking about this trip at all."

Boris spat into the river, then shook his head. "Not—? They'd better be! We were supposed to get an early start so we'd miss the storms."

I began to get irritated with this conversation. "They're not even negotiating. Which is exactly how I'd do it."

This brought Mo Briggle over the edge. "Not negotiating? First they are. Then they aren't. What the hell's going on?"

"Sounds silly," I answered, "but it works. Nobody gets mad."

Boris exploded. "Yes they do! I'm damned mad. You think I paid all this money to come down here and sit in a cramped canoe going nowhere? What are they talking about?"

"Monty knows Colombians. My guess is that they're talking about someone's family. Maybe the price of papayas. It's a game of words, not threats. Game of patience. We can all help Monty by keeping cool and not getting uptight."

Spider Webb sniffed. "I'm out of patience. How long do we sit here on our asses with no place to go? We got things to do down this river. It's time to get started."

The temperature rose steadily. Clouds continued their slow and silent expansion into dramatic billows.

Joe Muck shouted: "Hey! There's a piranha!"

The passengers lurched in their seats.

I said: "Joe, stop it!"

He slumped and flipped his big cowboy hat over his eyes. "I just wanted to change the subject."

CHAPTER 10

I brought them back up out of the canoe to stretch their legs and walk around a little. We were helpless. We couldn't commandeer the canoe and navigate the river ourselves. We didn't want to go back. We didn't want to wait any longer. It was one of those maddening, hopeless situations from a never-never world where reality evaporated.

Spider Webb saw things going wrong. She normally found something going wrong every day, but here on the dock at Puerto Lara, she was not one to wait and harbor her emotions. Getting out of the canoe, she motioned me to the other side of the dock. Keeping her voice low so that no one would overhear us, she said bluntly: "I don't trust Kolinski."

I paid attention to everyone's complaint. I listened. Sympathized. Nodded. I also tried to keep any matter in proper perspective, as gently as possible. "You scarcely know him."

"It's a feeling I have. He's not telling the truth about who he is."

"Does it matter?"

"It could."

"He's gruff. What of that?"

"He's too glib."

"Glib? Lots of people are glib. I'm glib."

"You're a detective. You have to be. He says he's an anthropologist. I don't believe it. He doesn't sound like an anthropologist."

I turned my head away. "Spider..."

"He could be fronting for something."

"Aren't you blowing this up a little—."

She leaned closer. "The man may be part of a drug cartel. Down here to check his cocaine plantations."

I tried to suppress a smile. "If that were so, he wouldn't be coming down here in a dugout canoe."

She frowned. "That's just my point. We don't know what we are getting into. Adams hasn't said much."

"There's not much to say. No one says much in the tropics. I kind of like it that way."

Her voice dropped to a whisper. "Besides, did you see the initials on his briefcase?"

"Yes."

"ILB. That's what they were."

I asked: "So?"

She took on the air of one who had discovered a sinister secret. "That's not his name. He's a fake."

"Spider, you're making a quantum leap. Could be a company's initials. Maybe the briefcase belongs to someone else."

"I don't believe it. Anyway, I didn't expect to be cramped in that canoe with a crook."

"I sympathize, Spider. But a man's not guilty till he's guilty."

"Not yet," she murmured, and walked away.

Carol Lynn Arden-Jones helped Lolita, the laundress, load her baskets of laundry on the donkey. The elegant Briton and the Colombian laundress embraced like lost friends. Lolita started down the road to Florencia.

Moments later, the Briggles hailed me. Mo had a worried frown.

"Didn't Monty say he wanted to get started early so we wouldn't get caught in a storm?"

"Something like that, Mo. Why?"

"Well, we're not starting early. We're so late now we'll probably get caught."

"Could be," I acknowledged. "I'm looking forward to it."

Mo stopped. He never expected *that* kind of a response. "We've been looking at that canoe. With canvas awning all wrapped around it, the whole thing is top heavy. In a storm with a lot of wind, don't you think it could blow over?"

I nodded. "It could."

"Well, then, I don't enjoy the prospect of putting my wife at risk."

I tried to be patient. "My guess is that they move to shore when a storm comes. We're all subject to one danger or another down there, but so what? It's worse at home."

"Granted, Barry. But I—."

"That's a heavy canoe. With us on board, it'll sit pretty low in the water."

"Well, that's a problem, too, isn't it?"

"Might tip a little. Otherwise, ought to be stable. These people down here usually know what they're doing."

"Usually? We don't have any evidence of that yet."

"They're pretty good at it, despite appearances. I don't think we'll have any rapids or high waves."

"You could be wrong, of course?"

I grinned. "Me?"

Joe suddenly shouted from the canoe. "They're loading! They're loading!"

Sure enough, Monty, Eduardo, José and the baggage handlers had sprung into action. They formed a line to load equipment. Bags, boxes and crates traveled from arm to arm and hand to hand.

Within minutes, the passengers had again taken their places in the canoe. I took a seat beside Joe.

Monty Adams came up, apologized for the delay, and uttered the understatement of the morning. "I guess it's time to go."

The Indian guide splashed through the water again. With one bound he leaped up onto the bow.

Eduardo came aboard and started the engine. Adams unhooked the chain from the post in the sandbank, coiled it, threw it in back. Then he took his seat on the pile of canvas beside Eduardo and the motor.

Spider Webb and Boris Kolinski tried to avoid looking at each other.

Two baggage handlers waded into the water and pushed the canoe out into the current. Then they went back to their loading.

"Aiyee—ee!" Joe yelled. "Go git 'em, cowboy!"

Our sleepy world sprang to life.

With a cloud of blue smoke, the motor burst into action. The back end of the canoe twisted around, pointing the bow downstream. The motor jumped and gave out a high-pitched whine. The canoe moved forward, gaining speed. Wind blew refreshingly against our sweaty faces.

Puerto Lara receded.

Eduardo steered the canoe out into the main stream, swerved to the left, and headed down the Orteguaza.

At the same time, thunderclouds, rising from the horizon nearly to the zenith, grew ponderous and blacker.

CHAPTER 11

The canoe glided swiftly, nudged by heaving currents and whirling vortices. As the prow thrust through surges and whirlpools, the vessel swayed and tipped, yawed and darted, bringing from Dana Briggle muffled cries of dismay. She held her husband's hand with a white-knuckled grip, watching in terror the roiling muddy morass inches away.

The Fishers sat transfixed in the front seats, taking notes furiously, absorbing every possible facet of a world unlike any they had ever seen. Beryl's transformation seemed complete, now that we were actually on the move, and she had obviously begun to recover. With binoculars they surveyed the massive wall of tropical forest, or, from time to time, the drooping, leaning trunks of giant bamboos clumped along the shore. Chris and Carol Lynn Arden-Jones, second back, scanned the landscape, amazed and bewildered. Nothing among the brown brick walls of Oxford prepared them for this world of violent water, giant forests, and shrieking parrots flying past on rapid wingbeats.

Not long after departure, Chris Arden-Jones spotted something on the distant shore and became agitated. Carol Lynn, following his gaze, said in astonishment: "It can't be."

Chris turned as best he could in his cramped position and called to the back of the canoe. "Monty!"

I answered. "He can't hear you. He's sitting beside the motor."

"Then would you ask him to come forward, please?"

"He can't, Chris. There's no aisle on this cruise boat. Something wrong?"

Chris pointed to the far bank. "See those children? Beyond there, swimming in the water?"

All eyes turned to the right. I responded: "Yes?"

Chris had a worried look on his face. "Aren't they in frightful danger? I mean, from all the deadly fish in these waters?"

"Deadly fish?" I asked.

"Yes. Piranhas. All that."

I saw what he meant. "Oh, well, I wouldn't worry too much."

Carol Lynn broke in. "I'm worried. Those children could be eaten alive. A horrible death."

This brought a smile to my face. "All right. Now would you note very carefully where they are swimming."

Carol Lynn turned her head toward the shore, then back to me. "They are swimming offshore from that little beach. What does it matter? They are in the water. Right in it. You see?"

"Yes, I see. And having a good time?"

"Quite."

"Now what do you know of piranha life styles?"

She laughed. "Goodness, Barry, you are putting me on..."

"No, I'm not. There's a little secret of which you are unaware."

She laughed. "Oh, Barry, there are many secrets with which I am unacquainted. Especially here. What are you talking about?"

"Piranhas are bottom feeders."

That stopped her. She digested the implications of the fact for a few moments, then said: "They live in the bottom of the river?"

"That's right."

"Well, be that as it may. I myself wouldn't swim there. Don't they know any better?"

Joe answered wryly: "It's a hot day. They must know something we don't."

Chris shook his head in disbelief and turned again to face the front. "So ends our first lesson in Amazon biology."

CHAPTER 12

We rounded a curve in the river and for a time floated beneath a high forest wall.

The tropical hardwoods, hundreds of species in every conceivable shape and form, grew in a formless meld. Each mast of tree trunk struggled upward or outward, pushing its green sails as far as possible to reach the sunlight. Nearly every tree competed and crowded to avoid the shade of its neighbors. Leaves small and large, pointed and rounded, hanging or erect, clung to limbs from the highest levels to the water's edge. Some even entered the water, attached to branches and trunks fallen part way into the river.

Where relentless torrents grazed the shore, night and day, year after year, they undercut the bank, toppling trees and tearing away chunks of soil. Where branches oscillated with the current, leaves rippled and fluttered in endless pirouettes. Massive palm trees raised their giant fronds toward the canopy. Clusters of lianas, long woody vines that also had struggled upward to reach the tree tops, hung by the hundreds, like dangling ropes on a three-masted schooner.

Very few openings, scarcely a leafy tunnel or cave, broke this mansion of green. Wherever we glimpsed within, the branches showed themselves festooned with epiphytes. These air plants buried their roots in the limbs and thrived there. They took energy from the sun, and absorbed water and nutrients that flowed along the limb. Joe Muck wished aloud that he could be a Tarzan swinging from limb to limb. That way, he said, he could *really* see what the forest held.

All at once, the woods receded. The great forest wall, hacked away by human hands, yielded for perhaps a minute as we glided by. In this opening perched a hut on stilts, built on a small terrace above the river. No steps had been gouged in the soil from river to door. A ladder of sorts, fashioned from bamboo lengths lashed with ropes, extended down the slope from its anchor at the top of the embankment.

Bamboo poles enclosed the space beneath the hut. A ladder led to a door on the main floor. Panels of bamboo slats walled in the living quarters. A thick mass of palm fronds covered the roof and spilled off the edge to form an overhang.

Swift passage of the canoe allowed us little time to study this almost forbidding outpost in the wilderness. We strained for a glimpse of life. Two small dark human heads with wide open white eyes appeared behind a shrub at the corner of the hut. Black-haired, dressed in white shirts, these shy figures stared as we passed only to disappear behind the the forest edge as the canoe slipped away.

Spider pouted, irritated at having to sit with Kolinski. She refused to look at the river bank on his side.

Joe suddenly pointed and shouted: "A caiman!"

Our eyes focused on a tiny cove at the water's edge. Spider cocked her hat so she could blot out Boris and still see the bank.

"A caiman," Joe repeated. "Crocodile. They're rare down here. Only small ones left."

The reptile could not have measured in length any more than tall, lanky Joe measured in height. It lay in an alert position: head raised, mouth open to reveal the gleaming sharp white teeth, banded tail curved to the left and held off the sand.

"Wow!" Joe shouted. "He's ready to move!"

Mo asked: "Move where? Toward us?"

"No, away from us. He's frightened."

Mo seemed puzzled. "Frightened? How come? My book says crocodiles are dangerous."

"To small fish and mammals mainly. If we get closer he'll probably leap in the water to escape."

"Don't they attack human beings?"

Joe grinned. "I suggest you back one into a corner and see what happens."

Mo looked away. "No, thanks."

We veered away, leaving the caiman astern, and headed out into the main stream.

Without warning, the canoe struck something and slowed with a jolt. We lurched in our seats. Loud scraping sounds, like the roar of a giant monster, engulfed us, amplified by the round wooden structure of the hull. Thrown off center, the canoe swerved and tipped toward the right.

Dana Briggle screamed, clasped her hands to her eyes, and pressed her head against Mo's shoulder.

The sounds of the monster roared for seconds that seemed like minutes to the uninitiated.

"Over we go!" shouted Joe.

The canoe jerked around again and bumped against something unseen in the water. Then, suddenly, the scraping ended. The keel stabilized. Currents carried the craft onward, as before, in a silent grip.

Carol Lynn Arden-Jones turned to look back with wide eyes.

"What was *that*?"

I tried to reassure her. "Gravel bar. Nothing serious."

Carol Lynn couldn't believe that I had described something so loud that it deafened us, and so forceful that it almost upset the boat, as "nothing serious."

"We were almost thrown out! Look at Dana. She's petrified. Can't we stop?"

I shook my head. "We're in open water again. It's okay. The river's shallow in spots. See that egret wading on a sand bank? That's how shallow it is. The current's strong. These sandbars and gravel bars change location almost daily. You can't memorize them. They shift. It's almost impossible for Eduardo, back at the motor, to see them, or steer around all of them."

Carol Lynn couldn't quite grasp all this. "Steer? Looks to me like he's at the mercy of the river. How can he steer when he's sitting back there? He can't see anything straight on."

"Well, Carol Lynn," I responded, "if you'll notice, he has his eye on the Indian up in the bow."

"Yes. I've noticed."

"The Indian is scouting sand or gravel bars near enough to the surface to be seen through the muddy water. He's also watching for water-soaked logs that could side-track us if we rammed into them."

"You mean pitch us into the river?" Carol Lynn looked quickly at the Indian scout. "I think you're considerably right. This chap has hardly moved a muscle since he came on board. He doesn't take his eyes off the water. But how does he communicate—?"

I had the same question until I watched the Indian closely. "Notice he's sitting sideways. He has his hands crossed in his lap. All he does is point a finger to port or a thumb to starboard. That's all the signal Eduardo needs. Don't be surprised at sudden swerves. Maybe a little tipping now and then."

Carol Lynn felt relieved. "Brilliant, Barry. Thank you."

Joe Muck narrowed his eyes in perplexity. "If the guy up front's so good and got X-ray vision, how come we hit a gravel bar?"

I smiled. "Joe, I can think of fifteen answers to that question. You want them all?"

Dana Briggle lifted her head in distress. "No! Please!"

The clouds grew darker. Lightning flashed above the river ahead.

A great blue heron, standing on a sandbank, seemed to ignore the passing canoe, then stretched its wings and rose when the craft drew near. A kingfisher flew over, voicing a piercing shriek. Another flock of parrots streaked past, this one in a random flight pattern rather than V-shaped. Their screeching chatter could barely be heard above the roar of the motor.

Spider bent over the edge, staring intently into the water. Joe called: "You sick?"

"Well, now that you ask, yes!"

"What's the matter? We're miles from a zoo."

"That's not it. We're going down through the world's biggest rain forest, full of wild animals, and we can't hear a goddamned thing. Ask Monty to turn off that blinkin' motor back there so we can float a while."

Dana Briggle, pale and upset, murmured: "No! Please!"

I answered. "We can do that on some tributary to the Orteguaza. We'll find a place even wilder than this."

Joe beamed. "That a promise?"

Spider: "Don't you forget."

"We'll ask Monty. Out here, at this speed, there's always a chance we could run into a mud bank. We'd need the engine for an extra burst of power to get off."

Joe scoffed. "That little engine? Buddy, we're loaded to the gunwales. We'd have to get out and push."

For a while, we floated in silence. Spider glared at Boris now and then, and Boris glared at Spider, but otherwise they said nothing.

Joe made a list of the wildlife observed on shore and river: iguanas, turtles, herons, egrets, doves, a black ibis, roseate spoonbill, wild turkey, anhingas and kites.

As the afternoon lengthened, the thunderheads seemed to stall. The wind died. The air grew oppressively humid.

After we had been on the river for an hour or so, the Indian on the prow raised his arm and pointed toward a sand bar near the river bank. The motor idled. The canoe turned.

Minutes later we found ourselves nudged against the sand and climbing out.

"Pit stop!" Joe yelled. "Don't get lost!"

By the time we returned to the canoe, José had arrived with the supply boat. Monty Adams set up a case of Cokes and a tin of cookies.

Boris Kolinski scowled. "Cookies? What happened to lunch? Dammit, Monty. We only had an orange for breakfast. You trying to starve us?"

Adams knew that the less one ate in the tropics, the better. He had said so last night at dinner. Now he said nothing and went back to the supply boat.

Joe Muck responded, irreverently: "Use your reserve, Boris."

"Oh, the hell, college boy. We paid good money for this trip, and it's supposed to include something to eat now and then."

He picked up a bottle of Coke and a fistful of cookies, patted his pocket flask, and stalked away.

Joe muttered: "I ain't a college boy, stupid. I'm a grad student."

Greg Fisher asked Adams: "Monty, we haven't seen any jaguars. Where are they?"

Adams swept his hand toward the forest. "They's asleep this time o' day."

"Bad news," Spider commented. "Aren't we going to see any at all?"

"Maybe tonight. In the river."

Joe asked, astonished: "In the what?"

"Watch for 'em along the bank, just their heads showin'."

Joe recoiled in disbelief. "Cats—swimming?"

"Do it all the time. If a capybara or a 'gouti—big rodents—or maybe a young tapir goes in the water, cat goes after 'em. If it don't, it don't eat."

Joe raised his eyebrows. "Fish, too?"

"A hungry jaguar goes after anything."

"All right," Spider said, "if they're here, let's see some. Monty, can we go out at night, along the river bank?"

"Well, they'd be hard to see in the dark."

"Can't we take a flashlight?"

"They'd see you comin' and go away."

Joe couldn't help saying: "Go to a zoo, Spider." She frowned and turned her back. "By the way, Monty," Joe went on, "what about piranhas? I mean, we get stuffed with stories about piranhas chewing up cows."

Monty stroked his chin. "They feed on fish down below."

"That's what Barry said. Now don't tell me they never eat a cow."

"If one falls into the water, bleedin', yeah. Piranhas attack in schools. They can clean everything down to the bones pretty quick."

Dana Briggle, pale and white, turned her head away and walked over to the canoe, holding Mo's arm.

Joe Muck persisted. "Haven't they ever eaten a human being? What about those kids we saw swimming?"

"Well, you get a lot of piranhas around meat cuttin' houses where they's lots of blood in the water. That gets 'em excited. If anyone goes into the water there—."

"Feeding frenzy?"

"Yep."

"I've seen that," Joe mused. "You ought to see the feeding frenzy when a vacancy occurs on the college faculty—."

Monty glanced at the ground for a moment, then said, in a gentle tone: "We got animals more dangerous than that in the river."

This stirred Joe's curiosity like nothing else. "More dangerous than piranhas? Name one."

"Anacondas."

"Right. Giant snakes. Thirty feet long."

"You ain't gonna find one that long any more."

Joe frowned. "Why not?"

"Huntin'."

"Do you see many?"

"Once in a while you see one with its head above the water. Maybe on the bank. I saw one last week hangin' over a limb."

"You did? What do they eat?"

"Anything along the bank. Young tapirs. Agoutis. Maybe even a bird."

Carol Lynn asked: "Children?"

Monty calculated a moment. "Anything up to 150 pounds."

Carol Lynn gasped. "That includes *me*! I weigh 150 pounds."

Beryl Fisher asked: "What do anacondas look like?"

"Very colorful," Monty answered. "Brown. Gold. Green."

Spider asked: "What else lives in the river?"

"Sting rays," Monty answered. "Indians tell me you get stabbed by one of them you're out of action for days."

Joe said: "My God! This place is *neat*!"

Chris: "I'd say the word is *priceless*, Joe."

"That's what 'neat' means!"

Spider persisted: "What else?"

Monty paused, his tone casual. "Well, electric eels."

It was precisely the answer Spider wanted. She led him on. "Here? In fresh water?"

"Millions of 'em in the Amazon country."

Joe smiled. "Oh, great! So next we get electrocuted. I hear they can do that to a man."

Monty nodded. "They can knock down a horse, even *kill* a man."

Joe shook his head. "My god, Monty, that would take an awful lot of current."

Monty grinned. "Some eels is six feet long. A thousand volts. Fifteen hundred, maybe."

Joe reared back. "Aiyee-ee!! That could ruin your whole day. If you get knocked out and then keeled over into the water, it's the end of the road, pal. Drowning will finish you off if the amps don't."

Spider said casually: "I hear they're using eels for medical research."

Monty made a noncommittal "Hm-m."

Spider would not let him get away with an answer like that. She asked bluntly: "Know anything about that?"

He looked up the river and said nothing.

Spider did not like people to ignore her questions. When they did that, she knew they were holding back something. She persisted. "Know anyone shipping eels out to hospitals?"

Monty answered matter-of-factly: "Lots of things shipped out of Leticia."

Evasive answers made her suspicious. She bored in. "Know who's doing it?"

Monty hesitated. "We'll be there in a few days."

This made her mad. She almost said something, but bit her lip instead, and said no more. On reflection, she decided that he had, in fact, answered her questions, at least partially. Monty knew all about eels and how they got shipped out of the country.

She was on the right track.

CHAPTER 13

Moving out again into the main current we could see José and the supply canoe fading into the distance downriver. The sky grew darker. The clouds became more ominous.

I turned sideways and said to Spider: "It may not be very easy to find out about eel shipments down here."

She looked me directly in the eye. "I'll find out."

"You're also going to have trouble wiping out zoos," I ventured. "They're pretty well established."

"Of course they are." She sounded like she'd been on this defensive track before. "It will take time. We know that."

"Some have become pretty well known as animal research centers. You have a problem with that?"

She sniffed contemptuously. "You can do a lot better research out in the wild."

"Not when rats eat all the eggs. The Puerto Rican parrot—."

"Oh, well, extreme cases, maybe. What can you learn from an animal in prison, not eating its natural food? Maybe shivering to death? Sick? Infected with parasites?"

"I take it that your policy is to bring people to animals instead of the other way around?"

"We just don't like to see animals in captivity. Period."

Boris, sitting beside Spider, spoke. "Ah, they don't have feelings."

She snapped back: "Ever own a dog?"

"Sure. I mean lions and tigers don't. All they ever do is produce more lions and tigers. They're just animals. How come you get so emotional about it?"

She preferred not to answer him, I could tell. But neither would she let him get away with that. "Emotional I'm not, buster boy. We just don't like to see *anything* caged, not even anthropologists. Although I could make an exception."

Boris clutched his poncho and rolled his eyes. "You cut me, dear madam! Well, I tell you this. You better get all the animals into the zoos as fast as you can, because people are spreading everywhere. They've filled up Europe and the U.S. Japan is loaded to the gills. South America's next."

Spider laughed. "Nature deals with overpopulation. Lemmings march to the sea. Famines wipe out millions of people. So do wars, diseases and plagues. These are great. Tobacco smoking is a voluntary method of population reduction. I'm for it. Very effective."

Boris shuddered. "Good God! When did they let you out of the goon saloon?"

Spider muttered something under her breath and turned away.

"You're wasting your time," Boris went on. "Look at that river. It's a highway. Every tributary down here is a highway. They take you back into every corner of the forest. People are comin' in. Lots of 'em. And you can't stop 'em."

Spider sniffed. "Well, fathead, people don't have to occupy every square inch!"

I didn't know exactly when I would have to step in and end all this. I had no way of knowing how rapidly these heated exchanges would escalate into violence. At the same time, I didn't see any harm in everyone airing his or her views. It was a sure way of getting to know your fellow passengers.

Boris was in good form. "One day this will all be opened up. All of it. People won't starve any more. You're out of date, sweetie. The forest was made to be *used*. Anybody knows that. Why do you think it was put here? We can ship out the logs, pump the oil, mine the gold..."

At that point, Joe Muck, sitting beside me, had taken all he could. "Beautiful! Just beautiful! The rivers are already running with mud and mercury. Who the hell do you think would *want* to live here? If they did, they'd choke. They'd starve. What would you do with the tapirs and caimans?"

Boris answered in a flash. "Sell 'em! Put 'em to use! Turn 'em into handbags. Make belts out of 'em. Haven't you seen crocodile boots in the stores? Get with the fashion, boy!"

That was all Mo Briggle could suffer. He turned. "What kind of perverted viewpoint is that?"

The Arden-Joneses turned. Chris scowled. "Is that chap real?"

Spider outshouted them all. "Where are the piranhas when we need them? You idiot! You're blind as well as dumb. Every law in every country is pointed in the other direction. You're the one who's obsolete."

A babble of angry voices erupted only to be cut off by a flash of lightning and deafening clap of thunder. Dana Briggle shrieked and buried her head again.

Joe Muck shouted: "There's your answer, Boris! Listen to that! The gods are after you!"

"They're on my side!" Kolinski shouted. "They're on the peoples' side!"

"Bullshit!" Joe shouted above the tumult. "They've come to take you out. I just hope they don't take us all out at the same time!"

From the black sky came another bolt of lightning and a deafening thunderclap.

The storm had arrived.

CHAPTER 14

Nothing could have so effectively drowned out the growing animosity between Boris and the other passengers. The "rain" in rain forest here is not the gentle drizzle that drifts into a temperate rain forest. Here the water falls by the ton—bashing, thrashing, battering and drowning.

A wall of heavy rain bore down upon us from behind, pushing violent gusts before it. The canvas canopy began to billow and thump, rocking the canoe. We clutched the edges to hold ourselves steady, but it was hopeless. Gusts of roaring wind threw us from side to side. Dana buried her head again.

The Indian pointed to the right. Eduardo turned the vessel and guided it toward shore.

José found an eddy within a sheltered cove and took refuge. Eduardo gripped the limb of a fallen tree, hoping to keep the canoe in place—a pitiful effort at best. The furious wind wrenched the limb from his hand. The canoe skewed sideways, end pointed to shore.

It was a perilous moment in which the canopied vessel, broadside to the winds, could have been blown over and all of us toppled into the whipping waves.

The Indian scout plunged into the water and swam ashore with a rope, which he lashed to a fallen trunk, securing the front end. Then he swam back and resumed his place on the prow.

Monty leaped into the water, clothes and all, and tied the stern to another tree limb. It was a precarious hold, but he had no choice. He hopped back aboard, just in time.

A powerful wind nearly blew the canoe against the bank. A liquid curtain deluged us like a waterfall. Heavy drops pelted the canvas with a roar. Torrents of rain splashed into the canoe at both ends, drenched the boatman, scout, and Adams, and roiled the river surface. The tropical Orteguaza had become a cauldron of exploding water.

No one could hear anyone else. The Fishers, up front at the edge of the overhanging canvas, recoiled and pulled jackets over their heads to keep out the heavy spray. They tried to shout, but the roar absorbed every decibel.

More lightning flashed, closer than ever. Thunder pounded, echoed, and reverberated, as in a vast celestial amphitheater. Tons of water fell on the sagging canopy and all around us. The roar intensified. The shore, close off the starboard bow, vanished from sight as if we had passed beneath a Niagara-like cascade.

Joe shouted "Whoopee!" but only the din of the rain could be heard.

Water began to flow along the bottom of the canoe beneath our feet. In the back, Adams bailed as fast as he could with a pitifully small can.

The canoe shifted and turned, pulled on the ropes, strained against the limbs to which it had been hastily attached, and tried to break free.

No one could see ahead, to the side, or behind. If a floating tree trunk, driven by wind and wave, came down the river on this side, no one would know until it hit. If the river rose suddenly, pushing a giant wave, we would scarcely have seen it until too late.

Under such a powerful onslaught, we could do nothing but sit, weak and helpless, victims of nature on the rampage. The water in the canoe became deeper, covering our feet. I cursed myself for not having brought a lightweight plastic or canvas bucket to help bail out the water. I should have thought of that.

The pounding pandemonium seemed unstoppable. By a miracle, the canvas held. Under such a downpour, weaker cloth would have ripped to shreds or blown away. If that had happened, the canoe would have rapidly filled and sunk.

The maelstrom moved on downstream. The torrent stopped abruptly, leaving us gasping, our ears ringing. The wall of water receded. The river bank reappeared. Then the river. Then the forest on the other side.

We sat with shoulders hunched, expecting another lightning bolt and claps of thunder. Only the sound of rain pounding the river came to our ears, and soon this faded.

"Well," Joe said, "*that* was a nice little shower. Are we sinking yet?"

In the back, Monty scraped furiously with the little can.

Mo had covered his wife's head with a jacket. She remained as though buried in a burrow.

The Fishers brought out their cameras to photograph the receding rain, but found the instruments wet and the battery compartments short-circuited. Greg cursed. "Plastic doesn't do it! Pull over to the nearest supermarket. We need a rubber bag."

Joe said: "Too late, my friend. The stores are closed."

Boris: "When are we going to stop for dinner?"

The river and forest absorbed this massive downpour as if nothing had happened. In the aftermath, we expected the river to be in a destructive flood stage. Not a sign of it. A few wisps of mist rose from the surface. Around us, the Orteguaza revealed no more eddies and whirlpools than before.

The cloudburst had been absorbed. Just like that.

The Indian swam ashore, released the rope, and carried it back to the prow. Monty went in again to untether the stern, and climbed back aboard. Eduardo revved up the motor. The canoe moved out again into the open current.

CHAPTER 15

For almost an hour we glided down the river, weary (or wary) of resuming our conversation. Or perhaps destabilized and exhausted after all the violence. This gentle aftermath would do us good. We could rejoice in a quiet float for a change. Passenger tempers cooling off.

Joe Muck tried to rev up the battle again, but without success. The others had had enough.

With Kolinski's resolve to turn caimans into purses, I could tell by Joe's angry eyes that he continued to seethe with resentment. Nor was he one to hold his emotions back.

"Why not turn every goddamned anaconda into suitcases?" he asked aloud, with acid bitterness. *"Or jaguars into fur coats?* If you do that, no biologist would ever again have a reason to come to the Amazon. No tourist either. Why pay good money to come see pineapple plantations? How could any idiot be so dumb?"

That almost threw Spider back into the tempest. She strived to lean farther away from Boris. He represented everything she had been fighting against for years. With their positions poles apart, I could tell that the more she brooded, the madder she got.

Yet their energy seemed sapped by the storm, the humidity, the heat. The battle had died, but I knew it was only a temporary respite.

Monty Adams continued his scrape-scrape with the little tin can. Eventually he lowered the level of water beneath our feet, leaned back on the canvas and fell into a snooze.

Greg and Beryl, from their front seat vantage post, followed the receding storm as long as they could see it. They peered into the fast-flowing river. Turbid sediments. Nothing more.

With the passing of the storm, the animals came back to life. The Fishers looked into the dark recesses of the forest, as though hoping any moment to see jaguars sleepily awake. Spider Webb looked into the water and fancied she saw headless eels swimming by the thousands deep in the murk...

The sun came out. The temperature rose rapidly. We all fought drowsiness. Eyelids drooped. Brains recessed. Anger faded. Heads nodded.

Nearly everyone napped. Dana slept at last. Even the Fishers dozed off, despite every effort to stay awake and see everything since five o'clock this morning...

The drone of the motor changed, slowed, cut off entirely. The canoe leaned over as it swerved. Eduardo guided the craft to shore.

Sudden silence waked us. We sat up. In a veil of drowsiness, we saw a house on stilts, set back from the bank above the river.

"Overnight stop," said Monty Adams.

Joe shouted: "Rouse up everybody! The Ramada Orteguaza welcomes you! Will someone ring for the porter, please?"

Boris snorted, squinting at the hut. "The saints preserve us! Is that where we stay tonight?"

Chris called back, with a trace of sarcasm in his voice:

"You wanted to meet the people."

They pulled up to a broken wooden dock with a small sign askew on the corner post:

FINCA BERMUDEZ

Someone asked: "Are they expecting us for dinner?"

Boris responded: "They look at us like any strangers. More pesos in their pockets."

The canoe nudged the dock. Eduardo leaped up and lashed a rope to the post.

Kolinski stumbled ponderously out on the planks, growling. "A shitty deal if I ever saw one." He offered his hand to Spider, who refused it and motioned for him to get out of the way.

CHAPTER 16

They led Dana, sallow-faced and barely able to walk, into the yard, Mo on one side, Carol Lynn Arden-Jones on the other.

The house at Finca Bermudez perched above an enclosure fenced by slender tree stems lashed to posts. From where we stood, the house appeared to have no more than one room with an alcove, less a house, perhaps, than a hut. It had been built on large tree trunks and elevated more than head-high above the ground. Rough-hewn planks placed vertically made up the walls. An opening in front faced the river; another in back faced a banana grove. Neither had screen nor shutter. Wide eaves extended above the walls and windows for more than an arm's length—extra protection where rain fell so often and so heavily. The roof consisted not of palm thatch, but of that other nearly universal topping in tropical settlements—rusting corrugated metal.

In the open space beneath the house, a milk cow lay tethered to one post, a horse to another. A flock of twenty chickens and two ducks pecked at the ground inside a makeshift pen. Two children watched the canoes being unloaded. Two dogs pranced around the newcomers as they came through an opening in the fence and climbed the wooden stairs.

I now began to get a gut feeling about this elevated hut, and it wasn't good. Friction among the passengers had already erupted in the cramped canoe. Now we would have to bunk ten people in a little room. And my premonition saw the friction getting worse as resentments grew.

"I'll sleep out under the stars," Joe offered. "That's what we do in Wyoming."

I asked: "What makes you think there are stars in the Amazon?"

He looked at me. "Rain at night?"

"Ask Monty."

"Never mind. I withdraw my offer."

Climbing the stairs and going inside, I saw the problem. The hut's main room amounted to a combination living-dining room, and was extended to an open anteroom for sleeping. At one corner, a table covered with a few bottles and cans of condiments made up the kitchen (a fire pit being on the ground underneath the hut). One small table and four crude chairs furnished the dining side. Floor pads at the far corner of the anteroom made up the bedroom. Into this they led Dana Briggle, prepared a resting place, and left her to sleep.

Señora Bermudez, a shy, dark-faced, dark-haired Colombian, withdrew to the fire pit downstairs. She fanned the coals into flame, added sticks, and suspended a battered black pot of water above the fire. She grasped a wandering chicken by the head, whirled it vigorously four or five times, and placed the carcass near the fire for plucking. With her other hand she kept a spindly dog away. Then another chicken, and another, until enough lay in the heap to feed more than a dozen people.

Señor Bermudez, as dark and shy as his wife, helped unload equipment from the supply canoe and carry it under the house. I brought up cases of Coke. I watched as Boris Kolinski steered Bermudez out of the compound and down the road toward the banana grove, talking in low tones.

Spider Webb watched, too, from the edge of the fence. Boris occasionally waved his hands in sweeping gestures toward the forest, then up and down the river.

She saw me on the other side of the compound and hurried over. She repeated that she hadn't trusted Boris Kolinski at Puerto Lara. She hadn't trusted him in the canoe. Now she didn't trust him here. What could he be doing? Asking for special favors? Soliciting extra food?

I set down the last of the Coke cases and came out from under the house to mop my face.

"Look down there." She pointed. "What does that shyster have to do with Bermudez?"

I smiled. "There you go. Spying again."

"I'm not. He's up to something. Like sabotaging this trip."

"Spider! What possible motive could he have?"

"I don't know how or why, but you know he couldn't care a thing for the rest of us. Doesn't even *think* like us. Looks to me like he's speaking Spanish. He never said anything about that before."

I laughed inwardly and said: "I didn't either."

"I know you speak Spanish."

"And French. And Chinese."

She turned abruptly toward me. "Then why don't you go down, friendly like, and join them? Just listen in?"

My answer was direct and simple. "Because it's none of my business."

"You said you were an investigative officer. Go down there and investigate!"

"I don't have to."

She frowned. "What do you mean?"

"I already know what they're talking about."

"You do?" For a moment Spider remained almost speechless.

"That's what I said. So would you, if you analyze it carefully."

"Now you *are* talking like a detective. For God's sake, let us all in on it."

"You'll find out soon enough what's going on. Knowing you, I imagine you'll find out sooner rather than later."

"I don't like being brushed off like that. I asked Monty about eels, and he gave me a brush off. Why?"

"He's not in the eel business."

She frowned. "What is that supposed to mean? He *knows* everybody down here. He knows what's going on."

"That's the obvious part of it. He respects their privacy. If you want to know about eels, go to the eel shippers and find out for yourself."

"How the hell am I going to find them?"

"Put your ear to the ground, Spider."

She was not amused. Her eyes grew darker, her scowl more fierce. Her voice rose a pitch. "Well, that son-of-a-bitch is up to something that could ruin our trip. I want him *off the boat*. I'd say everybody else wants him off, too. I want that bastard off the boat before he does any more damage to our peace of mind. I want you to tell Monty to send him back."

I watched her flashing eyes, her twitching fingertips, her jerking neck movements. She spelled trouble, and it was growing. I spread my hands in a helpless gesture. "Me? Why not do it yourself?"

"You have a helluva lot more authority than I have."

"Okay," I said. "You really want to put Monty on a spot, don't you?"

"I don't care. When one of his passengers is disturbing the peace, he has every right to get rid of the guy. True or false?"

"True."

"Then what does it take? Shall we vote on it?"

My voice lowered a notch, but I put an edge of steel to it. "Spider, I suggest that you calm down. Leave Monty out of this. It's really between us and Boris."

She snapped her head around. "All right. Then *you* throw him off. You've got an honorary Colombian police badge."

"You want me to use it for that?"

"Why not? That gives you more legal authority than Monty has."

"I don't think the Colombians had it in mind for me to—."

Spider stamped her foot. She had a short temper anyway, and now she was losing patience. "Well, then, Mr. Criminal Investigator, let me put it bluntly. I suggest that you get Boris Kolinski out of here for his own safety!"

Before I could respond, she turned and walked away.

That is exactly what I did not want to hear. My inner voice rose up at once: *You are going to have trouble with that one. Buddy, you had better defuse this keg of dynamite before it goes off in your face.*

The Fishers came up. "Did you see that ani flying past?" Greg asked.

I answered. "Yes. First one we've seen."

"Groove-billed ani," Beryl said excitedly, "cuckoo family. This place is terrific. We're going into the banana grove to look for birds. Give a whistle when dinner's ready."

Moments later, Joe Muck came up. "My legs have been cramped all day. Wanna jog?"

That was music to my ears. I joined him and away we ran.

As we loped alongside the banana trees, I saw Spider standing near the river bank, looking perplexed and uneasy.

CHAPTER 17

By the time darkness came—usually about six-thirty in the tropics—the Fishers had returned from birding, the Arden-Joneses from their walk, and Joe and I from jogging. Spider went in to the anteroom and approached Mo Briggle, then stopped.

Dana Briggle lay on the mat, sound asleep, oblivious to all the noise. That answered Spider's query and concern. She retreated.

Light from a single candle lit the room. Señora Bermudez brought a steaming pot of boiled chicken from below and placed it on the table. Nearby lay plates of pancakes, fried bananas, potatoes, and a bowl of boiled greens from a garden outside. The only persons missing were Boris and Señor Bermudez.

"Come and get it," Joe shouted in his melodic jesting tone. "And don't be piggy!"

Chris Arden-Jones laughed. "Can't help it, Joe. I'm famished."

We filled our plates, took coffee, tea or Coke, and sat on the floor along the edge of the room, backs to the wall.

Chris asked Adams: "Monty, where are we? Obviously, we didn't make it to the Indian village."

Monty replied: "Started too late. Be there tomorrow."

"Well, I'm glad the Bermudezes had this hostel handy. Saves us from sleeping with the crocodiles. What do these people do, actually? They're quite far out from civilization."

Adams answered very simply. "They think they're closer to it."

Carol Lynn: "What is that supposed to mean?"

Monty answered in a cryptic tone. "Think it over."

"That's silly. There is no running water."

Monty: "Whole river of it out there."

"It's not clean" She pointed to the river. Would you want to drink *that*? Lolita the laundress discharged three hours' worth of soap suds into it this morning."

"They can boil it if they need to."

"And they haven't any electricity. Just these lanterns and candles."

Monty grinned. "What would they use electricity for?"

Carol Lynn smiled in defeat. "A very interesting question, Monty. I would never have thought to ask it."

"They have plenty of free firewood. All they need."

Carol Lynn shook her head in dismay. "Then you actually think they're satisfied? Lolita didn't seem to be."

Monty shrugged his shoulders. "If they weren't, they probably wouldn't be here."

"You still haven't answered my question. What do they do?"

Monty responded. "You see the bananas? They run fruit up and down the river when they can find work. Or they take out logs."

Spider asked: "And animals?"

Adams didn't want to answer.

"What about eels?"

Monty shrugged. "I don't know."

She jumped on that. "Yes, you do!"

He shrugged again.

Beryl Fisher changed the subject. "Monty, have you ever heard of a white woman down here named Katherine

Messala?"

To that question, Monty had no answer. He lowered his eyes.

Beryl persisted. "Ever meet her?"

Still no answer.

"She was a friend of ours. She came down here to study the Huitoto. Do you know where she is?"

All eyes turned on Monty. Finally, he answered. "Best place to ask about people down here is the village."

She asked: "Why?"

Once again he evaded the question. "We'll be there tomorrow."

CHAPTER 18

Mo Briggle sat in a sullen mood, dabbing at his food. Spider asked about Dana.

"Better, thank you. We gave her some chicken broth. She's weak. We're going to try to get back to Florencia tomorrow."

"Back?" I asked. "You're giving up?"

All heads turned toward Mo.

"Yes, I've had to admit it. I was wrong to bring her here. Frankly, we hadn't expected all the hardships. She's just too fragile."

"Oh, bullshit," Spider erupted. "You men think every time a woman gets sick, you have to treat her like a hospital patient. Some women think that, too. She may be tougher than you are."

"Not tonight, she isn't," Mo responded. "She's sick."

"All right. What about in the morning? Every time a person makes a change from one culture to another, it takes a little getting used to. Is she homesick?"

"Not quite. Not that bad."

"Then let her speak for herself. She'll get better."

"Thanks, Spider. Nevertheless, we're going back." Mo seemed determined.

"Have you arranged it?" I asked.

"No. Not yet. Now, Barry, don't try to stop us again."

I ignored his admonition. "There's no taxi here. Not even a river taxi. No airport. No bus station."

"Maybe Monty can take us back."

I shook my head. "He's taking us downstream, Mo. Besides, it's a long pull upstream, against that current."

"Then maybe Bermudez. I don't care what it takes. I'm not going to endanger my wife..."

"Mo, she might be safer going on. Give that a little thought. The Indians have medicines. Then we eventually fly out of Leticia. She won't have to go back up the river at all."

Mo got up. "I still don't want any more of it! We're going back. Tomorrow! And that's that."

He went into the anteroom and sat beside his wife.

There was the sound of heavy feet on the steps and Boris came in, bellowing: "Where's the food?" He piled chicken, cakes and greens on a plate and sat on the floor.

Spider asked outright: "You're late. Where have you been?"

He answered between mouthfuls. "Went down to the corner drugstore."

"You lie. There's no drugstore within miles."

"No, honest. Nice place. Ice cold Budweiser—."

She scoffed. "You're hallucinating. You're going off the edge."

"I was talking with Bermudez. He owns this whole spread. Got it from the government last year in a coloniza- tion program. Raises bananas, sells hides, traps animals for zoos. The government is promoting settlement."

I held up a hand before Spider could explode. "Boris, I don't think you know yet that Spider is a member of an organization wanting to do away with zoos and keep ani- mals in the wild."

"Where nobody ever sees them?" Boris burped and looked at her. "You some kind of nut? Zoos are big money.

Animal trade's big money down here. There's millions of animals in the forest. Hell, they reproduce all the time. Bermudez has a contract, you might say, with the Indians. They go in and bring out what he needs, and he pays them for it."

Spider played it cool, out of character for her. "How does he know what he needs?"

"Market, sweetie. Market. Everybody wants everything. Zoos want live animals. Manufacturers want skins. Hospitals want animals to run tests on. Labs, pet stores, hell, it's a huge market out there. Worldwide. You're not going to stop that!"

Spider grinned and narrowed her eyes—body language for a serious threat. *"Oh, yes ... we ... will!"*

"Nuts. You're stupid, childish. Sentimental over a few monkeys. What are they? Nothing. Colombians don't care, and this is their country. They gotta eat. If you don't like it, get out!"

I cut in again before Spider could erupt. "I differ with you there, Boris. Colombians are damned proud of their country."

Boris: "That ain't what I heard."

"The people in Bogotá are setting up wildlife reserves all over the country. They've stopped the export of endangered species."

"That's a laugh! These guys can ship stuff out through channels the brass in Bogotá never heard of."

"Interesting. Tell us about it."

Spider had masked her fury long enough. "You stupid ass!"

Boris's head snapped toward her, eyes glowering. Before he could speak, Spider went on.

"I just came from Barranquilla, up north on the Caribbean coast. I went out to Isla de Salamanca National Park. They have a little museum there, and just inside the entrance is a big sign." She pulled a notebook from her pack, opened it up, flipped several pages and handed it to me. "I copied it down. Read this aloud so this bastard can understand what the hell is going on."

I read: *"Cuando la tecnología no tenga nada nuevo que ofrecer al hombre, aún continuará la naturaleza mostrándole sus maravillas.* Spider, this is terrific. Who wrote it?"

She kept her face straight. "Tell them what it says."

"Well it sounds better in Spanish. But it says, roughly, that when technology no longer has anything new to offer man, then nature will go right on showing him her wonders. Spider, who wrote this?"

"You want to know, but Boris doesn't."

"Go on," I urged. "Tell him anyway."

Boris snorted. Spider answered. "A government official named Eduardo Arango wrote it. A government *official*, you cheap shit. Did you get that? It's public policy. Now why don't you go some place and quietly drop dead!"

Boris spat out his response. "Sentimental trash. Just like you."

Spider started to move, as though to eviscerate him. I rose between them and spoke as gently as I could. "We didn't really come down here to tear each other apart. You've got a right to argue, but when you get physical you disturb the general peace, and I want it stopped. We have a big day tomorrow. We have to put up the hammocks before we can go to bed."

Spider retreated. Boris grumbled. The rest of the group sighed with relief.

We rose and strung hammocks on pegs in the anteroom, one above another, three high, in three rows.

When we finished, Joe Muck stepped back to look. "If someone on top falls out, he takes two others with him! Can I sleep under the house?"

I asked. "Have you slept with cows, chickens and dogs before?"

Joe answered: "Yes. Ruins your whole night. Forget I asked."

Within an hour the weary passengers had crawled into their hammocks and the candle had been extinguished.

Joe whispered so that all could hear. "Good night, Spider. May I hold your dagger for you?"

"Shut up!" she fired back. "And go to sleep!"

CHAPTER 19

For the next few hours, or at least after all the adjustments to hammock sleeping had been made, we all succumbed to exhaustion. The chickens, children, dogs and cows also slept soundly.

Until about three a.m...

It started with a dog coming up the stairs, its toenails clatter-clattering on the wooden steps. Silence. Sniffing sounds, as though the dog sought supper scraps on the floor. Another dog clattered up the steps, followed by sniffing and belligerent growling. They clattered down the steps again.

If this did not wake the sleeping humans, it must have lifted some of them part way up from the subconscious.

Then at three-thirty the questions began.

Perched somewhere outside, probably on the fence, a night bird of some kind—or was it a tree frog?—issued a short staccato call that resembled the human question "What?"

It may have taken some persons ten seconds or so to come from dream to reality and ask who's asking "What?" Or what's asking "What?"

The intervals between whats endured for perhaps twenty seconds, enough to sear the waking mind with the question "When is the next one?"

At four a rooster began to crow on the fence outside, demolishing the notion that roosters vocalized only at dawn. After a while, the calls of the first rooster set off the crowing of others, until a chorus split the night air.

At five, the horse neighed. Then the call of a young calf issued faintly from the direction of the banana grove. How nice, thought the groggy sleeper. How rustic. Within seconds, the call of the mother cow, directly beneath the house, reverberated in this alcove echo chamber like the roar of a fog horn ten feet distant.

Dawn came to an Amazon finca.

The "What?" bird went away. Roosters continued crowing. Cow and calf mooed at two-minute intervals until five thirty.

Joe Muck lay there and took it for as long as he could. Finally, he sat up and growled with the force of a grizzly bear: "SHUT UP!"

The others stirred.

Joe dived out of his high hammock in a graceful arc to land on his feet.

"Everybody up!" The cheerful, melodic voice again. "Form a line for your malaria pills!"

CHAPTER 20

I rose and went down the stairs out into the *madrugada*. This time of day, before dawn in the tropics, was a favorite with me. I wanted to get out and be swallowed up by these tangled woods.

Joe came up behind me. "Want to jog?"

"No, Joe," I replied. "I just want to walk slowly and listen."

"Me, too," he responded.

We ambled down the pathway past the banana trees and followed a faint trail in the darkness, using a small pocket flashlight when we couldn't see what was below, ahead, or above. Joe promptly ran into a huge spider web across the trail, one that had probably been woven some time during the night. He brushed off the cobwebs, and we watched the spider take refuge on the other side of the tree trunk.

We listened. Creatures that had slept all night were awakening. We could hear it. We couldn't see it. But it was happening all around us. Then the creatures that had been awake all night began to move to places of refuge where they could sleep all day.

At this hour, those night and day worlds overlapped. A sense of enormous energy pervaded the forest. Not a lyrical one, however—no joyous songs of finches, robins and orioles that wake the temperate deciduous forest.

The cool air, damp and reeking of decay, seemed to me refreshing. As daylight began, wisps of fog rode the breezes, sifted among trees, or curled across the river surface.

The endless high-pitched buzz of insects seemed, as always, distant and muted, mixed only with occasional chirps. Now and then we were startled by a loud crack, as though some heavy branch from the tree tops had fallen to the forest floor.

Or perhaps an echo of thunder after a distant rain. Or a muffled chorus of howler monkeys, their rhythmic chants distorted by distance and currents of air.

With better light, we turned and jogged along the river shore, over tricky and uneven footing. Returning through the forest, we found Spider and the Fishers, creeping among the giant trees, seeking glimpses of any night animals that might still prowl through the woods.

I asked Beryl: "Are you feeling better today?"

"Yes," she replied. "Much better, Barry. Thank you."

As we returned to the little hut, Spider saw Señor Bermudez going to the dock. Down she went to join him.

Climbing into the hut, we found Mo Briggle and the Arden-Joneses attending Dana, who appeared to have waked in good condition. Still pale, with shadows under her eyes, she rose.

"Barry," she said, "before you ask, I'm a lot better. I'm glad we came. And we're going all the rest of the way with you. So there!"

I grinned and gave her a thumbs-up sign. "Three cheers for you, Dana." I looked at Mo. He was grinning with obviously profound relief.

Helped by Carol Lynn, Dana walked down the steps and out along the river's edge.

Boris Kolinski remained in his hammock, unperturbed, oblivious to all the noise. We roused him and began to take down hammocks. All the others, except Spider, soon came back.

After Señora Bermudez had filled the breakfast table, we feasted: leftover scraps of chicken, scrambled eggs, fried bananas, coffee, tea and Coke.

Scarcely had we started when a furious shriek sounded from outside. Feet pounded heavily up the wooden steps, and Spider, beet red in the face, burst into the room. She drew herself up before us and spoke in a bold and imperious tone.

"We have an impostor among us!"

I shuddered.

We were so suddenly taken aback by the severity of the announcement that, for a few moments, no one said a word. Then Carol Lynn gasped. "What on earth are you talking about?"

I knew what was about to happen. I knew what she had discovered. It was something I had suspected all along but tried to keep it suppressed. My only course was to try to calm her before she exploded into bits and pieces. I waved my palm outward and down, in a calming gesture. "You'd better sit and have some breakfast."

Spider would not be calmed. "I knew it from the moment I laid eyes on him. I knew there was something wrong. He's a liar! That's what he is, a goddamned baldfaced liar! Barry can tell you."

All eyes turned to me. I simply stared Spider down and pointed toward the table. "Breakfast?"

She seemed on the verge of becoming incoherent. Rage filled her eyes. She trembled with fury. Then she pointed to Boris Kolinski.

"He's not an anthropologist. He never *was* an anthropologist. He told us he was, and *you* may have believed it. But I didn't. I knew there was something fishy about this son of a bitch. Now I've found out—."

Her words tumbled over one another. Joe Muck interrupted. "Spider, would you get hold of yourself? Calm down and speak slowly so we can understand. Are you talking about Boris?"

"Yes. I am talking about Mister Kolinski—if that is his real name. How are we to know *who* he is, when he lied to us about *what* he is?"

"All right!" Joe said. "Calm down! What's wrong? What's the matter?"

She turned to me and pointed a finger of accusation."Barry knew it all along. He knew something was wrong with this guy. Why didn't you say something? Why did you let it go on this long?"

I took my time to reply, letting her fume in silence for a moment. Then I said, speaking slowly and deliberately, with spaces between my words for effect: *"Because it was none of my business."*

She snorted. "Well, I'm making it *my* business! I'll tell all the rest of you what he is. He's a *land buyer*! A goddamned land buyer! Bermudez told me. With sign language. Maps drawn on the ground. I'll tell you what Mister Kolinski wants to do. He wants to buy these people out!"

She paused. The echoes of her blast and the meaning of her accusation reverberated around the room.

Carol Lynn: "What do you mean? Why should he want to buy this poor land?"

"It's *not* poor. It has trees. He wants to cut them down and sell them. Wipe out thousands of potential new medicines out there. The animals... You heard him. He wants to make belts and handbags out of their hides. He wants to find gold and oil."

"Here? Along the river?"

Spider's rage grew with every sentence. "Of course! That's why they're cutting everything down. The biggest tropical forest in the world that's what he's after. Wants to make it the *littlest* tropical forest. What do you think of that?"

She stopped, breathless.

No one said a word. All eyes drifted to Boris, who sat with aplomb, stuffing himself with chicken, as though he had heard nothing at all.

Finally, licking his fingers, he said: "Chicken's real good, don't you think?"

Mo exploded with laughter. "I can't help laughing. Spider, what the devil are you so screwed up for? So the guy's a bastard. I'm a bastard, too—to hear my associates tell it. I lie. Everybody lies at one time or other. So what's new? He sounds to me like a normal, red-blooded American capitalist. What are you going to do about it?"

Spider stamped her foot. "Get rid of him..."

Mo was in good form, unstoppable. "If he wants to kill animals down here, yes, I'd like to get rid of him, too. I want to examine those forests for new medicines. That's my business. I'll help you wrap an anaconda around him. But Spider, you gotta take into account one very important thing. He must be found guilty first. There has to be a crime."

Spider seemed like a balloon about to burst. "Crime against *humanity*. What bigger crime is there?"

Carol Lynn ventured, "Really, Spider, he's a human being. You can't go on like this. He has rights."

"Animals have rights, too!"

Greg Fisher spoke. "You want us to lynch him, Spider?"

It seemed a harsh idea for someone so gentle.

Beryl Fisher reinforced it. "We could tie him in vines and leave him in the forest for the jaguars he wants to kill. That would be poetic justice."

They were all mad. I thought the conversation a bit out of hand, gathering strength from Spider's outbursts. I held up my hand and used a moderate tone that, in this environment, garnered more attention than another shout.

"We thank you, Spider, for your revelation. I suggest that you pick up some breakfast and eat. We have a long ride, and we're about to leave."

She moved to speak, then controlled her anger, turned on her heel and took a plate. I went on.

"It is clear that Boris does not have the same objective on this trip that we do. Before we go any farther into ways to murder him, we ought to hear what he has to say. If he'd care to add his side to this frenzy."

Boris looked around at the rest of them. He wiped his fingers again. "Would it matter to these freaks?"

Joe growled, but said nothing.

I said: "It would matter to me."

Boris went on, as though addressing only me. "Yes, I've been a land buyer for a long time. I helped open big tracts south of the Amazon. Those lands have people on them now. Productive people. Hardworking Brazilians who have jobs at last. With money to feed their families. I haven't the slightest intention of buying up the whole tropical forest, for Christ's sake."

Spider sputtered: "*That's* a new policy!"

"I am only interested in land along rivers. That's where people live. Right now, they're farming and grazing—most useless thing you can do in the tropics. You know that!" He glanced at Spider fleetingly. "Anyone with an ounce of brains knows that. Cattle don't have a pound of meat on their bones. Nothing grows but papayas. Nobody buys papayas. Pineapple? Pitiful. Better pineapples elsewhere.

"No—the real treasure down here is the native forest. Wood's in demand everywhere. Animals in demand. I told you about pet stores, hospital labs. And what the hell? The forest grows back! Look at all the rain they get. The animals reproduce. What's all this bitching about? What the hell is wrong if we buy a few acres and leave the rest alone?"

To the other members of the group there seemed no way to answer him, and for a few moments his question met with silence. Even Spider had given up. But I could not let this pass.

"I think they feel, Boris, that yours would not be the only company to come down here. If you succeed, others will succeed. One road leads to more roads. One village leads to more villages. That's what will wipe out the rain forest."

Nobody moved, except Boris, who nonchalantly finished his plate of chicken. Spider wore a smile of grim satisfaction at my words.

Joe said: "That's telling him, buddy!"

Boris sneered: "Oh, grow up, kid."

Joe moved to rise. "I've taken all I'm going to take from—."

I put out a leg, over which Joe tripped and fell back to the floor.

Joe had a pained look. "What did you do that for?"

I answered: "I am not going to have any violence around here, and anyone who wants to test me on this can do so any time."

Joe subsided.

I rose. "We must go. But I want you all to keep in mind that the law says he can do what he's doing—whether we like it or not."

Spider got to her feet. "Well, Colombian law doesn't require me to ride in the same boat with him. Or in the same *seat*."

I tried again. "If you will just calm yourself. I think it is clear that Boris has nothing against any of us, and in good taste we should regard him as another member of our little group. Let him call you names. You only dignify them by getting mad. Attack him and you become the criminal, not him. If you don't want to go with us in the canoe, you can swim, but I think you'd find the crocodiles worse than Boris. If you want to rent a canoe and navigate the gravel bars yourself, we wish you luck. Or you can go back to Florencia, which I estimate is thirty miles behind us."

Now, of all people, Dana Briggle spoke. Her voice remained weak.

"No. Not that. I thought yesterday I would be the first to go back. Sometime during the night I got a grip on myself. I said if I went back, that would be proof that I can't stand up to anything. If I don't know how to swim, I'll learn right here in the Orteguaza. Piranhas be damned!"

The room filled with applause. The tension had broken.

Spider said: "Bravo, Dana!" She turned toward Mo. "You *see*! I told you that's what she'd say."

"All right," I said, "if Dana can pull herself together, so can everyone. Boris is only a messenger employed by a company ."

"Company?" Joe asked.

"ILB. International Land Buyers. He's in the Real Estate Division."

Joe repeated it slowly. "International Land Buyers Real Estate Division. ILBRED! Ha! Ha! Ha! That fits!"

Boris ignored the remark and continued eating.

We rose, put our dishes and Coke bottles on the table, picked up packs and descended the stairs. There we said adios to the Bermudezes, into whose hands Monty Adams pressed the requisite pesos. We went down the bank to the canoe.

Spider stopped. "Barry, I am willing to go along with you as far as I can. But I am not going to sit for another minute crammed in beside that bastard!"

I smiled. "If you want to change his mind, I'd think that would be the best place in the whole canoe to sit."

"Change his mind? Pshaw! He's hopeless."

"All right, trade seats then."

Spider gave up and went down the slope, fingers fiercely clamped to her wide-brimmed hat and dilapidated day pack. Then, suddenly, she stopped.

"Who is that?"

A bent old Indian, black hair cut with a bowl shape, a jaguar necklace around his neck, stood at the canoe, greeting each passenger as they exchanged names. Each time, he pointed to himself and said: "Palkuh."

Spider went down and shook hands with him. She pointed to herself and said, "Spider." Then she pointed to him. "You Correguaje?"

He nodded rapidly, and laughed, saying: "Correguaje! Correguaje!"

She boarded the canoe. I came up, shook hands with Palkuh, identified myself and got aboard. Monty said to us all: "This is Red Chief, Palkuh Mamha-uh. He is the chief of a village not far from where we're goin'. He's on his way from Bogotá back home. He'll be with us for a few days."

Monty turned and helped Palkuh aboard. The old Indian went to the rear of the canoe and sat on a coiled rope.

Joe Muck immediately rose. "No chief is going to sit on a rope while I'm around. Monty, he's a guest of honor. Tell him to come forward and take my seat."

He motioned for the chief to come forward. The chief bowed his head, smiled, waved his hand back and forth, and launched into a string of unintelligible words.

Joe repeated his offer, this time more firmly. Same response.

Monty interceded. "He says you'ins is important guests. He cain't take yer seat. But he 'preciates yer offer."

Joe bowed and sat down.

"That was a wonderful gesture," I said to Joe. "Red Chief will not forget it."

A few moments later, Boris came ambling down the slope. As he was about to board the canoe, he stopped dead still as he glimpsed the Red Chief in back. His eyes took on a frigid glare, his face wreathed in a scowl of contempt.

"That's Red Chief," said Joe. "Go back and introduce yourself, Boris."

Boris had frozen in position, scowling darkly. Then he looked at Monty and snarled. "What is that savage doing on this canoe?"

Monty's turned his eyes away and said nothing.

From the way he looked, I felt that Boris had met Palkuh somewhere before. It was only a feeling, but there was something sinister between those two... Boris snorted in contempt, climbed aboard and wedged himself in beside Spider.

The guide climbed up into the scout's seat on the prow. Eduardo left the supply boat, which José would pilot as he had yesterday, and took his place at the motor.

Bermudez poled us off, smiled and waved goodbye.

Up in the cottage built on stilts, we could see Señora Bermudez peering out the window, watching our departure.

CHAPTER 21

The journey down the Orteguaza River now became more tense. Boris and Spider did not talk at all. She tried to look in the opposite direction. He sat with an angry countenance. The rest of the passengers, glaring a bit themselves as the revelation about Boris sank in, could only puzzle, as I did, at his hostility toward the Red Chief.

Once again, the canoe glided beneath high walls of giant trees. Then it veered to the center of the river, and abruptly toward the opposite bank, following hidden channels and paths of least resistance.

Joe Muck, ever the optimist, broke the gloom. "I say, count your blessings. If we'd had a typical tropical downpour on that corrugated roof last night, we'd all be deaf today. Dana, you all right?"

Dana Briggle sat in an upright position, still pale and with shadows beneath her eyes. Head up, she watched the river with determination.

"Joe," she said, with a forward thrust of the lower lip, "I am going to enjoy every minute of today. Thank you very much."

"That's the spirit, kid!"

Spider forced a laugh. "Who's calling whom a 'kid'?"

"Spider," Joe countered, "you're just like a mother to me. Would you like to get off at the next stop?"

Spider leaned over the edge and watched for eels.

Carol Lynn Arden-Jones, elegant as ever with her string of pearls, turned to me with a puzzled look. "Palkuh seems distinguished. High born, as we would say. If we are to be guests of these people, how should we act?"

I smiled. "Very simple, Carol Lynn. Like guests."

"What are they like? How do we approach them?"

"Same as the Red Chief. With respect. He's a Correguaje."

She interrupted. "How did you pronounce that?"

"Corre-GWAH-hay," I responded. "The first thing you tell yourself is what they are not. They are not painted savages. Not dumb. I always approach them as equals."

Carol Lynn drew back in surprise. "Equals? Do you mean they've been educated?"

"A formal education is not required to make one equal."

Carol Lynn blushed slightly. "Please forgive me. I'm awfully sorry."

"There are probably schools down here. However, the Correguajes are undoubtedly very well versed in how to survive in the rain forest."

"Cheers, Barry! That's quite right."

"In their domain, we follow their rules."

"That's the point of my question. How shall we know what the rules are?"

She needed a lesson in conversing with Indians, so I did what I could. "Very simple. You just ask the Indians. Directly."

"How can we? Do they speak English?"

"Probably not. You can still ask."

"I see your point. Quite. We can all speak sign language."

"You two know how. Look puzzled. Use your fingers. Act out what you want to do."

Carol Lynn set about practicing quietly to herself. Mo Briggle, caught up by this exchange, asked: "Anyone know how many Indians live in the Amazon?"

I shrugged. I'd grappled with that problem myself. "The figure generally given is a million. This forest has thousands of rivers running through it. The people live sometimes way back where no one sees them, and they move every few years. Some are friendly to outsiders, some hostile. How can you get a census of that?"

Joe Muck had been waiting impatiently to ask his number one question. "Are they headhunters? Are they cannibals?"

I answered: "Some, maybe. Does the Red Chief look like a cannibal?"

"That's just it. Of course, he doesn't. How am I supposed to know what a cannibal looks like?"

Mo Briggle: "I can tell you. I have a few in my office."

I said: "All we have to do is relax. Do as we're told."

"Mix with the natives?"

"If they respond. Yes. We also pay attention to sacred spots—a tree, a spring, a burial plot. These people are probably as emotional about their ancestors as we are about ours, so we take care not to go where we aren't supposed to."

Carol Lynn dropped her shoulders. "How can we know all that?"

"You can't. Watch for piles of rock, painted sticks, bundles in trees—I'm guessing. I don't know. Just step lightly. Don't pick up things like that. Behave yourself."

Joe: "Behave? I don't like that."

I grinned. "I didn't think you would."

Boris: "Oh, come on. I've been among these people. You're just whistling up the wrong alley. Forget 'em. They're just naked savages. You can't do anything with 'em."

"Have you tried?" I asked.

No response.

Carol Lynn responded. "Why you can, too, do something with them. You can educate them."

"Why? Get 'em a college education, they come right back here. Waste of time."

Carol Lynn recoiled. "Boris! That's a beastly thing to say."

"They're all primitive. They want to stay that way. You ain't seen as many Indians as I have."

She shook her head and gave up. I watched what faces I could see and sensed a revulsion at Boris's callous attitude toward the natives. The conversation died. My mind began to smoulder at the implications of what he had said, and I felt that others were reacting the same way. It was getting to the point where we couldn't find anything constructive to talk about with Boris.

The hours passed. Erratic river currents bore us southward. Twice we grazed a gravel bar, startled by the sudden sound in our ears and swerve of the boat. Dana did not shriek this time. She clutched Mo's hand just the same.

Clouds rose again to the zenith, billowing above the trees in giant mushrooms. Rain soon fell, but more benignly than yesterday and not in such furious torrents. The curtain of falling water passed and went on down the river.

Joe Muck looked back at the Red Chief, asleep on the canvas. "I'm still not sure how we talk to these Amazon tribes people. I mean, there's a big gulf of language, customs, everything."

I answered: "We're human beings."

"Aw, Barry..."

"I'm serious. The frailties we have as human beings, they have, too. You get mad. They get mad. You laugh. They laugh. You get sick. They get sick. You have a bruised knee. They have bruised knees. Talk about these things. Show. Demonstrate. You have a lot in common."

Joe seemed a bit relieved. "Okay. I get the general thrust. But hell, I don't know a word of Correguaje."

"Language is not a barrier, it's only a tool. You find other ways to communicate. You can ask them their words for trees, river, and so on. They'll be glad to tell you. Get it?"

"I'm getting the message."

"If all else fails, try English. You just talked to the Red Chief."

"Come on. I'm serious!"

"So am I. Go right up to them. Speak any language you want. You'll think them shy and withdrawn at first. Everybody's like that. Talk to them. Laugh a little. Every human being can laugh. Make use of it. They'll warm up. So will we."

Joe hid his face. "I'm too shy."

Spider laughed loudly, her first laugh of the morning.

I asked: "Did you bring the gifts Monty suggested in his letter?"

Joe recounted the list. "Crayons, pens, pencils, drawing pads. Pictures of the houses and towns in which we live. Picture books. Earrings, combs, food seasonings. Fish hooks, nylon cord, matches..."

"They're human beings," I said. "What else? Different origin myths, maybe."

Joe brightened. "Hey! I want to know about that. Did they come from Big Anaconda?"

"Joe, you are hereby elected to find out."

He rolled his eyes to the trees above. "I walked right into that one all by myself."

We stopped on a sand bar and had a snack that passed for lunch. After that, an hour of sullen silence as we went on down stream, the canoe swerving from one channel to another.

About midafternoon we pulled up to a primitive dock on the left bank of the river. We saw other canoes, large and small, tied to posts, but no human beings, no village.

"Good news," Joe said. "Our supply canoe is here."

"The baggage and supplies are already taken to the village," Monty added.

Downstream, a small hut, on posts anchored to the bank, jutted out over the river. "What is that?" Joe asked.

I answered. "You want to ask in public?"

Joe responded. "That's a shit house?"

"In polite society we call it a loo, a Johnny can. I was trying to find a word suitable for our cultured society on this cruise ship."

"Where's the cultured society?"

Spider laughed and joked: "He wouldn't know it if he saw it!"

"Well, well, everybody!" Joe added, obsessed with the perched rest room. "Who says they don't have running water down here!"

With that introduction, we disembarked and started up the trail to meet the Correguajes.

CHAPTER 22

The trail led up into the forest along a small stream, whose crystal waters bounced over rocks and roots.

"Wow!" Joe exclaimed, taking position behind Monty and me. "It's sure good to be walking again! My legs are paralyzed."

We stepped over roots and rocks as well as places where the trail had been washed out by the almost daily torrential downpours. The forest was less dense and more shrubby than that along the river's edge. We could see some distance into it, but no sign of wildlife or of human habitation.

In half an hour we came to another log structure built on beams that spanned the creek.

Joe asked: "Another one?"

I nodded.

Behind the loo, the stream had been dammed by a collection of logs, and behind this structure lay a small pond.

"A swimmin' hole!" Joe said. "These people are civilized!"

We entered a clearing of hard-packed barren soil surrounded by raised thatch-roofed huts and large communal buildings closed at the end with bamboo slats. A small boy carrying a stick, on his way from one building to another, stopped to watch the newcomers. A girl in a knee-length gingham dress ran up to Joe Muck and took his hand.

"Well, I'll be damned." He lifted her up. "What's your name?"

No answer. He pointed a finger at himself. "Joe." He pointed a finger at her.

"Tiata," she said, trying to get a better look at his piranha tee shirt.

"What does that mean?"

Monty came up and answered. "She's well named, that 'un. *Tiata* means river. They call her that 'cuz she's always on the move."

A young man, probably in his late twenties, approached. He had pure black hair falling casually over his forehead. He wore a plain white tee shirt, shorts, and a ten-strand necklace of small beads. He walked up to Monty and they exchanged some words unintelligible to the rest of us. The Arden-Joneses pressed forward to listen. His language had a nasal and tonal aspect, some words ending on an upbeat, some down, some explosive.

Monty turned to us and said: "This is the chief. His name is Manyuco. He wants to shake hands with you, and learn your names."

We strode up and took turns shaking his hand, adding a few upbeat words of our own. He smiled. We smiled. Joe shifted little Tiata to his left side so he could shake hands.

The Wyoming cowboy stood in awe. The chief had a handsome face: dark, wide, high cheekbones, narrow nose with flaring nostrils, square jaw, and eyes that seemed little more than slits. Though short in stature, he had a stocky, well-muscled body, with powerful arms. He held himself straight-backed, with a princely bearing.

Manyuco smiled as he shook hands, saying one word in English to each guest: "Wel—come."

Other Correguajes arrived and stood behind the chief. With Monty's help, the chief introduced them in turn. The chief's wife, also short and dark, had a furrowed brow and dark serious eyes. Her upper teeth, though not visible, jutted out over the lower. Her long pure black hair flowed around her neck and chest and down her back. She wore a simple cotton dress printed with flowering roses.

"A floral print!" Dana Briggle whispered. "I'm home!"

Three strands of beads hung closely to her neck, one of dark wood balls, one of small shell sections, one of white plastic poppet beads. She smiled when she saw Carol Lynn, the only guest who also wore a necklace. They examined each other's adornments with great interest.

The chief next introduced his father, a short man with an infectious grin and merry slit eyes. His hair perched like a black bowl on his head, but his stubble of beard consisted of white hair. He bowed and smiled, revealing two remaining teeth, and spoke melodic words of welcome to which each arrival responded in melodic English, Boris included.

Suddenly a shout went up from the Indians. Behind them, the Red Chief came slowly up the trail, limping, walking with the help of a stick. They flocked to him, embraced him en masse, and led him to one of the huts.

That over, Monty said: "Chief Manyuco will lead you to yer huts. Tonight he will give us our dinner, which we will eat on the ground over there near the kitchen."

The chief led the newcomers to their quarters: Briggles a hut nearest the pond, Fishers next in line, Arden-Joneses third hut in the row. Next to that, at the apex of the clearing, sat the chief's hut. In this abode, larger than the others, Boris, Joe and I would set up floor pads and netting.

The chief led Spider to his father's hut, which sat just behind his own. The father showed her around. Then he grinned and bowed and went off to a large covered work space opposite the kitchen. There he and his grandchildren had set up hammocks for the duration of the visitors' stay.

Each Correguaje hut perched on posts about hip high. A log with steps hacked in it leaned against each entrance. A visitor climbing up to the hut had to negotiate these tricky gouged-out stairsteps with care.

Boris, Joe and I went into our hut, laid out our air mattresses on the floor and suspended mosquito netting from ropes attached to ceiling beams. Netting, tucked in on all sides, would be a good defense against mosquitoes as well as insects at floor level.

Boris departed. Joe and I each took a pocket full of gifts and went out to explore the village. Little Tiata leaped up on Joe again. A boy, nearly a teenager, led us around.

Joe pointed to himself. "Joe."

The boy pointed to himself. "Aunamunh."

Then they saw the white cakes, spread out on the roofs. "Pizza!" Joe exclaimed.

The cakes appeared at first to be pizza dough. If so, their diameter exceeded any pizza he had ever seen. They had been laid up on thatch roofs that came nearly to the ground.

"Probably some kind of bread," I corrected, "set out to dry in the sun. Looks like manioc to me."

Nearby, a wide shallow bowl, nestled in a structure of stick crosspieces, held a mass of the white material.

A group of children came running toward us, followed by their mothers.

"Oh, oh," Joe said, "the word is out. The visitors have presents!"

The mothers clutched up younger children and held them in their arms. Crayons, pens and paper exchanged hands. The children ran away, Tiata and Aunamunh included. Moments later, they returned.

I was fascinated by the handsome features of the Correguajes. The faces of the women, well rounded, had clear-cut lines, high cheekbones, flaring nostrils, and dark eyes that denoted compassion and understanding. Not unlike Spanish-speaking Colombians I'd met. All wore cotton dresses, sleeved or sleeveless. Each had a bearing as stately as the regal composure of their chief.

Yet they giggled and tittered and spoke their rapid-fire musical dialect, sometimes bursting out in a chorus of laughter. Men strode up, their bearing as stately. They wore white or printed shirts with khaki trousers. One had on a Colombian armed forces military cap, sharp-pointed in the front and back. The children wore mostly dresses or shorts; some sported headdresses of green parrot feathers. They watched every movement the newcomers made.

After a few moments the Arden-Joneses and Spider joined the group. For the next hour the village echoed with the sounds of squealing children, laughing adults, and barking dogs.

Spider came up to me. "Where's Kolinski?"

I shook my head. "He didn't tell us where he was headed."

She growled: "I know where that son-of-a-bitch has gone."

"No, you don't," I responded.

"Oh, yes I do. He's sizing up land to buy. Wildlife to make shoes out of."

"Spider," I tried to caution her, "if you start meddling in—."

Irritation showed from her temples to her jaw. Her face reddened with anger again. "I'm going out after him."

This charred my soul. "Spider! You just arrived. You don't know this forest. It's easy to get lost, and if you don't believe it, try it. You can get attacked by just about anything out there."

"Jaguars prowl at night, not in the daytime." she snapped back. "You heard Monty."

"Don't bet on it. When you're around, they go on red alert both day and night."

"Oh, thank you, Barry. That's the nicest thing anyone ever said to me."

"I suggest you confine your encounters with Boris to times when we are around to save him."

She harrumphed. "You're sweet. But I want to know what that bastard's up to, and I intend to find out. It's my job to handle this situation. You keep out of it."

She was getting too negative for comfort. Too asser-
tive. "Must I remind you ?"

"No, Mr. Criminal Investigator, you don't have to remind me of your authority. But I have rights, too, and where
I go is not everybody's business."

"Spider, if you are going to get into an encounter with
Boris, I am going to be there for the sake of safety. I will
not have violence on this trip."

"How will you stop me? Handcuff me?"

"I rely on your intelligence."

"You think I have some?"

"I certainly hope so."

She stopped, flustered. Abruptly she turned on her
heel and left without a word. This made me mad. Now my
trip had become one of watching over Spider. That is distinctly not what I came down here for.

Why don't you just let her go? my inner voice asked. *Let
her get into trouble? Serve her right. But no. You say she's too mad.
Incoherent. Don't kid yourself. She knows exactly what she's doing.*

That's what bothered me.

The Correguajes, having befriended everyone, showed
us around the village: the huge kitchen structure, with fires
and boiling pots attended by women on their haunches, huts
of the villagers, the bathing pool, and work rooms for food
processing. In one of the latter we saw a small dugout canoe, about as long as a hammock, filled with the same white
"corn meal" Joe and I had seen.

By the end of the tour, Joe had become convinced that
none of these people resembled what Boris had called a "naked savage."

"What a dumb ass," Joe muttered to himself. Then
he, too, realized that Kolinski had disappeared.

CHAPTER 23

Spider did not pursue Kolinski after all. It must have taken heroic effort to stay put. But I knew I could not control her for very long. After the tour of the village, I told her that I appreciated her staying with us.

"Just bidin' my time," she said, with a snarl on her lips. "I'm just deciding what to do if Kolinski shows up for dinner. Hit him with something? Dump ashes over his head? Or just get up and stomp out? No, that would offend the Indians. It's their dinner for us and he's an invited guest, too."

"You can't do anything about that."

"I can get up in a huff and go eat in my hut."

"That would be childish. It would give Boris a laugh to see you twitching with anger at him. Make him feel proud of what he'd done."

The more she thought about it, the madder she got. "You're right. Why must I use my valuable trip time thinking about that bastard?"

Bravo! You're making some headway cooling her down.

I didn't for a minute believe that.

At sundown, we converged on the kitchen compound. Joe, of all people, appeared wearing a bead necklace.

"Don't any one laugh," he cautioned as they broke out in laughter.

Carol Lynn, the resident necklace expert, asked: "Where did you get that?"

"This is a badge of great honor. The chief gave it to me."

"Jolly good! How did you rate that? You must be frightfully important."

"I gave him a picture of Yellowstone National Park, and he gave me this! I swore I'd never wear a necklace."

"Quite right. Marlboro men don't, do they?"

"Nah. But just you reckon! This makes me somebody. Nobody else on Mitchell Street—that's where I live in Laramie—will have one of *these*! Looks all right, huh?"

We arranged ourselves on the ground around a "table-cloth" of freshly cut banana leaves. All the visitors except one.

Spider informed them in cautious tones: "I'll tell you what I saw. I saw our Mister Kolinski leaving the village at four this afternoon. He went with two of the Indians down the trail toward the dock and the river. No doubt they will take him to see what neighboring fincas and villages he can buy."

Joe sighed: "There goes another thousand acres of rain forest."

Carol Lynn asked: "You're sure?"

Spider snarled. "What else would a land buyer be up to? He has to work fast. He has lots of territory to cover."

"Perhaps—."

"I'll tell you what else I saw. Just before he left the village, he took one of those ever-present bottles of you know what out of his briefcase. He gave each Indian a drink. They guzzled it down and giggled and guzzled another. Then they wrapped their arms around him and led him away as though he were Santa Claus."

Carol Lynn's disgust showed on her face. "That is really quite abhorrent. I must say I cannot imagine anyone so uncouth. It's very well known what spirits do to native tribes."

Spider slapped the leaf in front of her. "We've got to stop him. The world has lost too goddam much forest already. Somebody has got to make a stand, and this looks like one helluva good place to start. We may not be experts in getting rid of people, but I don't care. It must happen, and now is a perfect time."

Greg Fisher agreed. "I'll be glad to do it. But try to catch him. He's gone all the time."

Joe Muck frowned. "What do you want to do? Murder him?"

Beryl Fisher answered: "I'd love to!"

Dana Briggle echoed: "So would I."

Mo added: "Well, it wouldn't exactly be murder. Surely there's some quicksand around here. We can go on a walk with him, friendly like, while he's drunk, and—."

Spider didn't think much of that idea. "He'd catch on. He expects us to do something like that."

Joe had an idea. "If we can borrow a blow gun and get just the right kind of dart—." He left the sentence unfinished, but they got the meaning.

Spider didn't like that either. "That makes the Indians accomplices. We've got to do it ourselves. Shrewd-like."

Chris Arden-Jones registered surprise. "Spider! I believe you're getting serious. I think you'd really do such a thing!"

Spider: "This is no goddam time to be namby-pamby. You know what he's up to. Wouldn't you?"

"I thought you were joking at first. Now I'm not so sure."

"That was then," Joe answered. "This is now."

"Well, perhaps I would like to hear of it... I admit he's driving us barmy. He's not a savory character. Is there no other way to stop him?"

"Probably. What do you suggest?"

"Colombian government, that sort of thing?"

Joe answered. "Right now, the Colombian government is a thousand miles away."

"I know what we can do," Greg offered. "Let's find his rum and dump it. Without that he's done for."

Spider: "That is the best idea I've heard in—."

Secretly, I was enjoying this conversation. But it was beginning to get a bit too serious for my taste. I held up a hand to change the subject. "I would like to hear more about your plans for inflicting mayhem on Boris, but if you look over there toward the kitchen, dinner's coming."

CHAPTER 24

Three Correguaje women, including the chief's wife, laid before us fiber platters of—well, of what?

"That looks good!" Joe exclaimed. "What is it?"

When the baskets and trays of food had all been set down, Monty Adams named their contents. "That there's catfish. Pirarucú next to it—comes from a big fish three meters long. There's a bowl of boiled bananas. Them trays have pieces of yuca. These here dishes have seeds and fruit from the trees around here. Next to them's toasted grubs. Behind them, I think, well, I ain't sure."

Joe jumped in. "I'll tell you what they are. They look like ants to me."

I couldn't tell just how much Monty was putting us on. A conspicuous silence settled over the table.

Finally, Joe commented: "If anything moves, I'm going to shoot it."

I responded. "It's all very nutritious, Joe. You've seen how healthy the people are."

"I'm healthy, too, and I want to stay that way." He screwed up his face, and his voice turned plaintive. "Do we have to eat everything?"

Monty Adams pointed out that the Chief and his wife and father, along with Palkuh, would soon arrive and then the meal would commence.

Answering Joe, I said: "Manyuco and his family will be watching every move we make. This is a meal in our honor. Very elegant by their standards. Perhaps even by ours."

"You're comparing this to pizza?"

"Remember that you are a guest of honor. Would you like to know the penalty for not eating what the chief sets before you?"

"No. But I'd like to know the penalty for throwing up."

Spider asked: "Are we going to wait for Kolinski?"

I answered: "He may not even be here."

"Well, that's an insult to the Indians, isn't it?"

I thought for a moment. "Let's forgive him. Say he's on business."

Spider glowered. "I don't want to forgive him! I know what his business is."

The chief and his entourage, followed by Palkuh, arrived and sat opposite the guests.

Monty Adams leaned over and translated the exchange between Joe and me about throwing up. The Indians rocked with laughter. Then the chief filled his plate and motioned for the others to begin.

Everyone dug in with gusto. Except Joe. "Ants," he muttered. "Grubs. I'm from Wyoming, Barry. We're civilized up there. I've never—."

"They're civilized here, too, Joe. Help yourself. As you crunch down on the ants, I suggest you lick your lips as a sign of approval to the chief and the cooks."

"My lips," he responded, "are going to be so goddammed puckered I won't be able to move 'em."

I warned him: "Joe, you are perilously close to insulting the chief."

Joe's gaze fell slowly back to the plate in front of him. "Tell the chief to go first."

"You're stalling," I said, ladling on his plate a generous serving of ants and grubs.

Joe said: "Your eyes are bigger than my stomach. In fact, my stomach has shriveled to nothing. It just closed."

"Come on, Joe. The other people are eating."

Joe tried to suppress an intensifying sickly look. "Barry. I want the truth. Have you ever eaten grubs and ants?"

"Yes, with the aborigines in Australia. You get used to it. Watch me."

I swept the morsels in and crunched them with flair. Nodding to the chief, I washed them down with warm Coca Cola.

Joe looked away, his eyes sagging.

Spider delved into the grubs next, following my lead, with a smile to the chief and a look that said "Delicious."

Carol Lynn followed, saying: "I believe I've read somewhere that these are quite nutritious."

"My only regret," Joe commented, "is that Boris is not here enduring this with us. Now I know why he left."

I smiled. "It's the taste, Joe, the taste. It's your turn."

"Is there any chicken? They want to make us happy, don't they?"

Monty Adams punctured that hope. "They don't eat chicken. Tonight we eat their foods."

I nudged Joe. "You're still stalling."

"I sure am."

"You said you wanted adventure. I heard you."

Joe looked down at the plate, then up with forlorn eyes. "This is adventure?"

"Time's up." I frowned as I said it.

Joe: "One last question. When I eat these, where do I go to upchuck?"

Monty Adams responded. "Yer gittin' off easy, Joe. Wanta know what the Yanomami Indians serve over on the Rio Negro?"

Joe answered at once. "Tell me tomorrow."

Manyuco, the chief, observed Joe and hung his head to suppress a smile. The chief's father had no inhibition. Neither did Palkuh. They laughed uproariously as Joe popped into his mouth a handful of grubs and ants and gulped them down.

"Joe, you didn't even chew them."

When he could speak again, Joe squeaked, tears in his eyes: "You're damned right I didn't!"

After this ordeal was over and the color returned to Joe's face, Monty Adams said: "The little calabash in front of you is their own drink. They call it chicha. Ain't got much kick, less'n you drink it all night. They won't expect you to take much of it, maybe a sip."

"Hand me a quart," Joe said.

Greg Fisher asked: "Monty, we've been curious. What are these white cakes? Corn meal?"

"The yuca?" He pronounced it YOO-kuh. "Also called manioc and cassava. It's like bread. Everbody eats it down here. It has a poisonous oil—."

Joe Muck coughed and spat out as politely as possible the bite of yuca he had just taken.

Monty continued: "—which they remove by using a metapí or a cibucan. You'ins'll see tomorrow morning. The chief's going to take yuh to the yuca patch."

Joe regained his composure. "I kind of like it. Of course, anything would be good following...."

The more we ate, the more we relaxed. The more sips of chicha we took, the more we removed the diaphanous veil of uneasiness that pervaded the company since discovery of Boris Kolinski's secret.

Dinner ended, and no one regretted that during the entire evening, Kolinski never showed up. He would, though. He'd be back. Tomorrow the fight would go on. They would find some way to end his scheme...

CHAPTER 25

Sometime during the night, I came awake as the Indians carried Boris Kolinski up the steps of Manyuco's hut. They deposited him on his floor mattress and pulled the mosquito net around him.

Half conscious, I mused: a victim of gin and chicha. The stench of his breath permeated the hut.

I fell back to sleep immediately.

At breakfast next morning (catfish strips, fried bananas, coffee, tea and warm Coca Cola), Boris appeared, eyes red, jowls sagging.

"Well," Spider sneered, "shall we call an ambulance? How many settlers did you buy out yesterday?"

He snorted. "Give 'em time to think on it. Pesos change minds."

Her voice took on an even more acid tone. "And if pesos don't work? What do you use then? Overdose of sleeping pills?"

"I'm a great persuader. They can't resist."

"Especially when you get them drunk."

"I? Use the happy spirits as a tool of business? What the hell, woman, do you think I would—."

She interrupted. "I saw you giving them liquor yesterday. Right out in broad daylight. That's contemptible."

Carol Lynn: "Despicable is my word for it."

Boris sneered. "They ask for it. I give it to them. What's wrong with that?"

Spider barked: "That's no excuse."

"Got to be polite down here or would you know what that means? A little cultural exchange. They got me drunk on chicha!"

He belched and bellowed until his paunch heaved like a tethered balloon in the wind.

"I'm glad," said Spider. "Have you no principles at all?"

"Principles close the mind," he said. Then he assumed an injured tone. "I'm hospitable. Always have been. The Colombians drink more than they can take—that's part of their machismo makeup. I didn't invent it. I just help it along."

"Well, I hope they give you some yuca juice as well."

Boris spoke around a mouthful of fried bananas. "Add a little rum and lead me to it! Only, I wish I could stay."

"We'll miss you," Spider said in a mocking voice. "Going out to buy some more forest?"

"Yep. I got these people excited."

"Of course. Get up their hopes. Then shaft 'em. Ruin their lives. Why not just kill them off now and take their land without paying? Do them a favor."

Boris smirked. "Watch your words, prissy. Before you leave, this little village may be mine. Then I'll have the pleasure of kicking all of you out of it."

This angered the usually complacent Mo Briggle. "Not if we kick your ass out of here first."

"Is that a threat, Mister?" Boris belched again.

"If he doesn't," Spider growled, "I goddamned will. And *that's* a threat. You're going to be lucky to get out of this place alive."

Boris rose, his face red with anger. "Listen, you dim-witted witch. Just keep your tits outta my business or I'll bust your ass! Can your feeble mind understand that?" He turned to leave.

No insult imaginable could have been better calculated to shove Spider over the edge. She bared her teeth, screeched an unintelligible epithet, and rose faster than anyone had seen her move. With one circular motion she grabbed an empty gourd and flung it toward Boris's departing figure.

What superb aim! The gourd struck him squarely on the back of the head. I caught her arm on the backswing. Mo grabbed the other arm.

Boris stopped and turned, speaking slowly. "Nice shot, pussycat. It may be your last. I'll give you one final warning. All of you. Keep your goddamned noses out of my business. Nothing stops ILB. Anything happens to me, a company helicopter drops down on your asses faster'n you can say 'run for cover!' And that's a *threat*."

He left.

Spider called out: "Son of a bitch! I'll kill you! I'll—."

I grasped her arm with a solid lock and held her back, saying: "Stop it! Let him go. That man is dangerous. I don't want to have to haul your corpse back to Florencia."

Spider sat, her face flushed, her eyes flaring again.

Joe mused: "A bastard like that can ruin your whole day. We have *got* to do something."

Spider lurched and fumed. "Let me go! *Take your hands off me!* I've never, ever met such a goddamned pissant—." She became incoherent.

Mo muttered an oath. "Another remark and I would have clipped that bastard—." He stopped suddenly. "Oh, what the hell. Look what's happening. He's ruining our trip. Let's move to another village. Get him out of our hair. Or else remove him from this village. We didn't pay good money to come down here and fight an idiot like that."

"Capital idea," Chris commented.

Greg Fisher said: "No! We're not going to run away from him. He's not going to interfere. If he gets any worse, we'll do something in self defense. That's legal, isn't it? I'd rather just forget him. But he won't go away. Mo's right. We paid a lot of money for this trip. Let's get something out of it or else get rid of that bastard once and for all."

It was a pretty belligerent speech for such a gentle person. I could now no longer deny it: their tone was turning ugly.

Breakfast ended, we rose in time to meet the chief, who carried a machete, here called penilla, in his hand. A deep, brown net bag hung at his side, slung from a long loop around the neck.

Spider said: "Chief, give me that machete!"

CHAPTER 26

We left the village, moving along a narrow trail through the undergrowth. It was quite a procession. Spider just behind the chief in the lead with her wide-brimmed blue sun hat. Mo Briggle in his white shirt and blue slacks. Dana with pith helmet and wide designer sunglasses. Fishers with swinging cameras and binoculars. Chris and Carol Lynn Arden-Jones, she garbed as usual in travel dress with pearl necklace. Joe, bareheaded, in shorts and piranha tee shirt, which by now had become a sensation not just with little Tiata but with all the villagers.

I came last, forcing myself to amble, relieved that someone else had taken charge of the day's events. I could be thrust in charge if the Kolinski matter deteriorated. I looked at the chief's long knife for cutting yuca plants. Good blade for a murder.

The inner me spoke up. *Becoming obsessed already? You usually do. Where's your logic this time?*

What logic?

Somebody's about to get hurt, right?

Somebody already has. She hit him a good wallop.

They're mad at the guy. All of them. And you know perfectly well that collective mad is more ominous than individual mad.

Mad is a mild word. They're blind with rage. And it's getting worse.

Buddy, you're in trouble. Who's going to get whom? And when? When does anger turn into action?

When patience disappears. When patience turns into paranoia. So, logic suggests that they'll get him first.

That gives you two choices. One, the passengers do him in. Two, the Indians do it.

No, no. Not the Indians. They like him. Why not? All that money. All that gin...

Okay, then which passenger has the shortest fuse?

Spider. Anyone can see that.

Looks like it. Are you sure?

You have to ask? After this morning?

Don't be deceived. As you yourself have said, we can measure the fire in stars a billion light years away, but we cannot measure the fire in a human temper.

Very brilliant, Socrates. All right, then. What about Joe?

He's young, impetuous. Unpredictable today. Unpredictable tomorrow. Very likely murderer, though. Clean, Precise. He'd use strangling, that's my guess. He's an expert at roping a calf in the rodeo.

Greg? He's the silent type. Beryl, too. They're the caring type, not the killing type.

Must I remind you that quiet crusaders sometimes have the sharpest swords?

You may be right. What about Mo?

He doesn't say much. Watch him carefully. A man can conceal his thoughts but not his eyes.

How about Chris? And Carol Lynn? Are they too sophisticated to be drawn into this?

Very cultured. But you remember the Parradine Case? The cultured sometimes have short fuses.

What will they use? Poison? They don't usually carry poisons around.

There's plenty of poison right here...

I looked up from these reflections. The sun shone brightly, unlike the morning we started down the river from Puerto Lara. The Fishers, cameras dried out and working again, snapped pictures of the chief, the vegetation, the burned-over places.

We crossed a stream, the first clear spring water we'd seen in days.

Joe knelt. "This looks like Lodgepole Creek at home. Good to drink?"

"Test it and see," I answered. "Then let the rest of us know."

Joe rose. "No, thanks. I'm the Coke type."

Upstream we passed a fish trap made of bamboo slats arranged to pass small fish and hold larger ones in the current. We went by cashew trees, relative of poison ivy, with caustic liquid in the trunk. Shortly afterward, we passed a patch of pineapple plants not yet in fruit.

After half an hour we entered the yuca patch almost without knowing it. These slender plants, taller than lanky Joe himself, bore spindly stems with nodes at every hand-width up the trunk. The chief grasped three stems growing from the same root, slashed them away and pulled the roots from the sandy soil. In less than ten minutes he had filled his bag with roots that looked, for all their rough shape, like potato tubers.

Joe asked: "These the roots with poison in them?"

I responded: "That's what they say."

"Then save a bag for Boris."

The heat increased as the sun bore down. The chief wiped away perspiration.

As we sat to rest, Beryl Fisher immediately pulled out a notebook, drew a stick figure of a woman, and showed it to the Chief Manyuco. She pointed to the drawing, then swept her hands all about. "Messala?" she said, pointing to the drawing again. "Katherine Messala."

The chief looked at the drawing, mused for a moment, and said: "Katerina?"

Beryl almost jumped. "Katerina! Yes. Katerina. You know her?" She pointed to the figure, then to the chief.

He raised his hand and waved it from side to side, a negative response. Then he spoke a few sentences, unintelligible to them. Seeing their blank faces, he waved his hand toward the east and said one word: "Sonke."

Carol Lynn said: "Oh, this is frustrating. I haven't one word of Correguaje language recorded. What does Sonke mean?"

Chris: "It must mean a village."

Carol Lynn: "If it does, then how far away is it?" She turned to the chief and asked: "Sonke?"

Seeing their confusion, Manyuco took the pad and pencil and drew a stick figure of a man with feathers rising from his head.

Beryl said eagerly: "Sonke is a chief."

Manyuco drew the outlines of several huts near the figure of the chief.

"He's the chief of a village. And what he means is that Sonke knows about Katherine."

Manyuco nodded. "Katerina."

Carol Lynn made a sweep of her arms to take in their little group, then pointed to the east and said: "Sonke?"

Manyuco inquired with the same hand signals whether the group all wanted to go see Sonke. We nodded. He nodded. That settled it. On his face appeared the faint hint of a smile. I couldn't figure out why...

Carol Lynn held up her hand. "Now, wait! We are not going anywhere until I get some recordings of Correguaje words. If I had a list, we would get along much faster and more accurately with these people. When we get back to the village, we are to have a quick recording session. I absolutely insist on it. We are not going blind and deaf to see Chief Sonke."

"Key words?" Joe asked.

"Key words," she answered.

"Such as?"

"Oh—tree, village, hot, cold, day, night, you, me... that sort of thing. Do you understand?"

"Yeah," Joe replied. "Just be sure you find out the word for murder."

Carol Lynn laughed. "Come now, Joe. They may not have such a word. They're not savages."

CHAPTER 27

Manyuco led us back the way we'd come, and went directly to a food-processing hut at the edge of the village.

A woman sat inside, hair hanging to her shoulders, chain of beads around her neck. A child played in the corner. We crowded inside as the woman took the yuca roots handed her by Manyuco.

She washed them, grated them on a stone, and placed the mushy result in a small dugout canoe, which held perhaps a bushel of the meal already. There was a freshness to the dank odor of the mush, not unlike that of freshly scraped potatoes.

Grating completed, she took a pan of the mush over to a large metapí, a long cylinder of woven fibers hanging from the ceiling to the floor. Reaching up, she loaded the metapí with mush. It took several pans full of the damp meal, dropped in at the top, to fill the tube. The meal would have fallen out the bottom had the tube not been tied shut and looped around a horizontal log.

The weight of the meal squeezed downward. Yellowish oil began to drip into a bucket beneath the cylinder.

Joe asked quietly: "That the poisonous oil?"

Mo answered: "Save a cup. I've got a use for it."

I smiled inwardly. They're all obsessed.

When she had filled the fiber tube to the top with mush, the woman grasped the horizontal pole at the bottom. One end of it had been anchored to a post. The pole acted as a lever. By pressing down on the other end of it, she pulled down on the fiber tube containing the yuca meal. The device tightened, narrowed and exerted a prodigious squeeze on the contents. Oil poured.

"Some squeezer!" Joe said. "Wouldn't you like to get Kolinski's head in that?"

Beryl Fisher asked: "Anyone know what that oil is?"

I answered: "A vegetative hydrocyanide, I would presume. Most probably, prussic acid."

Joe responded: "Quick acting?"

I turned away. "I'm not going to answer that."

"Has Boris tried this with rum and Coke?"

They could not get Kolinski out of their minds. No matter what they did or what they saw, however interesting, he had become their focus of hatred.

When the poisonous drops had all but stopped, the woman rose, unhooked the squeezer from the ceiling, and poured the contents into another pot. The white meal, now much less damp, poured out easily. She molded it into crude flat cakes, which she carried in basket trays and spread out on the roof to dry.

"Well, there you have it," I commented. "Staple of the Amazon."

We thanked the woman, gave the child some crayons and paper, and returned to the kitchen.

Not without trepidation. No one knew what would happen if Boris Kolinski showed up to lunch with us.

CHAPTER 28

After a lunch of fish scraps, canned corned beef and canned potatoes, washed down with coffee, tea or Coke, the village became silent with the obligatory siesta. Spider and the Fishers left on a birding trip along the bank of the Orteguaza River. Chris and Carol Lynn walked to the spring. Joe went away jogging. Mo and Dana went to their cottage. None of the group caught a glimpse of Boris anywhere.

A few minutes later, Carol Lynn and Chris returned and gave the signal. They had assembled Monty Adams and Chief Manyuco around a pocket tape recorder in their hut. Joe, the Briggles, and I joined them. So did the Red Chief.

It was hot and humid in the hut, but I think we were beginning to get used to that.

"Please tell Manyuco," Chris urged Monty, "to speak very clearly because for us this is a difficult language. I will be comparing it to Balinese, Thai, and Chinese, and that takes a little time. As we tape, the chief should pronounce everything once at normal speed and a second time very slowly. I will give you the English word, you will give him the Spanish equivalent, and he will tell us the corresponding word in his language. Is that all right?"

Monty nodded. The rest of us looked on. Chris turned on the recorder. Carol Lynn made a chart as the words poured out.

ENGLISH	SPANISH	CORREGUAJE
Anaconda	Culebra grande	Anohal
Banana	Plátano	Aowuh
Bed	Cama	Caoweeh
Big	Grande	Buhal
Blue	Azul	Ahsoateh
Caiman	Caimán	Ohkohoteh
Canoe	Canoa	Tayawuh
Chief	Cacique	Palkuh
Clothing	Ropa	Tehalhohecah
Coffee	Café	[No word]
Cold	Frío	Nahsehsih
Cow	Vaca	[No word]
Down	Abajo	Tevah
Far	Lejos	Ho-oh
Father	Padre	Hakeh
Feet	Pie	Tehalcoapuh
Fire	Fuego	Ahpeteh
Food	Comida	Ahye
Foreigner	Extranjero	[No word]
Fruit	Fruta	Uhteh
God	Dios	[No word]
Grandfather	Abuelo	Wunehsaehmunh
Grandmother	Abuela	Wunehsaekuh
Green	Verde	Minanyeh
Head	Cabeza	Singhaopuh
High	Alto	Moo-oom
Horse	Caballo	[No word]
Hot	Caliente	Ahsih
Insect	Insecto	Kuhteh
Jaguar	Tigre	Pahl
Land	Tierra	Chivah

Little	Pequeño	Mamauh
Low	Bajo	Sihah
Monkey	Mico	Mahtoh
Moon	Luna	Piemayaunh
Mother	Madre	Hakoh
Mouth	Boca	Teehopoh
Nature	Naturaleza	[No word]
Near	Cerca	Alcoide
Palm	Palma	Uhneh
Parrot	Guacamayo	Ma-ah
Pineapple	Piña	Enhsih
Red	Rojo	Mamha-uh
River	Rio	Tiata
Sky	Cielo	Canaoumngh
Son	Hijo	Teohtee
Stars	Estrellas	Manyuco
Sun	Sol	Unseuh
Tree	Arbol	Sonke
Up	Arriba	Oomuh
Very hot	Muy caliente	Retibiahsih
Village	Pueblo	Wehoopah
Water	Agua	Ohcoh

When they had finished, Carol Lynn uttered exclamations of delight. "Capital! This is original stuff. We've got an awfully lot to work on. And now I can speak to these people in their own language."

It was a refreshing interlude. In half an hour, no one mentioned Boris Kolinski.

The guests poured out of the hut, intent on changing for a quick swim. Dana, the non-swimmer, arrived within minutes. She was first into the little shallow pool...and last to leave.

CHAPTER 29

I looked around. No sign of the villagers.

Hardly unusual, I thought. People in the tropics napped in the heat of the day. Exposed ground became a frying pan, too hot to touch, too hot to walk on with bare feet. Lizards avoided it. They and other reptiles retreated to shrubs or burrows. Animals with fur coats kept to the shadows, or immersed themselves in water. Even the hum of insects nearly hushed. The wind, reduced to a zephyr, barely stirred the leaves.

I climbed the steps to the chief's hut, crawled beneath the mosquito netting, and sprawled on my air mattress. Bathed in perspiration, I had trouble dropping into a doze.

I smiled at the thought of Spider and the Fishers hiking along the edge of the Orteguaza at mid-afternoon, absorbing the unchecked rays of the tropical sun. They would learn, as the Indians and animals had, how tropical heat and humidity sap energy.

I pitied Joe, trying to jog in a furnace. He, too, would learn.

I stared up through the netting. My eyes rested on the angular patterns of palm fronds laid on the roof beams.

Like attics anywhere, this one held a clutter of possessions, the contents typical of tropical rain forest households: hammocks, gourds and calabashes, baskets, feather headdresses, cloth, manioc trays, bows and arrows, darts, blowguns, reed flutes, drums—.

I fell into a kind of torpor. For a few blissful minutes, the world disappeared. Boris vanished. The ominous events that would almost surely transpire on his return receded from my mind.

My vision fuzzed, but I still tried to hang on. Tried in the waning moments of consciousness to figure out how I would handle an emergency so far from civilization. Without crime labs, without police. Monty would know. Perhaps I could rely on Monty to handle everything, and wash my hands of it.

Coward! Quitter! At such times my alter ego chastises me severely. *You know better than that. You're the one, boy. Let one thing go wrong, and you know exactly who they would all come running to. And it's going to happen. You know that. You'd better just get ready for it...*

I slept for a few minutes. The lassitude of a tropical afternoon, heat and all, erased everything. If I lay in a river of sweat, I could wash it off in the pool. Why worry?

Then, in the midst of this blackness, my drift through space was broken by a terrifying shriek.

Coming awake, I leaped up, jumped out the door of the chief's hut, ignored the log steps, and sailed through the air to the ground below. Joe ran up behind me.

"What the hell was that?" he asked.

So dizzy was I that I could not fix the direction from which the sound had come. The Arden-Joneses burst out of their hut, faces bewildered. "Who did that?"

"Which direction did it come from?" I asked.

The answer came in another scream.

We turned and raced to the pond. There we saw Dana Briggle standing transfixed, hands to her mouth, eyes focused on the water.

We followed her gaze to the body floating face down in the pool.

Mo Briggle ran up and took his wife by the arm, then saw the apparition in the water.

Carol Lynn spoke first: "Oh, no!"

I spread my arms. "Everybody step back. I would appreciate it, in fact, if you would go over to the kitchen and stay until I get there. Joe, would you see if you can find Monty Adams and ask him to come here? Mo, if you don't mind, I'd like you to bring your Polaroid camera and take a few pictures, please."

Dana, regaining her composure, asked: "Shall I administer CPR?"

Dana and I pulled the limp figure of Boris Kolinski out of the water, and Dana went to work.

CHAPTER 30

Chief Manyuco arrived. His face remained a mask. I nodded to him and looked around. By this time villagers had arrived but mothers herded children away when they saw what had happened. Spider and the Fishers could not be seen anywhere.

I studied the pool, which amounted to less a lazy swimming hole than a wide place in the flowing stream, dammed with a makeshift pile of rocks. The water could not have flowed more than knee deep at any point. A log lay at an angle from bank to bottom, its sloping surface a seat on which bathers could sit and wash. Kolinski's body had rested against this log, held in place by the current.

I scanned the jumble of stumps, logs and roots on the opposite bank. I could cross on a log placed a few yards downstream as a bridge. Farther downstream perched the loo on two logs over the stream. On the upstream side of the pond, a trail led off into the woods.

Pulling out my notebook, I glanced in all directions, examining the shadows, huts, and forest edges to find out whether anyone might be watching or fleeing.

I made a sign to the chief to remain there for a moment. Moving quickly down to the loo, I stepped up on the log, knocked on the side of the house as a warning, then looked within. No one there.

When I got back, Dana looked up as though to say: "It's no use."

I said: "Okay," and she stopped. Mo came up with the camera and I pointed out the angles from which I wanted pictures made of the corpse. With the chief assisting and Mo photographing, I pulled the clothing back, examined the hair, eyes, ears, mouth, and skin. No telltale marks. His fingertips, however, seemed abnormally bluish.

Except—. I went back to the mouth and pulled it open. I raised the lips and searched behind the teeth, uppers and lowers. Pushing my fingers as far down into the throat as possible, I retrieved some fragments of what appeared to be partially digested food regurgitated.

I got out my small pocket knife and held it up for the onlookers to see. "Now," I said to them, "please witness that I am going to make a small slit in the shoulder. I could do this anywhere on the body, but the shoulder is most convenient. The purpose is to determine the color of the flesh. Please picture this, Mo, because the incision must not be misconstrued as a stab wound that caused death."

Mo moved in close. I made the cut, less than a quarter of an inch in length, and peeled back the flesh. I found it unusually pink, although I had no way of determining what color his flesh had been when he was alive. I enlarged the slit to half an inch in order to make a closer examination. It was perhaps nothing more than a routine procedural step, but I made notes of the observations. Then I pulled the clothes back up.

Emptying the pockets of the coat and trousers I retrieved keys, knife, handkerchief, calling cards, sunglasses, pencils and pens. Nothing more.

Wiping my hands, I pulled out the notebook again and listed these items, then laid them out for Mo to photograph.

Monty Adams came up the trail from the direction of the dock on the Orteguaza. His eyes fixed on the corpse.

"Oh, Christ!" he said.

I asked: "Monty, one quick question—did you see Spider or the Fishers down at the river?"

"No. I've been gone."

"Where?"

"Next village over."

"Did you see anyone?"

"I was down the river till a little while ago. Went up to the other village about our trip there tomorrow. Just now got back. Ain't nobody at the dock."

"Do you know which Indians went out with Boris this morning?"

"No, I been at the other village."

"Any Indians go with you?"

"One. Not a guide. They was all out with Kolinkski."

I almost laughed at his mispronunciation, but said nothing.

He went on. "I know the way, so I only took young Aunamunh with me as a helper."

"Monty, I would appreciate it if you could find out eventually which of the Correguaje guides went out with Boris today. Right now, would you please tell the chief that, since this is his domain, I should like his permission to conduct an investigation into this matter. Tell him I have tacit authority under rules of the Policía and the Fuerzas Armadas Colombianas to investigate such instances as this. I should like him to approve it, as a courtesy, and you to be a witness to his response."

Adams translated. The chief looked at me and nodded solemnly, which I noted in writing.

"Monty, would you and the chief also search the huts? All of them. Let me know of the slightest thing unusual. For one thing, three items are missing: Kolinski's hat, briefcase and canteen. He usually took these with him. Would you describe these to the chief and ask him to see if they can be found anywhere? I'll look around, too, but I must first go over to the kitchen and talk to our group. After you finish with the chief, I'd like you to come with me, if you don't mind."

Adams translated. Monty and the chief went away. I strode to the chief's hut, climbed inside and went straight to Boris Kolinski's duffel bag. It seemed to be untouched. Nothing else remained at the bunk site except a toilet kit and liquor flask. I put these in the duffel bag, tied the top, and placed the bag under the mosquito netting on my own bed. Going back outside, I joined the others in the kitchen.

CHAPTER 31

I took roll mentally: the Briggles, Arden-Joneses, Joe Muck, and an assortment of Correguaje men, women and children.

"I am going to go ahead," I began, "without Spider and the Fishers, because there's a lot of work to do before it gets dark. I have permission from the chief, which adds to my authority to investigate this incident without a Colombian officer. This gives me the legal right to ask you to do anything that will help solve this matter and bring to justice the person or persons responsible for it."

Joe Muck listened to every word, his mouth half open. The Arden-Joneses sat with their backs against a post, contemplating the ground as I spoke. The Briggles lay on a piece of canvas, their eyes on me. The Indians understood none of the words but observed the proceedings with staring eyes and puzzled interest.

"Monty and the chief are searching the huts. The initial indication is that death occurred by drowning. I can detect no indication of violence. No suggestion of torture marks on the body. I have asked the chief to find out which of the Correguajes went with Boris this morning.

"At the moment there are three possibilities. One is that Boris died by accident. The second is that he succumbed to heat and exhaustion, exacerbated by drink and over-weight. The third is that he was murdered. Since I can't tell which, I must proceed with the assumption that foul play is involved. That means that I must investigate with due diligence, and I am going to do it. With many thanks for your help.

"You are all under suspicion. Therefore, I ask you to report to me if you wish to leave the village for any purpose.

"While this is a disturbing incident, we are going ahead with our activities. If you have anything to report to me any time, I ask you to do so. Any questions?"

Mo: "Need me to take any more pictures?"

"Yes, Mo, thank you. You and Dana can accompany me right after this meeting."

Joe asked with a worried frown: "Me, too?"

"Yes, I need your help."

Chris said: "We'll be in our hut if you need us."

Adams came up, reporting nothing amiss, but the chief still searched. I asked: "Monty, what about disposal of the corpse? Notifying the police?"

He replied: "I gotta report this soon as I can. Part of my agreement with the government. I'll get an Indian to take a message to San Antonio. People there will radio Florencia."

"How soon will the message get through to Bogotá?"

"There's no way of knowin'."

"A day, maybe?"

"Yeh, I think maybe."

"Okay. Until the police arrive, can you ask the Indians to wrap the body or bury it temporarily."

Adams nodded.

I turned again to the rest of the group. "If there is a killer among us, he or she could strike again. I'm investigating, so I could be the principal target. I don't want anyone gunning for me to get you. Just stay alert. Don't go out alone. Keep me informed."

Joe smiled. "We're not even going to get *near* you," he joked. "But since we don't know who did this, we are all probably targets anyway. What about the company? ILB? You heard Boris. They'll be on top of us. They'll think we all did him in. They may not stop to ask any questions."

I responded: " You're right about Boris's threat. I don't view that as braggadocio. ILBRED will find out what happened. Maybe tomorrow. We'll see what happens..."

They looked at each other. Without smiling.

CHAPTER 32

Joe, the Briggles and I headed down the trail to the river. No rays of the late afternoon sun penetrated the forest, so our path lay in shadow.

I tried to juxtapose a dozen people in front of a pond, huts, trails, forests, rivers, canoes. If a jaguar had ripped Boris apart, the matter would be simple. If a frenzied school of piranhas had chewed him up, there wouldn't have been much left. Had he been crushed by an anaconda, he would be at the bottom of the river. Or he had been electrocuted by an eel...

In the Amazon, there are dozens of ways to die. Hundreds.

Man Put to Electric Chair by Amazon Eel! Silly thought, *a priori.* Yet with murders, silly thoughts lead places. The "eel theory" could create a stir in Bogotá. Divine retribution! Man's murder of wildlife revenged! Offbeat homicide. No police force to take over, no labs to run tests, no fingerprinting. Nothing but—.

Joe's eyes were wide with excitement, and I could guess what went through his mind as we marched along at a brisk pace. He couldn't help being exhilarated. Never in Laramie, and not out on the ranch along the Sweetwater

River, in central Wyoming, had he ever been involved in a murder. Much less witnessed the events surrounding one. Now the *investigator* wanted his help. What luck! Or maybe *bad luck*... He could be standing within the target range next to me. Next to Ground Zero.

"Hello there!"

Spider and the Fishers approached us as they walked up the trail toward the village. I asked them straightaway: "Have you been walking along the river?"

Spider answered: "All afternoon. You should've come along."

Beryl Fisher added: "Yes! We saw a hoatzin, anis, egrets, a toucan, even a—."

I did not let her finish. "Did you notice anything unusual either along the river or in the forest? Or, for that matter, along the trail?"

Spider thought a moment. "Of course! To us, everything is unusual down here. I take it you mean human unusual?"

"Yes. For one thing, did you see Boris?"

"Don't mention that scum! No, thank heaven. Good thing we didn't, out like that. But I can assure you we weren't looking for him."

"Did you see any Indians?"

"A few, coming and going on the river. This is a lonely place."

"Did anyone pass you on the trail? Did you meet anyone?"

"Yes, a couple of Indian boys. We talked with them a few minutes. Then they went on."

"How old were they, could you tell?"

Spider grinned. "No one can tell how old an Indian boy is. They age early."

"Big little, or little little?"

"In between."

"Did you recognize them?"

"No. They weren't from our village, near as we could tell. I don't know where they came from."

"Were they carrying anything? Like knives? Sticks? Spears?"

"Nothing. Why? Why all these questions?"

"We found Boris floating face down in the pond an hour ago."

Spider croaked but couldn't say anything. Beryl Fisher gasped. Greg closed his eyes, threw up his hands and said: "There goes the whole damn trip. That bastard! How did it happen?"

I answered quickly. "We don't know. None of us appears to have seen what happened. Dana discovered the body."

Spider sighed in anger. "So what the hell do we do now?"

"With the chief's permission, I am looking into the matter."

Greg asked: "Screw up our trip?"

"Not if I can help it."

"Well," Spider said, relieved. "I'm glad somebody's in charge. I don't mind saying Hallelujah! That son of a bitch is dead!"

I answered: "A murder is a murder, whether we liked the guy or not."

"It could have been a heart attack."

"I don't think so," I said.

Spider looked puzzled. "So where does that leave us?"

"Innocent, for now. Everybody in our group had a motive, especially you three. You probably hated his guts more than anyone else, and maybe that's a badge of honor. I am going to find out what happened and, if it was murder, who did it."

Spider spoke: "You're sure it was murder?"

"I'm not sure of anything."

"How'd it happen? Bullet hole? Claw marks?"

"No marks on the body. Did you see Monty Adams on the dock at any time?"

"No."

"All right, you're free to go where you wish around the village. Don't go far. Report to me anything unusual. I will contact you later. And stay alert. Could be there's a murderer after all of us. Not to mention ILB."

Spider paled. "Comforting thought!" She and the Fishers walked on up the trail to the village.

With Mo and Dana, we went on down to the river. Mo started photographing the dock and canoes. Monty arrived shortly with an Indian, whom he dispatched upriver with a note for the authorities at San Antonio.

I asked whether Monty had found anything suspicious in the village. He shook his head. "Nothin'."

Briefcase?

Same response.

"Did you talk to the Indians about Kolinski?"

"Not the ones who went with him today. They went fishin' right after they got back."

"Did anyone else see where Boris went after he left the dock?"

"Don't reckon. They don't usually pay no attention to what tourists do."

"Any indication Boris was sick or staggering drunk?"

"Didn't think to ask. He was always a little looped."

"Okay, Monty. I'm going to look around here for a few minutes, then go back. But there is one problem. Something very important is missing. Have you seen that straw hat he usually wore?"

"No. Not down here."

"How about his briefcase—leather, very worn?"

"Haven't seen it."

"The aluminum notebook he carried around and wrote in?"

"No."

"Thanks, Monty. Let's keep on the move."

Adams nodded and left.

I looked around. The dock, the canoes, the boat house showed no sign of life. Neither did the loo, perched out over the water. The river banks upstream and down, all empty of human activity, had been tinted orange by the afternoon sun.

Joe asked: "What are you looking for?"

"Anything unusual," I answered. "Out of place. Color clash. Odd movement. Trouble is, like Spider said, everything down here is unusual."

"Okay, but a tree's a tree. A dock's a dock. You can still find something."

"Maybe. Let's find that briefcase."

We looked around the dock. The little canoes of the Indians had lots of blood in them, dried blood. Joe saw it first.

"How do you account for this?"

I examined the dark red stains and drippings. "Either they commit a lot of murders or they clean a lot of fish here."

Joe scowled. "You're making fun of me."

"That is the last thing I'd do to anybody. The sun is setting. I want to do three things—look along the river here, check the pond again back at the village, and go out to the yuca field. Want to run?"

Joe's eyes brightened. "Lead on."

We jogged upstream along the river bank as far as we could at shore level. Then we leaped up on the embankment and went a short way along the trail that Spider and the Fishers had said they used.

Returning from this, we headed downstream, first along the shore, then up on the embankment, and finally to the loo, which I checked.

Nothing. No aluminum notebook. No straw hat. No worn leather briefcase.

I muttered aloud: "We're not getting anywhere here. You ready?"

"Like a bronc in a chute," Joe said.

We turned and ran up the trail to the village.

CHAPTER 33

By the time we reached the pond, the sun had almost set.

We waded into the water, lifted logs, peered behind stumps, kicked through fallen leaves, scanned the lower branches of trees, examined the bottom of the stream. No notebook, no briefcase, no hat.

I looked at Joe. "Ready?"

Joe leaped away, sped past the huts and out along the trail to the yuca field. I ran behind, both ducking branches and sidestepping roots.

When we got there, we examined the yuca plants, the disturbed soil from which Manyuco had pulled the plants, crude planks for prying out roots, an old woven carrying bag, and a rusted penilla.

Nothing else.

We jogged back, slowing before we reached the huts. I pondered.

"There were four trails where someone could have encountered Kolinski. One upstream, one down, one to the yuca field, one to the spring."

We looked at each other. Joe said: "We haven't been to the spring."

Away we went, past the kitchen and into the forest, ducking, sidestepping, dodging. In this dim light I couldn't be sure we would find the spring. Or see the trail well enough to get back if we did.

A side trail veered off. We followed it, only to meet a dead end. Back to the main trail. Another side trail. Another dead end.

I stopped. "Any farther, and we'll have to grope our way back in the dark. Night comes fast down here."

Joe, dancing, said: "Let's go on. Another minute."

We encountered another side trail, took it, and discovered the spring.

Nothing there. We ran back. For all our running, we'd discovered absolutely nothing.

Puffing as we climbed into the chief's hut, I said: "That is distinctly not the speed with which I usually investigate matters. But we had to cover the countryside tonight, as soon as possible after discovery of the body."

I opened the mosquito netting over Kolinski's bed, and hauled out the duffel bag that had belonged to Boris.

"Joe, I want you to witness my opening this bag, and list the contents. Here are pen and paper. List the items exactly as I state them."

I flicked on the fluorescent side of my flashlight and set it on a bench, then bent low to the duffel bag. Reaching in, I took out a padded cloth bag, and opened it.

"Take these down," I said to Joe. "One quart of rum, another quart of rum, a quart of Scotch, a quart of zubrovka, all nested in plastic and rubber."

"This guy didn't take chances."

"A broken bottle would be a strategic disaster. In his work he needed a good supply."

"Yeah. To brain-damage the natives."

"Careful with your comments, Joe."

"I don't give a fuck. I think the way I think. Liquor was one of this shmuck's weapons. Used it to get whatever he wanted."

"Did he get what he wanted?"

"Obviously. He wouldn't be down here in the Amazon unless he'd been good at it somewhere else. This is tough country."

Next came a bag of pens, pencils, miniature dolls, hard candies and balloons. Joe sneered: "This jerk went straight to the kids."

"So did you."

"Shut up."

"We all have things like this. Monty told us to bring them. We use them to make friends. Boris was just a professional in a different way."

I next pulled out a travel kit and listed the items within: "Toiletries. Small bath towel. Wash cloth. Travel alarm. Bottle of orange pills marked Hydrochlorothiazide 50mg, Dr. Lovegren, Collins Avenue Pharmacy, one tablet per day."

"What was that for?"

"Hypertension. I'm not surprised. The guy had high blood pressure."

"Maybe that's what killed him. Overdose of pills. Where's Collins Avenue?"

"Which Collins Avenue? What city? Maybe the one on Miami Beach. Next. Bottle of sleeping pills. Two pairs of rolled socks. Two boxer-type underwear. Two white cotton tank tops. Two bottle openers. Ten small plastic glasses. Bottle of water purification tablets. Peanuts. Caramels. Antacid tablets."

"No surprise that!" commented Joe. "By day's end he needed a new stomach."

I dug deeper and came to the last item in the duffel bag. "This is what I was waiting for."

I pulled out a bulging leather wallet tied with a boot lace.

Joe's brow lifted. "His money. He must have a bundle in there."

He did. I took out a wad of bills and counted. Fifteen million pesos in crisp new bills.

Joe issued a slow, drawn-out whistle. "Jesus! A walking bank."

I frowned. "This presents a problem. Florencia is two days away. This stuff needs to be stashed."

"Right," Joe agreed. "Where we going to spend it?"

"We give it back before someone tries to spend it."

"Give it back? To ILBRED? Come on..."

"It's their money."

"There's no safe deposit box in this village."

"I have no choice. You must witness the opening of this wallet and state the nature of its content. I will write out a separate note to that effect, and you will sign it."

This done, Joe signed it.

I began returning items to the duffel bag.

An idea occurred to Joe. "The guy must have had a wad in his briefcase, too. A 'working bundle,' you could call it. He must have taken some petty cash out each day to seal deals."

I nodded. "Good assumption. We have to find the briefcase. If it has no money in it, and we assume there should have been, then robbery is added to the motives for murder."

After replacing each item in the duffel bag, I reached over to my own duffel, took out a length of cord and tied the Kolinski bag shut. Taking out a roll of filament tape I cut off a strip about thirty inches long with a small knife. Wrapping this around the center of Kolinski's duffel bag, I withdrew a marker pen from my pocket and wrote "SEALED BY POLICE" on the strip.

Joe smiled. "That's not going to keep out a thief."

I grinned. "Locks keep out the honest."

Joe tried to decipher that as I put Boris's duffel back on his own bunk, dropped the mosquito netting, and rose.

"Dinner should be ready by now."

CHAPTER 34

The diners had seated themselves on palm leaves, talking with the two strangers.

"Barry! Joe!" Mo Briggle called. "Meet the new guests. Dr. José Martín Garcia, of the Agostín Codazzi Research Institute, and Dr. Melvin Jackson of the Smithsonian Institution in Washington. Gentlemen, this is Dr. Barry Ross, an investigative officer associated with the United Nations, and Joe Muck, a graduate student at the University of Wyoming."

What a surprise to see new faces! Joe and I shook hands with the newcomers. Then I asked myself: was it a coincidence that they arrived on the day of the murder?

"What brings you to this part of the world?" I asked.

Jackson spoke through a gray-and-white beard. "I'm an entomologist. My field is nocturnal flying insects. Dr. Garcia has been good enough to accompany me in my field research."

Spider added eagerly: "Dr. Jackson agrees with me about zoos."

I smiled. "Well, Dr. Jackson, you have an avid fan right off. Are you staying in the village?"

"We've strung our hammocks for tonight in the supply room behind the kitchen. Tomorrow we'll set up our station in the woods some distance down the river. We have to sleep there, in a quiet place, because we work at night and sleep in the daytime."

Mo could not control himself, blurting out an avalanche of questions. "Can we come see your setup? Can we come out some night and watch what you're doing? Are you after moths, or what?"

Dr. Jackson replied: "We're after certain species, yes. Anything new, of course. Dr. Garcia and I would be delighted to have you as guests. Someone here could guide you, once they know where we've located."

I sat and became the professional detective again. "Tell me, Dr. Jackson, when did you arrive?"

"Just at sundown."

"You came from Florencia?"

"Yes. It's quite a long trip, you know. We were in two small canoes, and we fairly flew across the water."

"Did you see any other Americans? Any tourists?"

Jackson looked at Dr. Garcia briefly, then answered.

"No. I can't say we did. Not many natives, either, for that matter. Why do you ask? Are you expecting somebody?"

"We're involved in a number of projects," I said vaguely.

"You are an investigating officer with the UN."

"Right now," I said, "I'm a student of Amazon biology. I think my fellow passengers would be as interested in your work as I."

"Well, Dr. Ross, if we can assist in that effort, please know you can count on us."

"Thank you."

Dana Briggle had no inhibitions about discussing the matter of land acquisition. "I don't mind telling you, Dr. Jackson, that we like to see your kind of research going on. We've seen people down here buying up land for logging and mining. I hope you find something more valuable in your insects than they find in oil and gold."

Jackson nodded. "Something of a race, I suppose."

Carol Lynn Arden-Jones, in travel dress and pearls, asked: "Their intent, as we understand, is to change the tropical forest into farm plots and gold mines. Haven't you scientists anything to combat that?"

Jackson said: "This forest is a difficult place in which to work, as I'm sure you know. Few people want to stay here long enough to conduct tests. We need research badly. That's the best way to fight the miners. Everyone knows there are medical discoveries waiting out there. But the hardships are formidable."

Joe responded: "Especially when you have to eat ants."

Jackson raised his eyebrows. "Oh, you've had some already? I find them tasty."

"I fell into that one!" Joe said. "Sorry, Doctor."

Garcia, dark haired with the bearing of a professor, spoke for the first time, in impeccable English. "Alas, Mr. Muck, you are all too right. Most students of biology prefer more familiar foods."

Joe asked: "What about Colombian students?"

"We have good ones, but I fear not enough money."

A flash of light glowed in the darkness outside. Chief Manyuco and Monty Adams entered. They sat on the ground, and placed in front of them three items: a worn leather briefcase, aluminum notebook, and planter's hat.

Joe sputtered: "Yipe! Uh, what the... Where in the hell did you find those?"

Monty answered simply. "Steps of the hut nearest the pond."

Amid gasps of astonishment and gulps of surprise, all eyes turned toward the Briggles.

CHAPTER 35

Soaking wet, we left at dawn for the neighboring village.

Thunder, lightning and the roar of rain diminished. Dense banks of fog clung to the river like shrouds as the canoes glided across the water. We stayed close to shore. In the gloom we saw only occasional limbs clutching toward an absent sun. Once we barely missed a low limb that emerged without warning from the mist and scraped low over our heads.

The damp air—cool, clammy, perfumed with growth and decay—enveloped and chilled us. Carol Lynn had learned what to wear from that shivery morning at Puerto Lara. Now she met the rush of river air in Joe's ruana, her hat pulled around her ears, sunglasses cinched in place. Insulated like an astronaut, Joe had said as we boarded the canoes.

This time we traveled in two small open canoes, Briggles, Fishers and Arden-Joneses in one, Spider, Joe, Monty and me in the other. Spider still wanted the motors silenced, and Joe still wanted to paddle. As we turned up the Pinilla River, however, the need for motors became apparent.

It was the first wild tributary we'd seen. The water seemed at first glance to be gently flowing, less muddy, less

treacherous than the main river. Not so. The current put
our little motors to the test. Ascending the Pinilla, "this
tunnel through the woods" as Chris called it, resembled
passage through an obstacle course. Huge trees fallen into
the water lay at angles from shore, their branches obstructing passage. Living trees, bent over the water and sagging
to its surface, forced us to sweep away limbs. The canoes
scraped over and against fallen limbs, their progress helped
by hands that reached out and pushed or pulled.

In this wild backwater, we passed no huts along either bank. No fincas, docks or boat houses. Only dense forest, giant and shadowy, the towering treetops far beyond
our view.

Joe, elated, thumped his piranha tee shirt and gave a
Tarzan yell, which the roaring motors swallowed. I knew
how he must have felt. "This is the real stuff!" No doubt he
wanted to remind Monty Adams that we hadn't yet had a
walk in undisturbed forest, but the motor's noise would
have drowned him out.

For an hour the boatmen steered the canoes the only
way they could: darting, glancing, backing off, gunning
the motors, often barely able to squeeze beneath a tangle of
trunks and fallen vines.

Spider cursed as she tried to keep her wide-brimmed
hat from being snagged by a limb and ripped away. She
could have pulled off the hat entirely. Forest and clouds
screened out the sun. Yet the hat offered some protection
against limbs and lianas. At least she had one great advan-
tage today: she didn't have to sit beside Boris Kolinski.

I pondered our fortune in retrieving Kolinski's possessions the night before. I had wanted desperately to examine the contents of the aluminum notebook. The Briggles
and I, in the presence of the others, all of whom signed a
witness report, emptied the contents of the briefcase out
onto a bunk: a pint canteen (empty but the odor within
suggested that it had been filled with Coca Cola), chewing
gum, compass, bottle opener, ballpoint pen, checkbook,

small packet of pens and pencils, miniature dolls, hard candies and balloons, deodorant, raincoat, pocket English-Spanish dictionary, and a wallet with air tickets, travelers checks, credit cards, and five million Colombian pesos.

Joe had let out his long, descending whistle of astonishment. "That could make a down payment on a lot of rain forest."

After Joe had retired for the night, I examined the writings in the aluminum notebook—names, figures, doodles, and nearly illegible scribbling. By flashlight in bed, I read page after page, as best the pages could be deciphered. On some pages the ink was smudged. On others, the ink had been paled by absorption of water.

The notebook revealed more than anyone needed to know about Boris's business life, his thoughts, his plans, his comments admiring, snide, hateful. Some of the entries were in Spanish. A few disjointed Spanish phrases seemed to mean that he was fond of certain terminology and intended to use it again. The word *paulatinamente*, for example, which means slowly. I wasn't quite sure how he would use the word. At this hour, I wasn't anxious to go farther into Boris's mind.

I sealed the briefcase but did not put the notebook back inside.

As the canoes nosed their way up the river, I reduced the possibility of robbery as a motive. The thief could easily have taken the money, in the belief that he deserved the whole wad for his trouble. Or that society had done him wrong and now had to repay him. Logic suggested that not a peso should be left but long experience told me that logic did not always accompany murder. In this case, it was no help at all.

At length shafts of sunlight filtered down through the trees. The lead canoe drifted to starboard and nudged the muddy bank. We extricated ourselves, stepped over the side, and, slipping and sliding, crawled up crude steps cut in the embankment.

Emerging from the forest gloom, we came out upon a broad sunlit grassy expanse, as large as a football field. After the confinement of the river, it seemed like a Shangri-La. Indian huts, elevated on stilts, lined both sides. The familiar logs with notched steps leaned against the door of each. At the far end, to everyone's surprise, sat a long low building constructed of adobe-like bricks. Steel posts supported it. Corrugated metal capped the roof.

A piercing shriek filled the air: "Aki—eeee!"

The celestial blare came from somewhere within the nearest hut. Monty Adams grinned. "This here chief ain't like other chiefs in these parts. Better git ready—."

Before he could finish, the chief appeared at the door, leaped down the steps and bounded forward. A perfectly round bowl of black hair sat atop a handsome dark face wreathed in smiles. I guessed he could have been an uncle of Chief Manyuco. For all his age, he had the lithesome agility of a jungle cat. Adams introduced him as Chief Sonke.

The chief burst among us, laughing, giggling, shaking hands. He repeated our names in an awkward, lyrical Correguaje accent. Each time, he said something in return, probably "Welcome! Welcome!".

He stopped and gazed admiringly at Carol Lynn's pearls. Giggling, he examined the Fishers' Jungle Republic camera bags, thumped Joe's piranha tee, and put my baseball cap on his head for a moment, laughing all the while.

At Sonke's invitation, we sat on the ground in a circle, after which he passed around a gourd filled with chicha. Following the first round, Beryl Fisher got down to business. "Do you know a girl named Katerina?"

Sonke's eyes lighted. "Katerina!"

Beryl's eyes lit in happy surprise: "He *does* know her!" Then to the chief: "Where is she?"

The chief's face became puzzled. Carol Lynn got out her list of Correguaje words and spoke: "Katerina *alcoide?* Katerina *ho-oh?*"

At these words, the Chief jumped with delight, reached over and took her hand, then launched a stream of sentences toward her.

"No, no, chief!" she said, with a laugh. "I don't know *that* much Correguaje. All I want to know is, Katerina *alcoide*? Or Katerina *ho-oh*?"

Sonke giggled. "Hee-hee, hah, ho-oh!"

Beryl: "What's he saying?"

"Well, he knows Katerina, and she's here in the Amazon, but far away."

"Where, then? Ask him if she lives in a village somewhere? She may be captive."

Carol Lynn turned to the chief. "Katerina... *wehoopah*?"

Sonke became animated again, nodding vigorously. "*Wehoopah! Wehoopah Huitoto!*"

Gasps around the circle.

"Oh, my God!" Beryl blurted. "She's in a Huitoto village."

Greg let out a sigh of despair. "So ends *that* matter."

Carol Lynn now became animated. "It doesn't! We'll go find her. I'll get the chief to take us there."

Chris spoke up at once. "Why should we? You will remember, my dear, that they are a hostile tribe. They shoot people with arrows, or whatever."

Carol Lynn scoffed. "I'm interested in their language. Why should they want to shoot me? Not in the company of a friendly chief."

"How do you know he's friendly? How do you know he'll take you?"

Carol Lynn turned to Sonke, pointing to him. "You," then pointing to the circle, "take us, *tayawuh... wehoopah*?"

Beryl: "What did you say?"

"I asked if he'd take us to the village in a canoe."

We all looked at Sonke. He sat still for a moment, his eyes moving from one person to the other. Then he began to point methodically at each of the men, and wave his hand back and forth to indicate a negative.

Carol Lynn: "He's saying that he can't take men. Must be a taboo."

The chief then pointed to Carol Lynn and Beryl, smiled and nodded.

Chris immediately rose to his knees. "That is the end of *this* conversation. My wife is not going into hostile Huitoto country without me!"

Greg Fisher echoed: "Beryl, just say no!"

At this, Spider could not keep silent. "Will you two superior males calm down. What could you do if you went with them? You heard the chief. This is one situation in which they will be better off *without* you. They don't want any white warriors coming into their territory."

Carol Lynn raised her hand. "Let's not get started on that track. Beryl and I both have work to do in the Huitoto village. She will talk with Katherine, and I will get someone to take me around naming children, huts, trees and so on in their language. Now I will ask the chief if he will take us."

I held up a hand. "Before you start off into the wild unknown, I have two questions. One is why you are so anxious to find this woman."

Beryl answered: "She's my cousin."

"Well, then," I went on, "we have to consider that Monty has prepared our itinerary pretty closely. And it's a tight schedule. We are already disrupted by the Boris problem. That throws a wrench of uncertainty into this."

Beryl protested my line of reasoning. "Monty himself said we'd have a little flexibility to do the things we wanted."

"All right, then," I responded, "before you start making arrangements to go with Sonke and be gone for a couple days, you should clear your plans with Monty."

Chris said abruptly: "I think you should just drop the whole thing."

Beryl looked at Monty, who said: "Well, t'morruh we'll be near Huitoto country. If you'ins kin go 'n' come in two days, I don't reckon it'll hurt none. Long as you go with Sonke."

Carol Lynn turned to Sonke, pointed to Beryl, then herself, and said, *"Sonke Tayawuh ho-oh wehoopah Katerina?"*

Sonke smiled and raised his eyebrows in a way that said, "Well, I could be bought."

Chris: "This has gone far enough!"

Spider: "Sit down!"

Carol Lynn took out some Colombian pesos and held them in front of Sonke.

He pushed her pesos back and began looking around the group. His eyes lighted on Joe's piranha tee shirt and his face took on a leering expression.

Joe squirmed. "Oh, *no you don't*! You're not going to hold me hostage in this business."

Sonke rose. Everybody got up. The chief said: "Aki eeee!" and pointed to the piranha, laughing uproariously. Then, leaning forward, he peered closely, giggling all the while.

The pair made quite a picture—tall, blond cowboy and short, dark Indian chief, both in shorts. Cameras came out and started clicking. When Sonke saw that, he abruptly held up a finger, instructing the photographers to wait. Dashing to the hut, he leaped up the ladder in two bounds.

Joe, awestruck, whistled. "Great shit! What kind of a fink-o is this?"

Monty said: "After you and the chief are through, you can look around the village. If the chief wants to show you'all around himself, stay with him. If you walk away, he'll be hurt."

Joe laughed. "Gotcha! Insult the chief and he'll have you for lunch. Didn't you say these people had once been cannibals?"

CHAPTER 36

Sonke came out again, this time sedately descending the steps.

Joe whistled in astonishment. "Whee-ee-you! Will you look at that! What a quick-change artist!"

The chief, though still barefoot and clad in shorts, had placed over his shoulders a pure white flannel-like toga. Around his neck he wore multiple strands of blue and red beads. Beneath these, strands of seed pods cut in half spread out over the shoulders and fell part way down his back. Beneath these hung the prize display: a string of nearly two dozen jaguar teeth, all of different sizes.

Into a large hole in each ear he had inserted a bright red feather as long as a plumed pen. These pointed out front like the sweeping wings of a flying hawk.

Joe fell to his knees and started snapping at upward angles to accentuate the regal bearing. The Fishers pushed forward for closeups. Mo Briggle brought up his Polaroid camera and shot both portraits and profiles.

Sonke suppressed a grin. He stood in all his glory, savoring every moment of this mass veneration.

When they finished, Joe went forward to stroke the jaguar teeth. He gave the chief a postcard of Yellowstone.

Sonke again touched the piranha on Joe's shirt, and broke into a drawn-out musical laugh. Stopping abruptly, he rushed up into the hut, and came back down with another necklace of jaguar teeth. He raised it ceremoniously over Joe's head and brought the teeth down on the beads that Manyuco had earlier bestowed.

Joe went wild, jumping and turning. "For me? For me? Chief, you mustn't do this! Oh, yes you should! I'll never take it off. I'll wear it to class every day. Wear it home. I'll show it to all the——."

Then he stopped. The chief's black eyes still focused on the piranha shirt. An innocent face, half smiling, expectant...

Joe straightened, twisted his face, and spoke in slow, imperious tones.

"What I do now, I do in great pain." He placed his hand on his brow as a martyr. "Never has one man sacrificed so much to honor his people."

He choked up, the actor in him at its zenith.

With that he lifted his piranha tee shirt, eased it around the necklaces, and removed it. Coming forward, he knelt before Sonke, and with great ceremony presented it to the chief.

Sonke's eyes opened wide in mock surprise. His mouth spread in an ear-to-ear grin. He took the shirt with all the poise and dignity he could manage, whirled and dashed up the steps. When he returned, the toga had been replaced by the shirt. Now the giant jaws of the piranha met the teeth of the jaguar. No monarch ever showed a wider smile.

Sonke clapped his hand to Joe's shoulder, laughing in high-pitched glee. He let out a stream of musical words unintelligible to the visitors, and led the lanky cowboy off on a tour of the village. Joe made a departing comment. "Well, as Rick said in Casablanca, I think this is the beginning of a beautiful friendship."

Beryl and Carol Lynn stood with jaws agape. "Does that mean what I think it does?"

Monty said: "Joe just paid for your trip."

Spider said: "I'm glad. I want you to ask your cousin about Huitoto attitudes toward wildlife, about hunting. About selling animals."

Carol Lynn looked at me. "Barry?"

"All right," I responded. "Go with it. But you must follow Monty's and Sonke's instructions implicitly. In fact, I would myself like to know if ILB has gone that far inland to buy out the people. I doubt it, but I want to know for sure."

I acquiesced, but I still had misgivings. If anything went wrong, I didn't need two distraught husbands on my hands.

By this time of the morning, the tropical heat had removed the chill of the river trip. The visitors wandered among the huts, interacting with villagers in sign language, and watched the ubiquitous grating and squeezing of yuca.

Walking with the Briggles, I brought up the subject of Boris's briefcase on the steps of their hut. "We can't ignore that."

"No, sir," responded Mo in a humble tone.

I got out my notebook. "Tell me about it. Your remarks are on the record."

Mo spread his hands. "We have no idea how it got there, if that's what you want to know. You'll have to ask Monty. We never saw it. Maybe they found it under the hut. Maybe someone watched us go to dinner. It was after dark and we used a flashlight. They could have come up and dumped the stuff on our steps after we left."

"You definitely did not see it in or near your hut at any time?"

"Definitely. We would have reported it."

I jotted in my notebook. "All right. Now, with regard to the discovery of the body..."

Dana shook her head helplessly. "The sight startled me. I couldn't help screaming. It was silly of me."

"Not really," I said. "It was a sudden reaction. You got attention. Do you remember seeing anything unusual at the pond *besides* the body?"

"No, I was so shocked. What do you mean?"

"Anyone disappearing in the woods, for example? Anyone watching you? Walking away from the pond as you came up?"

She shook her head. "Nothing. I do remember thinking as I came back that everything was so quiet. I just said to myself that the village was still asleep."

I frowned. "Came back?"

Dana lowered her eyes. "I went on a walk in the woods."

Mo looked at her sharply. "You did what?"

"I crossed the river and went into the trees. There was a faint path. I was just curious."

Mo scowled. "After all we've been told about going in there alone."

I asked: "How long were you gone?"

Dana. "I can't honestly say. Maybe twenty minutes."

"In that time, Boris got to the pond. Did you see anyone as you came back?"

"Nothing."

"Okay. Did you ever have any intuition, any inkling, that this might happen?"

"I have a good imagination. Coming down the river in the canoe, I imagined that we would all drown! The more everybody talked about Boris, the more I began to imagine how someone might put an end to him."

"Did you ever, either of you, have such thoughts yourselves?"

Each answered, hesitantly, yes. "I guess we all had," Dana replied. "Boris did that to you."

We reached the brick building at the end of the grassy area and looked in the door: desks, maps, globes and a blackboard.

"A schoolhouse!" Dana remarked.

"Probably established by missionaries," I mused.

Mo said: "Must be a tough job to get building material all the way down the Orteguaza and up that little tributary."

Out front a concrete bunker supported a tall flag pole, but the pole had no flag. At the edge of the building we saw a small tag that read: "Treated with DDT," and gave the date.

Dana commented: "Must be a lot of cancer around here."

"Where's the teacher?" Mo asked.

"Gone, probably," I replied. "Difficult to get teachers down here."

"If these villagers move around a lot, how come the school?"

This puzzled me, too. "Hard to say. Someone may be trying to stabilize their nomadic patterns."

We passed Joe and Chief Sonke. The latter gestured wildly and pointed to the huts during a lengthy peroration apparently about Correguaje life.

Lunch consisted of canned Spam and biscuits, of which Chief Sonke partook as though savoring a repast of sirloin tips. Between bites, he wandered up to everyone in sight, showing off his new tee shirt.

After lunch, we reloaded into the canoes. Carol Lynn was last in, pleading with Sonke to take her and Beryl into Huitoto country. He agreed, bobbing his head up and down vigorously.

When?

Tomorrow.

I now began to take this matter seriously. A deviation from our scheduled itinerary could disrupt Monty's schedule, deal us a blow if the Americans got captured, and put my investigation into Kolinski's death on hold. If anything happened to Beryl or Carol Lynn, I would have two distraught husbands on my back, and we would have no choice but to go after the the captives. This could risk the ire of the entire tribe, and we would have a pitched battle on our hands.

Maybe I was overdoing it. Sonke would protect them. He had no problem as long as they were women.

Still, I couldn't help perceiving our trip as starting to come apart. While Monty had promised to try to cater to individual needs, I doubted if that encompassed entry into hostile Indian territory.

There was no way of knowing exactly how hostile the Huitotos were. Or why. I could guess. Perhaps a massacre of their ancestors decades ago. Ruination of their lands by petroleum exploration. Desecration of sacred grounds. It had all happened before.

As we shoved off, Sonke stood on the bank, a genuine monarch of the rain forest: beads, seed pods, jaguar teeth, piranha shirt, and a grin as wide as the Amazon.

Joe waved for as long as he could see the chief. Then he settled back in his seat, smiled to himself, and caressed the jaguar teeth.

Moments later he sat upright. "Listen! What's that?"

The canoe motors made less noise now as the current carried them downstream.

Spider asked: "What's what?"

"I thought I heard a helicopter."

"Here? Can't be."

"Remember Boris? 'If anything happens to me, an ILBRED helicopter will be down on you quicker than—.'"

"Joe!" She waved her hand to shut him off. "It's too soon. They couldn't get here this soon. They don't even know about it yet."

"Monty sent a message yesterday, you know."

"Things don't happen that fast in the jungle. You're just hearing things."

"Okay." He went back to the necklace. "I'm just hearing things."

CHAPTER 37

Returning in the orange glow of sunset, we walked up the trail from the dock, Joe as much on clouds as on the path. With the trade of a single sweat-encrusted tee shirt he had become an Amazon chieftain, replete with fangs of the tigre.

Approaching the village, he called out: "Where is my little welcoming committee?"

Chris said: "Well, you don't have your piranha shirt anymore, Joe. You'll jolly well be out of favor now. Sorry, old boy."

Joe called: "Tiata! Tee-ah-h-h-ta!"

No answer. Nowhere a sound of village voices. Silence. No dogs barking. No feet running across the plaza to greet the arrivals.

"See? I told you," said Chris. "My sympathy, old chap. Tough to lose a girl."

Joe looked around. "We've lost everybody."

It was true. We found the kitchen, usually a bustling social center at this hour, vacant and silent. Embers glowed beneath cooking pots. Faint wisps of smoke spiraled up through the opening in the roof. New picnic tables made by Manyuco's father had been placed near the kitchen entrance. No one sat at them.

Dana said: "Dinner should be in preparation. They're late."

I looked around. "Will all of you seat yourselves at these tables and stay here until I get back. Do not go into your huts. Monty, would you come with me?"

Joe asked: "Where are you going? Can I go?"

Monty and I disappeared into the blackness. Dana found a candle in the kitchen, lighted it, and set it on the table.

We went into each hut, checked the yuca house, the workshop, storage rooms, and, finding nothing, returned to the kitchen.

It was an eerie situation, totally unexpected. I told the group: "The village is deserted."

Spider: "Something is wrong. Why should they be gone?"

I asked Monty. "Has this ever happened before?"

"No, sir. Not while I been here."

"Could it be a dance somewhere? A ceremony? A death in the tribe?"

"Dunno. They wouldn't be gone with tourists to feed. That's a law with them."

"Well," Spider said, "it's a ghost town now."

Dana: "Something has happened to them."

Joe scowled. "I want to know where my little girl is."

Carol Lynn: "She'll be back, Joe. They'll all be back."

Dana: "People just don't disappear. There has to be an explanation."

Spider: "Boris. It's related to Boris. He's come back from the grave."

I saw a movement at the edge of the clearing. "I don't think Boris has come back. But someone sent his agents. There are two men with submachine guns coming up just behind you. I suggest you sit still and let me do the talking."

Beryl blanched. Joe sat upright. Carol Lynn shook her head in disgust. The Fishers closed their eyes. Dana turned and looked around.

Sure enough, two shadowy figures, dressed in black, against the black of the night, came into the dim circle of light. One fat and round-faced with stubble, the other burly and square-jawed.

Each carried, almost casually, a Uzi submachine gun slung over the shoulder.

I was the first to speak. "You're late."

Square Jaw said: "Everybody here?"

"Yes. We've been expecting you. Did you get Boris?"

"Yeah."

"The duffel bag?"

"Yeah."

"The briefcase?"

"Yeah. Only, they's one other thing—."

I cut in. "I don't think these people know your names. Maybe we ought to get better acquainted."

Square Jaw: "What? Get off it!"

"Well, why don't we just call you Square Jaw and your buddy Fatso? How would that be?"

Square Jaw responded: "Stop the stupid talk. Don't make us nervous or you'll..."

I interrupted: "You're already nervous."

"I said cut it. Which of youse done in Boris?"

I suppressed an epithet. "Good question. I just started the investigation here. And I don't like no guys musclin' in on my territory. I ain't through yet."

Square Jaw looked at the other passengers and repeated: "Which of youse done in Boris?"

"Who wants to know?"

Square Jaw said nothing for a few seconds, obviously seething with impatience. "Come on, Buddy. Stop buttin' out."

"The name's Barry, case you're interested. I asked you who wants to know?"

"It don't matter to you. We want the one who done it. Now just shut up and turn 'im over."

"Like I told you. I don't know who did it. Go back and tell that to your bosses. ILB, right?"

"All they want is bodies. Dead or alive, it don't matter. We want 'em now." He pointed to the group. "These people know. Whoever done Boris in, stand up. We'll let the rest of youse go."

A moment of silence. No one moved. I watched the thugs place their hands on their guns.

Slowly, Joe Muck got to his feet.

I had never seen such daring and ignorance. You might call it bravery, but I could see him being cut down without warning in a hail of machine-gun slugs.

While I was pondering this, and watching Square Jaw very closely, Dana rose. The whole gang was crazy.

Mo got up. Chris and Carol Lynn stood. The Fishers rose. Finally Spider.

Square Jaw seemed too astounded to move. In his feeble brain there must have been the question that they couldn't all have done the job. That they dared to make fun of him.

This display of drama had to be stopped. I said quietly: "All right. You've made your point. Square Jaw thanks you. I thank you. Now you may sit back down."

They sat.

"Shish!" Joe muttered. "Just like in Spartacus! I always wanted to do that."

For the first time, Fatso spoke. "Come on, boss. I'm gettin' fed up with this."

I asked: "What makes you think he was murdered?"

"Dead, ain't he?"

"Sure he's dead. Drank too much. Had a heat stroke."

Abruptly Fatso snarled, pointed his gun into the tree next to the kitchen and let off a fiery burst. The suddenness of the movement and the deafening explosions so close to our ears startled us all. Twigs and shattered leaves darted into the night sky, then fell in a shower of debris.

When the echoes had faded, Fatso cast glaring eyes over us. "I can settle the whole thing, Boss. Just like that. Can I?"

These guys were getting edgy. It was time to play my hole card.

"I don't think your boss wants to," I said. "He ain't got what he came for."

Fatso turned and looked directly at me, puzzled, almost stupefied.

Square Jaw slowly put his finger to his nose and brushed away an imaginary fly. Looking straight at me, he said: "That so?"

I remained perfectly calm, almost nonchalant. "Yeh. That's so."

For a whole minute, Square Jaw and I glared at each other. Nobody moved. Nobody said anything. Some in the group scarcely dared to breathe. I had to suppress a smile, noting that both Joe and Spider were completely silent. I also hoped against hope that Joe would not lash out and try to tackle these guys as he would on the gridiron.

Fatso turned away in disgust and faced the dark.

Joe glanced furtively at me, waiting for some kind of signal. I shook my head almost imperceptibly. Spider stirred uncomfortably. The rest sat granite still.

Square Jaw blinked, shifted on his feet, and broke the silence. "All right. Where is it?"

I grinned. "You two bastards can just hie your asses out of here and go back to ILBRED. Tell them I've been reading Boris's notebook. I know all about your activities in Puerto Asis. You know about that? Your bosses will. The Colombian government doesn't. The government has been trying to find out what's going on in Puerto Asis. I now know the name of your mole in the *Ministerio de Agricultura*, too. Boris wrote a lot. The notebook names another agent in the *Instituto de Recursos Naturales Renovables*. This could break open your whole goddam outfit, buddy. Ever heard of Lucio La Palma? No? Very few people have. Tell your bosses you heard about Lucio La Palma. Tell them where you heard his name. Then ask for instructions. Tell them there's a lot of other stuff in there, and they're not going to like it being made public. Do you understand that?"

Square Jaw's face remained completely emotionless. He waited to reply, and when he did, the voice contained no hint of emotion.

"We'll take one of these people back with us. For safekeepin'."

The effect on the people at the table could scarcely be observed. Chris and Carol Lynn sat looking off toward the kitchen. Spider fiddled with the big hat in her lap. Joe shifted so that he could watch the faces of the speakers, his eyes darting from one to the other of them. The Fishers sat looking almost nonchalantly at each other, as though resigned to being blown up.

When I spoke, I delivered the words very slowly, with an icy edge.

"You won't lay a hand on any of these people. You may as well get that shitty idea out of your heads right *now*."

The thugs did not move. Their reaction could not be perceived in the darkness. Square Jaw replied: "That so?"

I came down hard and fast on the heels of that response. "Yeah, *that's so*. And you won't get the notebook, either. I sealed it and sent it to San Antonio to be mailed to my office. Tell your bosses that nobody in Colombia knows where my office is just in case ILB gets interested. With one phone call I can have the notebook either opened or thrown away."

I paused for a moment. The thugs had become edgy, sneaking looks at one another, shifting on their feet. I went on: "Tell them I'm about to find out who killed Boris. And when I find out, I sure as hell am not going to tell ILB. The police will let ILB know soon enough. Now take it from me. Get back to Bogotá as fast as you can and get new instructions. Now, anything else I can help you with?"

Square Jaw seemed like a statue of granite. Fatso shook his head in disgust. I turned my back on them and sat beside Spider. I leaned forward, put my elbows on the table, and glanced at Joe.

Never had I seen anyone in such a state of paralysis. Joe seemed almost on the verge of exploding with pent-up agitation, ready to unleash a flying tackle to bring both men down at once. Spider's face had a combination of half grimace and half exultation. The rest, if they expected a barrage of flying lead out of the darkness, betrayed no hint of it. No fear. No panic.

Finally, Carol Lynn, looking around, whispered: "They're gone."

Before Joe could erupt, I held up a finger, shook my head, and said softly: "No."

They watched me as an orchestra watches a conductor. They all obeyed, remaining as silent as stalking *tigres*, listening, hearing nothing, saying nothing. They peered into the dark and saw only emptiness.

Minutes went by, accompanied by the buzz of insects that now seemed all out of proportion in the noises of the night. We listened for the slightest footfall. An intruder brushing against a tree branch. The clank of metal...

This much on edge, we became vulnerable. When a tree frog suddenly screeched in the darkness beyond the edge of the kitchen, it sounded like a screech of a suddenly stilettoed murder victim. We jerked involuntarily. We couldn't help it. This unanimous action instantly loosened tension, and provoked a reaction of laughter, which came out stifled, choked and almost throttled. I laughed, too, but held up my hand.

Silence settled again. There was no hint of rain in the air, but we could see the glow of lightning somewhere beyond the horizon. Had the thugs gone into a huddle and decided to come back shooting? We had not known such moments of tension since leaving Florencia. It was almost unbearable. Our ears groped for the slightest sound.

At length, I said quietly: "Dana, do you think we could use another candle on the table?"

She rose without answering and went into the kitchen. As she returned, an enormous roar filled the night air.

Joe shouted at the top of his lungs: "Helicopter! They're taking off!"

The loudness increased. Above the treetops to the south we glimpsed a flashing red light rise, then diminish in size as the craft flew away. The roar of the engine faded.

Pandemonium broke loose around us. The circle of candlelight filled with people. Correguaje cooks came out of the darkness and went into the kitchen. Chief Manyuco appeared on the scene with Monty. Spider, the Fishers, and the Arden-Joneses seemed all to be talking at once. The Briggles shouted: "Hooray for Barry!" They all came to me and hugged, and slapped, rejoicing in their sudden release from tension.

Out of the dark came a tiny cry. Little Tiata ran straight to Joe and leaped up into his arms.

CHAPTER 38

Next morning we headed up the Micalla River.

We were drowsy. We had stayed up late. My incorrigible fellow passengers wanted nothing more than to cheer our victory over the ILB thugs. I warned them not to do that. We weren't out of the jungle yet. They wouldn't listen, steeped as they were in Coke and chicha.

Joe had offered the first toast: "To the bravest bastard this side of San Antonio!" They applauded and lifted their cups.

Spider rose: "I offer a cup to the smartest son-of-a-bitch I know!"

The Arden-Joneses rose, and Carol Lynn extolled: "Cheers to a professor of murder and a Roman conqueror of the first order!"

The Fishers followed, then the Briggles, then Joe started the whole process over again. They couldn't stop. They danced on the banana leaves, sang more praises to their hero of the night, and eventually devoured boiled chicken, cheering and probing me mercilessly about my tactics. I brushed them off, saying I wasn't going to give away operational secrets. They laughed and shouted, and eventually wandered off in the darkness to their huts.

At sunrise, Monty had crowded us into a single canoe, fulfilling his promise to take us, especially Spider, into some wild country. We were crowded because Sonke and Aunamunh, the nearly a teenager, were along to accompany Beryl and Carol Lynn into Huitoto country. The Briggles had opted not to accompany us, but rather to go into the forest with Drs. Jackson and Garcia.

Entering the mouth of the Micalla and starting upstream, we discovered at once that the Micalla had even more obstacles than the Pinilla River. So many, in fact, that vegetation, dense and obstructing, very nearly blocked our passage. For two hours before the accident occurred, the Indian guides cut repeatedly through vines and fallen limbs so that the canoe could get through.

This only proved to Spider that we had definitely gone into the wild Amazon, beyond the beaten path. Our destination: somewhere upstream to discharge Sonke, Aunamunh, Beryl and Carol Lynn into the forest for their trek to Huitoto country. That argument had mingled with all the celebrations last night. The wives crushed all their husbands' opposition, with some spirited help from Spider. Now, accompanied by only a chief and a boy, they were off into territory unknown to them.

"Where no one has gone before," Joe observed. With such a load, the small motor strained to make headway against the powerful current.

The usual nighttime thunderstorm had struck at dawn. The heavy downpour left water dripping from leaves and vines. With high humidity along the river, much of this moisture remained in the trees, even in midmorning. When the canoe squeezed through a mass of vegetation, we came out dripping, our clothing soaked.

Spider didn't care. She had no complaints. She had asked for this. Whatever happened, she'd gotten what she'd been begging for. If only Monty could silence the motor and let them listen to the real forest...

Chris and Greg sat sullenly, about to lose their wives into the depths of the forest with Sonke. Neither trusted an

Indian chief they barely knew, especially in the territory of hostile Indians. This could be the last they would ever see their wives alive, and each fed his imagination with images of horror at the hands of...

Twenty minutes up the river, Joe shouted: "A morpho!"

Everybody followed his gaze and glimpsed what he identified as a rare sight in the Amazon. A huge morpho butterfly passed directly over us, its iridescent purple wings flashing in the filtered sunlight. The creature appeared to be about the size of two human hands spread out, fingers extended.

Amid our exclamations, Joe said in disgust: "Take a good look! People use those wings to decorate serving trays, picture frames, mirrors, everything you can think of. We're lucky to see one alive."

We craned our necks to observe the morpho as long as we could. Then it continued downstream and disappeared.

From time to time we glimpsed the hanging baskets of oropendola nests, some ten feet long, attached to the tips of tree limbs. We saw a bird fly to one of the suspended masses and work its way within.

The motor on the canoe labored and whined like a chain saw. Progress up the river continued slow and erratic, but we didn't mind. Joe called it a green canyon with a floor of brown water. For a ceiling we had the brilliant blue of sky and white of billowing clouds. On either side, a nearly impenetrable mass of limbs, trunks and leaves walled us in. Tiny openings gave tantalizing glimpses beyond, but the forest gloom contrasted with the glare of the sun, so we saw no objects inside.

After we had struggled up the river for an hour, Monty Adams pointed out some abandoned huts set back from the river bank. "Huitoto," he shouted.

Chris and Greg frowned, glancing at their wives, simmering with indignation.

Another hour of winding and struggling went by, the motor laboring, stopping, getting restarted, whining and sputtering. The river narrowed even more. The obstructions became thicker, passage in places almost impenetrable, even with machetes. Spider wondered how much farther they would be able to—.

A loud bang broke the noise. The motor stopped. The little canoe lurched. A small object sailed through the air and splashed into the muddy river.

Free to float on its own, the canoe turned crosswise in the current, and began to spin out of control downstream.

CHAPTER 39

"Motor's out!" Monty shouted. "Get the oars."

He, Eduardo and Aunamunh picked up paddles attached to gunwales of the canoe, plunged them into the water and pulled mightily to steer the canoe to shore. It drifted rapidly, snagged a fallen tree, listed to port, and brushed the edge of a mass of vines.

The passengers reached out and flailed their arms to disentangle from the clutching stems. Leaves slapped their faces. Limbs knocked Spider's hat askew We were all forced to bend double. Joe and I pushed as hard as we could against a fallen trunk. Eventually all these efforts freed us from the tangle.

Out on open water, the paddlers could maneuver. They didn't have much time before they would strike the next tangle of vines. Monty searched the wall of green for an opening, some embankment where we might haul ashore. No luck.

Spider, at least, became elated. No motor! That infernal racket she had tried for days to silence no longer disturbed the quiet.

Once the river current carried us into a thicket. We reached out, grabbed limbs, and shoved, trying to get the canoe pointed out into open water.

It was no use. The current dragged us even farther into the morass of limbs and lianas and held us there.

As she fought the overhanging snags that reached out and clawed at her, Spider, I fancied, began to see some advantages of motors on canoes.

I reflected on what would happen if a sharp limb gored the hull and sank the canoe. If someone got injured and had to be rushed to a hospital three days away. And what would happen if the hostile Huitotos caught us helpless like this?

Our arms flailed wildly. Progress came in inches. Around a tree trunk. Over a submerged log. Under the vines and through a watery thicket. Into and out of vine-covered tunnels. Plunging paddles sent up spray that struck our faces without warning.

Monty shouted instructions. Eduardo shouted instructions. Aunamunh put his feet against a limb to steer the bow into open water. He stretched so far out, with only his fingertips grasping the canoe, that his feet slipped and he fell into the river. Grasping a vine, he flung himself lithely up over the edge and back into the canoe.

These chaotic efforts finally succeeded in getting the prow pointed toward open water. With desperate paddling, the canoe broke free. Everybody cheered.

Drifting at the will of the current, the paddlers tried to avoid thickets. Around another bend, and then another, they finally discovered a muddy bank and edged over to it. Aunamunh leaped on shore, secured a rope to the nearest tree, and hauled the craft as far out on shore as he could.

CHAPTER 40

"What happened?" Joe asked, getting to his feet. In the furious battle with the lianas no one had had time to ask what brought this all on.

Monty and the crew converged on the motor and soon had the problem defined: the cam shaft had broken and sent a part of the device out over the river and down twenty feet to the muddy bottom. Somewhere back upstream.

"Repairable?" I asked.

"Maybe," Monty replied. "Be a while."

"Terrific," Joe said in delight. "We're marooned! In hostile Indian territory! Wait'll I tell *this* to the folks back home."

"Don't," cautioned Spider. "You'll have a credibility problem."

"I already have."

Stranded on a wild river, Joe and Spider realized their dream to see the uncut Amazon forest at last. See cannibals, too, Joe thought. He grabbed his pack and leaped out on the bank. Spider flung her hat into the canoe, and would have plunged through the shrubbery and into the woods had I not held her back. I raised a finger, suggesting she wait a moment.

Chief Sonke analyzed the situation. Seeing Monty and Eduardo working on the engine, he tapped Carol Lynn on the shoulder and motioned to Beryl and Aunamunh. He picked up his backpack, pointed to theirs, and swung his hands toward the woods. They would leave for the Huitoto village from here. Now.

Without further word, he and Aunamunh stepped through the shrubbery and disappeared into the gloom beyond.

"Here's where we separate," said Carol Lynn, picking up her pack and embracing Chris. Beryl and Greg said their goodbyes. Joe, Spider and I embraced the departees. Against my better judgement.

Chris and Greg had heavy scowls on their faces. "I distinctly dislike committing my wife to unfriendly Indian country alone," growled Chris to Carol Lynn. "You have one more chance to abort this mission. I suggest you do it now."

Spider's voice grew in volume. "What do you want her to do? Call Sonke back and tell him she's changed her mind? That now she's afraid to go? Is that the kind of wife you married? There's a twelve-year-old boy in there dying to go. What the hell do you think your wife is made of? Sponge rubber?"

Chris suffered this outburst all the while looking at his wife. When Spider finished, he asked: "Well?"

"We shan't be alone," Carol Lynn responded for what seemed like the twentieth time. "We'll be in quite good hands. Besides, I transcribed my new Correguaje words. With them I can converse with the chief. Gives me a chance to try them out and add new ones. Brilliant, don't you think?"

"Why don't you simply give up the whole idea? You don't have to go, you know."

"Because it's dangerous? Because I'm frail? Because—."

Chris slapped his trouser leg with a resounding *splat!* "Oh, skip it. Skip it. I know you're tough. I know you can take it. Spider's right. Go on!"

"Thank you."

"But remember this: don't play the foolish heroine. Give them your pearls if you have to."

Carol Lynn took offense. *"I will not!"*

Spider barked: "Of course she won't. Now leave her alone." To Carol Lynn she said, tenderly but forcefully: "Don't give 'em anything, honey!"

Carol Lynn followed this with more hugs all around, then picked up her pack, gave Chris a wink and a playful cuff on the shoulder, and disappeared into the tomb of darkness behind the great wall of forest.

Greg held Beryl's hand as long as he could. "You're putting an awful lot of trust in one man."

"I've done that before," she said, a sly look on her face.

He frowned. "That's not what I mean. How do you know Sonke and the Huitotos are on good terms? I mean, this week?"

"I don't," she replied. "Sometimes you have to trust people you don't know very well. Makes life exciting, right?"

Then she, too, embraced the others, entered the wild woods and was gone.

CHAPTER 41

I waited until Chris and Greg joined us, then, with Joe and Spider, started upstream.

"Watch for *tigres*," Monty called. "Big cats in there. Not many, maybe, but some."

"Only takes one," I called back. "We won't go far."

As Monty and the boatmen began to hammer on the broken engine, I took my pack, pointed to a hole in the forest wall, and led the way through. The thick vegetation at the river's edge, nourished by sunlight, gave way to a forest much less thick.

Inside, our eyes began to adapt to the dim light.

Spider said: "There's nothing in here."

I answered: "You're almost right."

Tree trunks rose in the gloom like columns in a dimly lighted mosque or cathedral. They reached straight upward until they disappeared in a mass of leaves that filtered out nearly all light. Each tree trunk stood far enough from its neighbors to allow us easy passage. Few shrubs, thickets or lianas blocked our passage. No carpets of flowers. Very little grass. Only a vine or two, trailing from above.

"Too shady for much to grow," I said. "The sun never shines down here. Well, maybe a little spotlight at a time. Most vegetation needs more sunlight than this."

We shuffled our feet among huge dry leaves, resulting in a rustle that seemed out of place in a rain forest.

"It rained this morning!" Greg commented. "How can all this be dry?"

"Well, it rained out on the river, and up there," I answered, pointing to the forest canopy. "Not much trickled through. Water ran along the leaves and into moss or air plants growing along the limbs. Most of it got pretty well absorbed. Besides, it rained five hours ago. That's time enough for excess water to drain away. There's some evaporation, though the air is very humid."

"I don't see any flowers," Greg mused. "We haven't seen many on our whole trip. This isn't what you'd call a garden of Eden."

I waved my hand toward the tree tops. "Flowers grow up there. Way up. That's where the sunlight is. Lots of orchids. Heliconias. Bromeliads. Very beautiful. Even cactuses."

"You're kidding!"

"When you get back home, find a copy of Margaret Mee's book, *In Search of Flowers of the Amazon Forest*. She was a British artist who explored the Amazon for years and painted the flowers, birds, Indians and landscapes. She traveled the rivers. Indians brought flowers to her, sometimes from high up in the trees. Flowers like you never saw."

Greg wrote the title down in his notebook.

We came to tree trunks festooned with sharp spines, gigantic thorns, and shelf fungus. We stopped and listened. Beyond the hum of insects we heard an ebbing and flowing chant of guttural tones that seemed to come, stereo-like, from several directions at once.

"Jaguars?" Spider whispered.

"Howler monkeys," I offered. "You hear them all over the tropics. Try to see one. That's something else..."

The sound of the distant growling rose and fell again, then faded.

"If you're right beneath them," I added, "it's quite a racket."

An ear-piercing shriek punctured the quiet. From the direction of the river came a loud and unexpected cascade of musical notes, explosive and liquid.

"Oropendola," Greg said. "We heard it yesterday. They're the birds that make those long hanging nests. What a song!"

It came again, piercing the silence with sharp melodic bursts like clanging bells, beeping horns and a murder victim shrieking all at once. Greg raised his binoculars in vain.

"You won't see it," I said. "Except maybe flying down the river where the forest is more open and there's more light."

Greg, still worried, asked: "Where will they sleep tonight? I mean, our wives. On the ground? On a limb? It gets cool in here."

I answered: "My guess is that there are hundreds of places to sleep. Holes here and there. Caves. Old shelters or huts built by Indians. Most likely would be in a pile of leaves on the ground."

Greg: "Now I *am* worried!"

"Beryl, I assume, is an outdoor person. She'll enjoy it. What about Carol Lynn?"

Chris answered: "Not much camping, I'm afraid. But stubborn. Adaptable. Durable. She'll get along."

We moved out of range of the hammering sounds that came from the motor under repair.

I wanted to investigate the forest more closely, but I had another investigation to conduct. We were under threat by the thugs of ILB. I did not underestimate their ability to make life miserable for us. There was no assurance that my bluff would work. I was out on a limb. If all those items in Boris's notebook were common knowledge, then my ruse would fail. Nothing could keep the thugs from finding us again, and, with guns trained, start some kind of torture.

If my ruse worked, then they would leave us alone. Nice hope. I didn't believe it. Meanwhile, I had to continue probing the minds of the passengers.

I held Greg back as the others walked ahead. Then I asked softly: "What did you see on your river excursion the other day? You and Beryl went up the river bank with Spider. Did you see Boris?"

"No," Greg replied. "He was gone all day, as you know."

"Evidently he came back before you did. He would have had to reach the dock while you three walked up or down the river. Did you see any boat out on the river, or tied up at the dock?"

"We must have been too far upriver. Didn't intend to go that far. Kept seeing so many things—hummingbirds, hoatzins, even a toucan. Just kept going without realizing how far we'd walked. When we got back, only a couple canoes were at the dock."

"Then most of the time you were out of sight of the dock?"

"Yes. Anyway, if we'd heard anything, we wouldn't have paid any attention."

"Why not?"

"We had our eyes and ears tuned to discovering birds, mammals, reptiles, anything in the trees around us."

"Did anyone go with you?"

"Yes, an Indian boy. Spider had some lemon drops and gave him some, and he thought they were out of this world."

"How long did he stay with you?"

"Half an hour, maybe. He went back to the village by a shortcut."

I turned my head. "A shortcut?"

"Yes."

"Did you go along it?"

"We assumed it led to the village. The boy took off into the woods. We saw it was a trail. Primitive, but passable."

"Did you go along it?"

"A few minutes, that's all. We wanted to see where it went."

"Did you?"

"No."

"Then you came back?"

"Yes."

"How did you know it was a trail to the village?"

"We just put two and two together. We presumed the boy was going home."

"Very interesting," I mused, hand to chin. "That may be the trail Dana took. Was there any way to tell why they had another trail to the village?"

Greg spread his arms. "There are trails all around there. Not constructed trails like we build at the nature center in Wisconsin. Just paths where you see the leaves trampled down. You can follow them if you keep close watch. All I can say is that it just looked like a shorter way for the boy to get back home. Why? Does it mean something?"

"Could be," I answered. "As far as the river is concerned, did you see anything unusual out there? Anyone you knew?"

"Nothing more than canoes now and then with Colombians or Indians in them. Maybe both."

"What were they carrying, if anything? Fishing poles?"

"Not that we could see."

"Packs? Bodies?"

Greg hastened to point out that underneath the canvas in the canoes the occupants could have been carrying anything.

I went on. "When you got back to the dock, did you notice anything unusual?"

"No. We were still looking for flowers, birds and things."

"In the time that you were gone, Kolinski returned. Who was at the dock when you came back?"

"Adams and some Indians."

"What were they doing?"

"Talking. I guess we should have known that something was up, because you had discovered the body by then. Monty was always talking with the Indians. We don't like to interfere."

"Could you hear what they were saying?"

"Too far away."

"How do you feel about what happened?"

"Beryl and I were relieved. I don't mind saying it. I don't know what would have happened if that had gone on another day."

"Explain."

"That last insult to Spider was all I needed. If I had seen that bastard one more time pumping gin down the Correguajes... Well, I don't think I'd have been accountable for my actions."

"How do you feel about the Indians?"

"Protective. I think we all do. They are wonderful people. I admire them for opening themselves and their villages to us. Sonke yesterday was a real highlight of the trip. He made it all worthwhile. They're indigenous. They belong here. Boris's comments about them and plans to move them out just added to our resentment. It was all piling up. I'm not surprised at what happened. Heck. I'm glad it happened!"

A call came through the woods and we made our way back to the river bank. "Is it fixed?" Spider asked.

Monty nodded.

Spider added: "Ingenious. How did you do it?"

"Always take an extra motor when we go out in one canoe. Took parts we needed from one and put 'em in the other."

Spider smiled. "You make it sound so damned simple! We could have been marooned out here for God knows how long!"

Joe Muck held up a finger and said: "So what? We'd have had lots of turtle eggs to eat!"

"Oh, shut up!" she said.

The passengers reboarded. Chris and Greg took one more forlorn look into the forest where their wives had disappeared. They glanced briefly at each other and scowled. I could see fear and uncertainty in their faces. Their wives had disappeared into unknown territory with no phones, no radio, no telephone. No contact whatever. All very well to say "Forget it, forget them, they'll be all right." But from their disturbed minds they could not erase the fact that their wives had been severed almost completely from them. For an undetermined amount of time, with a tribe antisocial, to say the least...

Eduardo steered the canoe downstream. The motor wheezed and clanked. Which didn't matter. Everyone aboard had a new respect for it. We steered right past a tangle of trunks and vines dipped into the water.

Best of all, we hadn't heard a single helicopter all day long.

CHAPTER 42

Returning to the village, we found the Red Chief sick. Tiata led us to the hammock in the Chief's hut. The old man's eyes had closed as though in death, his wrinkled face at rest. He breathed steadily, however, which led us to conclude that he had only entered a deep sleep.

I asked Monty: "What's the matter?"

Shake of the head.

That response broke my patience, rang an alarm bell in my inner sensor banks . I wanted to ask: "Don't you know? Why not? If you're so well acquainted with these people, what gives?"

Monty *did* know. Monty lived with the Correguajes. Learned their language. Helped through crises. Talked frequently with Manyuco.

Then why this secrecy? Enough of it! I took Monty's arm. "Would you come over to the kitchen table for a little while, please?"

Adams nodded. We descended the steps and left the old chief's hut. Outside, we encountered Jackson, Garcia and the Briggles, just returned from their trip into the forest. After the greetings, I said: "I'd like all of us to gather around the kitchen table. It'll soon be supper time anyway. If you would, please."

Before the meal began, Dr. Jackson asked: "Has anyone given the chief any treatment, any medicine?"

Monty answered. "Someone has gone to look for something."

"Where? San Antonio? Florencia?"

"No. Into the forest."

Mo Briggle asked immediately: "The forest? What are they looking for?" Monty remained calm. "Y'all can see when they git back."

Mo persisted. "Do you know what it is?"

"No."

"Do you know what's wrong with the chief?"

Monty lowered his head. I scowled and was about to speak.

Anger crept into Mo's voice: "You ought to know. You've been living with these people, working with them. Manyuco must have told you why he's sick."

Monty still didn't answer, which made Mo madder.

"Look, you promised to show us the Amazon. Now show us what's going on with Palkuh. I run computer tests on medicines. That's one of the reasons I came. I need to know."

Spider spoke up, her voice also tinged with impatience. "Monty, I have the same bitch. I ask you if anybody ships eels out of the Amazon. You almost ignore the question. The hell with that! You said you'd help us. In all your years down here, you're not blind—."

I interrupted. "I think we can all understand that if Monty pried his nose into everybody's business on this river, then blathered it all around, he'd lose respect. He has to get along with people. Anybody who reveals secrets is no longer trusted. He's dead in the water."

Spider: "Okay. So?"

"So he plays his cards close. I would, too. I haven't much to go on, but I suspect that if Monty answers your questions, he indicts someone. My guess is that there is something really bad behind the chief's being sick, and Monty's reluctant to get you all upset—."

"Reluctant be damned!" Spider barked. "If something bad is going on down here, it's goddammed time we all found it out."

Joe added: "That goes for me, too. I'm getting a little tired of all this secrecy and run-around."

In the ensuing silence, they waited for Monty to respond. He held his head down. No one spoke. No one interrupted his thoughts, in the hope of letting him respond in his own good time. A minute passed. Then he said, softly: "I guess I ought to apologize to you. I don't mean to ignore y'all. Tain't my way. I have to, sometimes, like Barry says, but I don't like it. Most of the time, I don't have no trouble. Folks I bring down here keeps to themselves except when they want to know about *tigres* and things like that. But I got to say this. You're not like most people I bring down here. Christ! They ain't nothin' you ain't asked me about. Sometimes I don't know. I just as well wait for people to find things out for theirselves..."

Spider barked: "How? You're the only source of information we have down here. We ask about fish. You tell us. We ask about jaguars. You're full of information. I ask about shipping eels to hospitals, you clam up. We want to know what's wrong with Palkuh. You give us a stone wall. I'm getting pissed off, and I don't mind saying so."

Monty lapsed into silence again.

I said: "Monty, I understand what you're saying. I think you're right. I sympathize. But I also think these are valid complaints. If you're trying to hide something to protect somebody, I can appreciate that. But there is one element that makes this a little different right now."

Monty looked up. "Yes, sir?"

"I'm trying to investigate a murder. To do it right, I need to become at least partly as knowledgeable as you about this country and its people. I always require a lot more knowledge than I use. Everyone in our group is under suspicion. They have a right to know what is going on. I would like you to tell us what you are hiding. I respect your desire to keep your thoughts private on this river. I will resolve not to say who divulged anything, and I will ask the people around this table to consider the source of any information you give us as not to be revealed. Unless, of course, it is widely known to all but us. Am I clear?"

Nods around the table.

Monty waited for a while, first with head down, then looking around at all the other faces, and finally back at me. He said, softly: "You ain't going to like it."

Spider looked at me, then back to Monty.

"Go ahead," she said.

CHAPTER 43

Monty spoke softly, looking mostly at the candlelight and at his plate.

"Palkuh is chief of a village on the Rio Ramón, a tributary of the Caquetá River. Day after tomorrow, we'ins will go down the Caquetá to the Tres Esquinas air field, but we ain't got plans to go to Palkuh's village."

Spider: "Why not?"

Monty went on. "Awhile ago, maybe a year, some miners came to the village and found gold in the river banks just upstream. They tried to buy the land all around, includin' the village. That way, they could own it and make their operations legal. ILB tried to help them."

Mo: "Palkuh wouldn't sell?"

"ILB offered him and his people everthing. Money. Transportation to a new location. Land. New start in life. But it didn't work. The Indians didn't want it. Palkuh wouldn't sell."

"Why?" I asked.

"'Cuz, he said, it was his home. The home of his people. He didn't want to move."

Chris: "Bully for him."

"Miners got real mad. But before they did anythin' real drastic, they went to the guvmint. Tried to get the bigwigs in Bogotá to force the Indians out. For the good of the ee-conomy, they said. That didn't work. They come to the end of their rope. So then, they began to be very nice to the people in the village..."

"Uh, oh," said Joe. "This is getting ominous."

Monty went on. "I warned yuh. Yuh ain't goin' to like this. The people like sugar a lot. 'Specially the little kids. The miners brought sugar to the kids. To the people. They ate it up. Got used to it. Everbody in the village became friends with the miners..."

He paused, as though finding it too painful to proceed.

Spider: "Sounds like a Boris Kolinski trick. What then?"

Monty stopped. "Are you'ins sure you wants t'know this?"

"Yes!" Mo almost shouted it.

Spider said quietly: "We can take it."

I commented: "I don't want you to hold anything back."

The food came. Monty waited, looking at his plate for a few moments without saying anything. Then he went on, measuring his words carefully.

"After they got everybody used to eating sugar, they started putting little amounts of arsenic in it."

For a moment there was silence, the empty silence of total disbelief.

Spider gasped. "Oh, my God."

Mo said: "Monty! You have to be kidding."

Joe choked, sagging in his seat, putting his hand to his forehead. "Great shit!"

Dana: "I can't believe this."

Monty continued. "It wa'n't much, at first. Nobody noticed. Kids only got a little sick. Then, later, the people in the village, as they ate more arsenic, got real sick. Started dying."

Joe blurted: "What a goddamn cruel trick. Monty, how could anyone do that to those kids?"

"They's only a few of the original people left out there now. Palkuh didn't eat much of the sugar, but ever since then, he's been sick off and on. And that's what's the matter now. He went to Bogotá and got the guvmint to tell ILB to stop trying to buy the land. He won. And now they're after him. Personal like ... The chief hisself."

I asked: "ILB?"

Monty stopped and would say no more. He got up and left.

CHAPTER 44

I rose at dawn and looked over at Palkuh's hammock. The old chief was gone.

This sent a chill down my spine.

I sat up. If he had died, there would no predicting what kind of uprising might explode against white intruders into these realms. Vengeance knew no limits.

Pushing it a little, aren't you? my inner voice scolded.

I certainly was. Dressing in a hurry, I went out the door. Dropping down the steps of the hut, I ran toward the kitchen and saw Palkuh playing with Tiata.

What a relief!

See, you're a little edgy.

I went over to them and joined the game. I launched a puzzled look at the chief, who grasped my shoulder with one hand and with the other executed a wave to mean "I'm all right, thank you."

Manyuco had brought the medicines yesterday, administered them, left the old chief alone. The remedies in those leaves and strips of bark had worked overnight.

Mo Briggle, the medical imaging engineer, had selected samples from the little pouch and put them into a plastic bag—handling them as though they were a cure for cancer. Mo had said something like *"This* time *we'll* be the ones to beat Forward Imaging."

I looked at Palkuh quizzically and asked about Sonke. No news. Sonke and Aunamunh and Beryl and Carol Lynn could be on another planet as far as we were concerned.

I looked around and listened for any kind of helicopter. Anyone slinking through the woods. Maybe I *was* getting edgy. I was playing a deadly game. How long, or even whether, I could hold the upper hand kept me in a pool of anxiety. I was banking solely on the secrets in Boris Kolinski's notebook.

If this didn't work, we were in trouble. I had little in the way of fighting tools. No heavy guns. No ammo. No reinforcements. Nothing.

The enemy had everything.

And the enemy was scared. Boiling mad. Blind with rage.

If I didn't find out soon who murdered Boris, I'd be facing Fatso and Square Jaw again. Returned with new instructions. An ugly thought.

I decided to walk the shortcut trail a little way. Crossing the stream on the log, I entered the forest and found the trail primitive, as the Fishers had said, but obviously well used by the Correguajes.

I followed it for ten minutes. It yielded nothing, leaving me where I began. Wondering how the body got to the pond.

If not by the shortcut, then up the main trail from the river. Quite a job. Boris as a dead weight would have been very heavy. Hauled in a cart? The Correguajes apparently had no carts. I'd seen no cart tracks. Had two people carried him in order to share the weight?

This supposition stopped me. It implicated at least two persons in the crime. Which two? The Briggles? Fishers? Arden-Joneses? Spider and Joe? Or had the killer *hired* someone to help carry the corpse?

A voice in the back of my brain kept asking about Boris's briefcase. Something missing from it. What?

Where had the briefcase *been* the afternoon of the murder?

After breakfast, I asked Chris: "You were walking during the siesta?"

"Half hour at the most. Got a bit too hot for us. We found the trail to the spring. When we got there, it looked so enticing that we splashed a little water on our faces and arms. Terribly refreshing."

"Then you came back to your hut?"

"Not directly. We got back to the village to find people in hammocks or in huts, hardly anybody awake."

"Notice anything unusual?"

"Yes. The quiet."

"If you didn't go to your hut, where did you go?"

Chris explained. "The yuca grinding process still captivated us. We also thought we might be able to engage one of the Correguajes to name additional things around the village in their language. They've a tonal language, you know, almost like Chinese. We wanted to hear them speak it more."

"Did you find anyone in the yuca house?"

"No. We looked around a little, examined the metapí at close hand. The grating board. Supply of meal in the little canoe. Actually, nothing seemed amiss. Nobody hiding in there, if that's any help to you. Eventually we left and returned to our hut."

"Did you get a look at the pond as you returned?"

"No. When you come from the yuca hut past the chief's house, the three huts on that side blind your view of the pond."

I thought of the hut construction on stilts and asked: "Could you see under the huts? I mean, any legs or feet moving?"

Chris shrugged. "I don't suppose we were alert enough to notice. After all, it was a lazy afternoon. Nothing had happened yet. We probably wouldn't have paid any attention if we had seen legs moving back there. We started setting up for the recording so we were occupied for the next half hour or so."

"Tell me about your conversations with Kolinski."

"That's rather painful, you know."

"Yes. For everybody."

"We tried to remain neutral. If we got wrought up, our trip would be affected. Our focus is on languages and the Indians. We asked him about his work. He asked us about England. I thought we were going to get along swimmingly. Then the more details we learned about his work, the more we thought about our children."

"Children?"

"We haven't any now. But we will. Some day, we thought, when they come here they would see only fincas instead of wild forests if Boris had his way. That meant he was taking something away from them, just for greed. It began to settle heavily on me, I can tell you."

"What else?"

"We came to dislike the chap intensely."

"Because he was corrupting the natives?"

"That, and for other reasons."

"Ripping up the forest?"

"Yes."

"Depriving your children?"

"All that. We take seriously this business about upsetting global balances of oxygen and all. The scientists make quite a good case of it."

"Then Boris was an enemy? On several counts?"

"What the hell, Barry. Any civilized person would look upon his work with at least some repugnance, don't you think? Barbaric, really."

"Have you ever hunted foxes in England?"

The question startled Chris. It came so suddenly, so out of context. "Well, yes, we both have. Why do you ask?"

I smiled. "I can imagine Spider calling that barbaric."

Chris grinned. "She already has. I see you've turned the tables on me. I suppose we are none of us without guilt.

Foxes? Yes. Killing something wild has a sort of fashion to it. Look at your deer hunters. Though I have to confess that polls show most Englishmen against fox hunting. There've been some frightening rallies against it. Anyway, my feeling about Kolinski was that there are too many of him."

"So kill him?"

"Waste of time. Why murder a messenger? Or, as you chaps say, a leg man. Go to the top. Go to ILBRED. Complain. Badger government officials. Tell them they'll lose tourist money if they don't get rid of these people. Boris? Why wipe out a mere pawn in the game?"

I nodded in admiration. "I've got to hand it to you. That's the most sensible thing I've heard yet. Just the same, we have a murder on our——."

Chris stopped me. "Is it really a murder?"

I looked puzzled. "What do you mean?"

"Could it have been a combination of gin coco and chicha at forty degrees Centigrade and ninety percent humidity?"

"Go on."

"Well, I mean, those are powerful ingredients, are they not?"

I laughed. "Chris, you'd do well in Scotland Yard. Ever think of changing professions?"

He smiled. "Barry, you are positively maddening."

"Thank you," I responded. "I try to be."

He showed no outward emotion about his wife being in Huitoto country a world away. Stoic British character.

"By the way," he said, "will you be able to take time out for our trip tonight?"

"Wouldn't miss it! And you?"

He paused. "Do piranhas swim at night?"

CHAPTER 45

In short order, I had queried everyone except Spider and Joe, the chief suspects.

I'd made exactly zero progress. A corpse comes out of the blue and lands in a pool of water and no one sees it happen. Anybody could have done the job. They had all become so obsessed, so polarized on the subjects of wildlife and land preservation, they could be dangerous. To them, the defense of nature was a crusade, if not a profession.

By default, the whole matter had fallen into my lap. Monty's hands were tied as a tour leader. Besides, Monty had no expertise in managing a crisis like this. The police were miles away. Fatso and Square Jaw could be heading back even now.

Then there were Beryl and Carol-Lynn, off on a tangent in Huitoto country. I did not have time to manage that distraction. The ladies could take care of themselves, but safety among hostile tribes could never be guaranteed. This could very easily descend into a no-way-out agenda.

A fishing trip ought to be good for all of us. What could go wrong?

At seven-thirty, the tropics turn into inky blackness, intensified by clouds building up for a night storm. With flashlights, we walked down the trail to the landing, and from there set out in two canoes up the Orteguaza.

Joe Muck, ever the optimist, congratulated the Briggles.

"You've come a long way, Dana," he said. "Now you're going out at *night*."

"What's so tough about that?" she asked.

"Fatso and Square Jaw," he answered.

Mo commented: "Forget them. This is our last night with the Correguajes."

We traveled without lights. Joe leaned over to me and asked why.

"Size up the situation yourself," I answered.

He growled: "I knew you'd say that. Okay, we have the best guides. They go out day and night fishing. They've memorized every inch of the river. And they want to scare the shit out of us."

No other lights showed out on the river or along the banks on either side. The boatmen sat fore and aft, watching for whatever logs they could see floating toward us. The canoes proceeded slowly, never very far from the black wall of trees that rose from the river bank. On the other hand, that would seem very far out if the thugs flew back tonight. With searchlights. We would be helpless.

Less than five minutes after leaving the dock, one canoe jolted to a stop and threw its passengers forward. Monty and Eduardo leaped out in the ankle-deep water, pulled the canoe off a sand bar, and leaped back in.

Joe muttered to himself: "Well, there goes my theory. As Osgood said in *Some Like It Hot*, 'Nobody's perfect.'"

After half an hour the motors idled, then quit. The canoes began to drift back down the river. Monty and Eduardo threw out an anchor, then lit two torches so that the flare of light would attract fish.

Joe Muck stood up. "Lead us to the biggies!"

One Indian took up a four-pronged spear. Joe examined it with keen interest. "Palm wood," Monty told him.

"Palm wood? Can't be. It's hard as steel."

"Could be *Ireartea* palm wood" I offered. "Bolivians and Ecuadoreans use the wood of *Ireartea* palm for bows, arrows and lances. Tough stuff."

"Can I?" Joe asked, anxious to try out the system.

"Okay," Monty said. "Watch."

The Indian grasped the spear, took a position in front, and peered into the circle of water illuminated by the flares. Joe peered, too. How, he wondered, could they see anything in muddy water like...?

Something moved at the surface. The canoe jerked as the Indian hurled his spear.

Connect!

"Ai-yee!" Joe shouted. "You got 'im!"

The Indian slipped into the water, took the spear with fish impaled, handed it up, and climbed back aboard.

"What kind of fish is that?" Joe asked.

Monty answered: "Arawana."

"Hand me a spear."

"Joe!" Spider snapped. "Fishing is for the Indians."

"It's okay," he answered. "My grandpa always said I was part Shoshone."

"It's still killing," she scolded.

"I'm catching this for the Correguajes."

He grasped the spear with a tight-fisted grip, spread his legs as widely as he could in an attempt to brace himself, and peered into the water.

For nearly a minute, nothing happened.

At the first sign of movement, he reared back and hurled the spear with a fierce lunge. Thrown off balance, he teetered out over the edge of the canoe.

With a loud "Ai-yee-ee!" he fell into the river and disappeared.

Dana screamed. Monty Adams grabbed a rope. I half rose, ready to dive.

Joe's face appeared in the light. He came up sputtering and shouted: "Bring on the piranhas! Bring on the eels!"

I doubt if anybody ever reboarded a canoe faster than Joe did that night. He grabbed the spear before it could float away and shot out of the water like a flying fish. Grasping the edge of the canoe, he hurled his long legs over, threw in the spear, and landed with a thump about where he'd departed.

Righting himself and sitting up, dripping and smiling, he said: "How's that for scouting the premises? No fish in there, guys!"

As it turned out, there weren't very many. At least the fish didn't respond. Even with hook and line, success eluded the would-be anglers. The thrill of night fishing, though, caught us in its spell, and we fished for an hour.

I put away my fishing rod. "Well, it's all right. We landed one big fish anyway."

Joe groaned. "I'm not going to hear the last of this."

"Right," said Spider.

"Wait," Joe went on. "You come up on the Madison River. I'll show you a real blue-ribbon—."

He stopped. "What's that sound?"

This time they all heard the helicopter at once. Looking up, they saw its flashing lights upriver, coming toward them.

CHAPTER 46

Instantly, the scouts dashed the flares into the river.

Darkness enveloped the canoes. The motors roared. Spinning the vessels in a sharp circle, the boatmen moved them under massive trees that hung out over the water. Hands reached out to grasp the limbs and hold the canoes in place. The motors were shut off, but I knew that telltale wisps of smoke from them lingered above the water.

Flashing lights came closer. The chop of the rotor blades grew louder. Searchlights came on. Blinding beams of light swept the water, bank, and wall of trees.

The intruders slowed almost to a stop, hovering off-shore. Joe peered through the leaves and for an instant saw the ILB symbol on the side. "Square Jaw's back!" he shouted. "They saw our lights!"

We could only wait. We had no idea what they wanted. Had they returned to negotiate or to wipe us out?

If the two small canoes tried to escape from behind this veil of leaves, spotlighted in the open water, the hovering helicopter's guns could riddle us in seconds.

I reached into my backpack, drew out my 9mm Parabellum pistol, and loaded a magazine. I didn't want to use it. In the face of death, however, I always felt more comfortable armed and aiming. If I had to go down, I'd go down firing.

At what? Glare of searchlights nearly blinded us, even though filtered by thrashing leaves. I couldn't begin to get a fix on the windows of the chopper.

Seconds passed. The whole scene seemed to be paralyzed. Square Jaw or Fatso, if that's who it was, had not yet raked the sheltering tree with lead. They must be uncertain. Could any part of either canoe be seen? I looked over the side. Only speckled moving patterns of light struck the canoe. Perhaps I should feel grateful for the foliage.

The helicopter edged closer. Beams searched the bank and wall of trees. A good sign. If the beams stopped and locked on to us, the game would be over. It flashed through my mind that if they did spray the trees with lead, my ploy about the notebook would be considered dead.

So why this return of the thugs? Stepped up terrorism? Harass us until we coughed up the murderer? They might have a new message for me. Perhaps an ultimatum. A more chilling thought: new thugs replaced the old. Gunslingers with less patience. Ones who shot first. How easy it would be to wipe out *all* the suspects...

Gusts of wind thrashed the trees furiously. Limbs and trunks above us whipped and bent in uneven circles. Leaves and twigs began to fly off. When would the limbs or trunks snap off? I tried not to think of it. Which would get us first? A ten-ton tree? Or a hail of lead?

It seemed like a nightmare that would never end.

Abruptly, the light beams veered to the east. The 'copter eased off downstream. The winds died and limbs stopped thrashing. Darkness enveloped the canoes again.

Farther down, the powerful lights searched bank and forest, sweeping out across the water and back toward the hidden canoes. Sounds of the whirling blades faded. Searchlight beams grew smaller. As the craft rose and flew downstream, the lights disappeared altogether.

In the silence and darkness, our ears still rang from the racket.

Greg Fisher broke the silence. "This is the most relaxing vacation I've ever been on."

Laughter burst out spontaneously. Joe said: "Comes with all the other freebies like ants and grubs."

Mo asked: "Barry—your assessment?"

"No way to be sure," I answered. "Harassment perhaps. We're all threats to ILB now. We know the company's secrets."

"*You* do," Joe said. "We're innocent."

Spider spoke. "Remember what Barry said. If they gun for him, they get us, too."

"Greg's right," Dana said. "The Amazon's so peaceful!"

For ten more minutes we waited and listened. The sounds of river ripples and nocturnal insects came to our ears.

"All right," I said. "Let's go."

CHAPTER 47

Motors started. The scouts took their places.

In the darkness, we could see very little. No floating logs, gravel bars, hanging limbs. Nor could we send sudden messages to the boatman in back. We decided to use illumination, no matter how it might give away our location. But no flares. The Indian at the prow would use a flashlight, turning it on for very brief periods. He would flash a signal to starboard to command a right turn, or to port for a swerve to the left.

For fifteen minutes we followed this procedure, moving slowly along the edge of the river. Dodging right. Swerving left. Bumping gravel. Knocking against floating logs.

"If those guys come back," Joe whispered, "I'm swimming ashore!"

Suddenly, the motors idled. The canoes drifted toward the river bank.

"This isn't the village," Joe said. "Where we going now?"

I answered. "They have a surprise for us."

"*That's* the understatement of the night!" Joe responded. "What do you think we've been having?"

The passengers drew out their flashlights and clambered up freshly cut steps in the embankment. We resembled nothing more than a parade of glow worms inching up a cliff. Any aircraft within visible range could have seen us with ease.

Never mind. In the sheltering forest we found a refuge safer than any on shore.

Reaching the top of the embankment, the Indians led us into the woods. Their lights fell on new obstacles: exposed roots and fallen limbs along a primitive pathway.

Moments after we reached the top of the bank, Joe, second in line, rammed his face directly into a huge spider web built across the path. The strands covered his hair, wrapped around his ears, masked his eyes. He flailed wildly and brushed his head and shoulders to remove the presumed denizens of the web.

I said: "Watch where you're going, Joe."

"I was!" he answered. "That's the trouble. I was looking down. How do you shine a flashlight up and down at the same time?"

Spider called forward: "Joe, you're a foot taller than the rest of us. We thank you for taking out all the webs as we go along."

Joe snorted and started again along the trail, holding a stick in front as a shield.

The sweeping arcs of flashlight beams caught a distant pair of red eyes peering at us.

"A jaguar!" Joe blurted.

"Probably a 'gouti," said Monty.

Joe grumbled. "Aw, killjoy. I hear the jaguar usually waits for its prey to come within range."

"Probably so," Monty responded.

Spider added: "That's why you're in front, Joe."

After we had walked in silence for perhaps five minutes, Joe stopped and pointed ahead. "What is that?"

We stopped and peered ahead in the stygian gloom.

Spider said: "What is what? I can't see a thing."

"Up ahead," Joe responded. "Very faint. Purple light of some kind."

"Careful, Joe," cautioned Chris, "they're ghosts. Speak reverently. It may be ancestors of the Correguajes come to haunt us. Devour the weak who fall out of canoes. "

Joe said: "Shut up. See it? Hear anything? I know. It's witches."

"Only the wail of banshees, Joe."

We changed to a slower pace. Soon everyone saw the ultraviolet glow through the trees.

"Good God," whispered Greg, "if that's a glow worm it has to be the biggest on earth."

Joe responded: "Why not? Everything's bigger in the Amazon."

Drawing closer, we saw, strung across the trail between two trees, what appeared to be a bed sheet. We passed banks of batteries beside the trail, connected to a powerful light that cast a vivid purple glow on the sheet.

"You were on the mark, Chris," Joe said. "It's ghosts all right."

A voice came from behind the sheet. "Greetings, friends."

Two familiar faces peered around the edge of the sheet.

I went forward. "Doctors Jackson and Garcia, we presume."

Jackson said: "We've been expecting you. Stay where you are and we'll show you what's happening."

We formed a circle in front of the sheet. Drawing closer, we were able to discern movement across the face of the sheet, as though it had come to life. Hundreds of moths and other night-flying insects crawled across the surface. Jackson reached up, grasped a moth by the wings and pulled it away from the sheet.

"Look at this. You thought moths dull and drab, perhaps?"

We moved in close and shined our lights on a moth of greenish color, with white, red, and golden spots.

"Tiger moth," Jackson went on, "*Evius albiscripta*, I think. We can never be sure of species names down here. So much of what we collect is new to science. I'd say most of what we have on that sheet is new. I can't even tell what family they belong to. Or whether they might even be part of a new family."

Dana pointed to the glittering green moth in his hand and said: "Are there night birds? Do animals eat these?"

Jackson laughed. "I'm afraid not this one. The tiger moth contains a toxic substance that potential enemies avoid."

He reached over, unscrewed the lid of a jar, and dropped the moth inside.

Joe whistled. "I've never seen so many different moths in my life."

Jackson explained: "The lepidopterous fauna consists of both moths and butterflies. This neotropical forest contains remarkable populations of many insects. Outstanding. One family alone, the Erycinidae, contains more species than can be found anywhere else on earth. There is a greater biomass of invertebrates—the little things you see crawling on the sheet there—than of all the mammals put together."

Joe wiped his brow. "Whew! Do you need an assistant?" He walked over to get a closer view of the glowing sheet. "What are the rest of these things? Why do you use ultraviolet light?"

"Carries farther through the forest than white light. Attracts twice the number of insects. The other things there are beetles, flies, and smaller species we'd have to put under a magnifying glass to identify."

At Jackson's invitation, they examined collecting jars and traps, thumbed through note pads bulging with scrawls and unintelligible words, and poked their heads into tents where the scientists slept each day. On tables protected by mosquito nets, they saw instruments, mounted specimens, textbooks, and more note pads.

Afterward, as they walked back through the forest, astonished, reflective, trying to get their thoughts together, I spoke. "You see how rich in life one little spot in this forest is. It's the same with other life forms. This region supports more than two hundred kinds of hummingbirds..."

Joe whistled again. "We only have fifteen in the whole U.S.A."

"Do you know how many species of trees there are on every hectare in some parts of the forest? I mean *different* species?"

"A lot," said Joe.

"Three hundred."

Joe reacted. "On two and a half acres? Why from our ranch, we can only see one kind of tree for miles and miles. That's the lodgepole pine. There's no comparison! My god! This place is neat!"

Spider said: "This is what our land buyer wanted to wipe out."

Joe asked Adams, who walked in front of him: "Monty, we've only got started. How many months did you say we were going to stay down here?"

Monty said quietly: "We leave tomorrow."

CHAPTER 48

Next morning: no word from Huitoto country.

Greg and Chris cut me off on my way to breakfast, their faces creased with angry frowns.

"When are you leaving?" Chris asked.

I answered. "Right after breakfast. Are you packed?"

"You can all go down the river. We're not leaving until our wives get back!"

"And that's that," Greg added. "We've talked this over. We've decided. No argument about it. And no talking us out of it."

They left little doubt, by the grim determination in their voices, that they were adamant. I had prepared myself, and knew exactly what to say, but before I could speak, Chris went on in indignant tones.

"We don't know where they are. They don't know where they are. They could be anywhere out in that giant forest, lost, with no landmarks. If they got separated from Sonke, how would they find their way back?"

Greg added: "Anything can happen with hostile tribes. You know that as well as we do. Yes or no?"

I gauged at once their stubborn intent and made no effort to fight it. I understood their feelings. I also knew how utterly helpless they were. And how futile to argue. I asked calmly: "Where will you wait?"

It was not a response they expected. It took Chris by surprise. He had thrusted and parried with me before and lost every skirmish. He vowed not to lose this time.

"Right here," he answered firmly.

Greg scowled. "Where else did you think we'd wait?"

I went on. "How will you help?"

Chris almost replied, but stopped and cocked his head. "What do you mean by that?"

"Just what I said," I replied. "If they don't return...will you go after them?"

Greg had a puzzled look. "We?"

Chris looked me in the eye. "We jolly shall if we must. Look, Barry, we didn't want them to go in the first place."

"How does that help now?" I asked. "It was their decision, was it not?"

Greg: "We'll go in a canoe. We'll get a helicopter if we have to. We'll get the army..."

"And if the ILB men come back?" I asked. "They're here now, somewhere. You saw them last night."

Chris's ire rose. "Damn it all. These are our wives. We are serious."

"So am I. I happen to be very much concerned about the safe return of all four of them."

"When will that be?"

"We don't know. No one knows."

"We are not going to leave them behind. You think we're that callous? Cavalier? We're waiting for them. Right here. In this village. As long as we must. You may take it or leave it."

Finishing this, Chris started to walk away.

I answered quietly. "As you wish. The rest of us will go on to Tres Esquinas. Down the Caquetá River. That's where Sonke is expected to meet us. We'll be there tonight. May I take a message for your wives?"

I guess I have a mean streak in me. I savored the moment. I didn't mean to tease them. Concern for loved ones is a serious thing. They had to be respected for that. I just wanted them to learn one of the basic rules of foreign travel: trust the natives.

They stood rock still, eyes almost closed, a sheepish look spreading slowly over their sagging faces. Neither spoke a word. They reddened. Greg turned slowly away, and both drifted off without looking back.

Little Tiata raced across the compound and leaped up on Joe, almost knocking him down. He grabbed her to keep her from falling.

"Hey! What do you think I am? A lady doesn't jump up on a gentleman."

Spider asked mockingly. "So where's the gentleman?"

"Shut up!"

Little Tiata pulled admiringly at the jaguar tooth necklace.

"Oh, no you don't! Your Uncle Sonke gave me this and you're not getting it."

Ahniyah took Dana's hand and showed off her new mixture of toys: stick figurines with bits of cloth wrapped around them, a rubber ball, a Star Wars rocket, crayons and a small metallic mirror. She had studied her image ever since the Arden-Joneses gave her the mirror—when was it? A week ago?

Time had gone so fast, Dana could not believe it. We had not had enough of the musical voices, like wind chimes in the breeze. Not enough time with the Correguajes. Now, at departure, what could we say to Ahniyah? We had not learned the word for goodbye or even if the Correguajes had ever invented so sorrowful a word.

Mo looked at Dana, then to the ground. "I could get to like these people."

She responded briefly: "You already have."

Mo walked away and stood looking off into the woods.

An entourage of four young Correguajes surrounded Greg and Spider. One played a new tin flute. One held aloft a picture book on dinosaurs. Another sported wristlets and anklets of red beads.

Spider picked up Ahmoomah. "Why don't we take one of these little charmers with us?"

Joe recoiled in mock surprise. "What! And put her in a zoo?"

I warned them. "You are getting too attached to these people. It's a good thing we are leaving—for their sake!"

I wandered over to the fateful pond for a final look. Something still bothered me, and I gazed steadily as though mere looking would bring up some missing piece of the puzzle. I was still plagued by one persistent question. How did Boris get here?

Monty Adams shouted instructions to start walking down to the river.

Spider gave her back pack to young Amaunh to carry, and picked up his sister.

"You're just spoiled, Ahmoomah! You want a ride to the river! It's a long way. I'm not sure we'll make it."

Tiata rode on Joe's shoulders. The Red Chief walked beside them.

I tore myself away from the pond and joined the rear of the column.

When we reached the dock, Mo went to Monty. "Is Aunamunh coming to Tres Esquinas and Leticia?"

"We ain't planned on it. He's s'posed to come back here."

"Well, I... Mrs.Briggle and I have kind of taken a liking to him. Could he come down with Beryl and Carol Lynn when they return from Huitoto country? I'll be responsible for him. He can come back upriver in the canoe with Eduardo or José. He's an orphan and..."

Monty translated for Chief Manyuco, who nodded assent.

Mo smiled the biggest smile I'd seen on him.

Dana grinned and said to me: "This is not the same Mo Briggle who came slumping home that night after the loss to Forward Imaging."

"So I gathered," I answered.

"You said it," Mo responded vigorously. "Wait till I get home this time. With the medicines the chief gave me, and the moths Dr. Martin prepared, we won't be the same company again."

Chief Manyuco's wife carried a small, two-foot-long version of the yuca-squeezing tube, the metapí or cibucan. Since the Arden-Joneses had showed such an interest in yuca production, the chief's wife handed to Chris this miniature version as a souvenir.

Chris looked upon it with surprise. "For us? This can't be for us. Oh, but what a memento of your village. Monty, tell her how very much we appreciate this. They are just so kind..."

Tiata hugged Joe for the last time, uttering a stream of words that Joe interpreted as "Next time you come down here, you big cowboy, bring me a piranha tee shirt, or else."

He had difficulty tearing her away and setting her down on the dock.

Minutes later the canoe slid out into the Orteguaza River. We watched the old broken dock for as long as we could see it. And as long as we remained in sight, we saw the villagers waving—Ahniyah, little Tiata, Ahmoomah, Amaunh...

No one talked for a while. I saw Dana brush a tear away. Spider hid her eyes behind sunglasses. Joe's eyes glazed as he watched the swirling waters pass. His gaze wandered idly to the egrets and herons on the passing sand bars, the caimans in the coves, the flutter of a morpho, the distant swaying nests of oropendolas. He closed his eyes.

CHAPTER 49

The river became wider and deeper, with fewer sand and gravel bars. We stayed close to shore for the sake of safety and quick retreat.

Monty sat on the canvas, as usual. This time, however, he faced the rear. This gave him a good view of any aircraft that might come downriver. If he spotted any, he could issue immediate commands to Eduardo to dash for the shore. Palkuh sat beside Monty. The old Red Chief smiled and laughed, all trace of his sickness apparently gone. The canoe took him closer to home.

José, in the supply canoe, followed behind, alert for air traffic.

At length, Joe broke the silence.

"Do you realize we never saw a single dance? They never danced for us. Not once. How come?"

Chris responded. "We asked the same question. I'd been terribly curious about their rituals and ceremonies and whether we would witness one. I asked Monty, and his answer was vague. Something about ceremonies being sacred, and it wasn't the time of year for rituals, and they were private family affairs anyway."

Mo asked: "Did anyone hear about their origin myths?"

Joe answered. "I was asked to look into that. As near as I could find out, they believe that their first ancestors emerged as anacondas from rocks in rivers."

"Pretty simple, I guess," Mo responded.

Chris said: "Spider, we didn't see any animals. Well, maybe a pet monkey, and some birds. But no jaguars, no tapirs, no pacas."

"That's right. So?"

"You keep saying that we should dispense with zoos and safari parks and go see animals in the wild. Well, we can't. Not here, anyway. The forest is too thick. The beasts are too far up, too far back, too deep in the river, or asleep when we're awake. How can you tell people to come here and see the wildlife when we don't see much?"

"You *could* have."

"I beg your pardon."

"Did you go swimming along the river banks last night?"

"No, ma'am..."

"Hike way back in the forest?"

"No..."

"Well, you didn't go where the jaguars are. How can you expect to see any?"

"Spider, you've made your point. This also says that I have to go to a zoo if I'm to see them at all."

"You don't have to do anything of the sort," Spider snapped. "You don't care what it costs the animal, just so you can see it. That's cruel. If you don't see them down here it should be your tough luck and not theirs. It's no reason to imprison them for life just so you can have a quick look in a zoo. Go to books! Go to museums!"

"I appreciate your thought, Spider, but books and museums aren't enough."

"The hell they aren't! Books are enough for dinosaurs. You can't see dinosaurs in the wild. There aren't any left.

No one can dig the Grand Canyon out of the ground and put it in on display in New York. Nobody complains about that. A book satisfies people because it has to satisfy them. I say treat jaguars the same way. Take pictures of them instead of tying a noose around their necks and hauling them off to some stinking cage."

"You are going to make a believer of me yet, Spider."

"Besides, what's wrong with books? Pictures are enough for ninety-eight per cent of the population."

Joe asked: "Where did you get *that* figure?"

Dana rescued Spider. "I asked the other day about fish and the Indian diet. Did anyone find out about that?"

Joe answered. "I talked with Manyuco and his father. They rank fish number one. Anyway, must be a main source of protein. And the best fishing isn't now, it's in the dry season."

That astonished Chris. "They have a dry season down here?"

"Well, call it a season of lesser rain."

"That's the best fishing?"

"Sure. Rains taper off. Streams dry up. Fish flounder. Easy to catch. The people use not only flares and multipronged spears like we did—."

Chris laughed: "Like who did?"

Joe: "Stop that laughing—but hooks, lines, bows and arrows. They also use basket traps, hand nets, and poisons. The hook and line system is neat. They hang a line from a limb out over the water, bait it with worms or berries, and go back to inspect the line from time to time. Smart cookies, these guys. When the rainy season begins again, the streams fill. Fish ascend the streams and fishing may rev up some, but after a while the fish disperse."

Dana commented: "The Indians had better adapt themselves to the life style of the fish."

Joe snorted. "That's what pisses me off about this whole situation down here. Gold miners come in and use tons of mercury in their mining. Mercury gets in the water.

Then in the fish. Then, maybe miles away, little Tiata eats some fish and drops dead. You don't have to murder these people directly. All you have to do is fuck up their ecosystems. Their whole neighborhood becomes uninhabitable. How'd you like to have that happen to Oxford?"

Chris applauded. "Bully, Joe!"

"No applause. Throw coins, please!"

About mid morning Monty passed the word from in back to look up ahead.

"Ee—yow!" Joe shrieked, astounded. "We've come to the ocean!"

"No," I said. "We're entering the Río Caquetá."

The river was so wide, we could scarcely see the other bank. As we glided out onto the huge river, we could see water in all directions, upstream and down, without apparent confinement.

Joe whistled. "Barry, this surely is the Mississippi?"

"You're getting closer, Joe. The Caquetá flows another eight hundred miles to the east before it reaches the Amazon."

Chris looked on aghast. "I never imagined this much water in one river."

"We can't go out across there," Joe said. "We'll lose the protection of the river bank."

I answered: "Monty's open to suggestions."

"What if we get caught? Do we *have* to cross?"

"Tres Esquinas is on the other side."

"Cross at midnight? Wait 'till tomorrow? As Indiana Jones would say, we have to think of something."

I pointed up the Orteguaza. "Too late, Joe."

The helicopter flew just above the water, approaching from the northwest.

"Oh, oh," said Joe, "here comes the gun ship. Goodbye, guys."

As the craft approached, we saw the green and brown colors. When it turned, we glimpsed the letters on the side: I L B.

Peering closely, we saw the pilot and two dark figures inside. The craft circled, its downdraft forcing hurricane winds against the canoe, tipping it to starboard. Eduardo gunned the motor and turned downstream, coaxing all the speed he could from the little motor.

The helicopter followed, first on one side, then on the other. Wind gusts lifted the canvas and banged it against the ribs. Water and spray flew up, drenching Eduardo, Palkuh and Monty and showering the rest of us with spray.

Combined noises of the canoe motor, the helicopter engine, and the chopping blades deafened us. I reached into my pack and circled my fingers around the Parabellum.

The aircraft went ahead, turned, flew on its side, and came directly toward us, lifting in time to avoid a collision. The canoe tipped. Water flew up from the river. Spray drenched us again.

Then the helicopter left. As suddenly as it arrived, it turned and flew downriver, soon only a speck in the distance.

Joe raised his fist. "Come back, you bastards! Come back and fight!"

CHAPTER 50

We reached Tres Esquinas by noon. On an apron back from the river bank stood a DC-3, its fuselage painted with the insignia of FAC, Fuerza Aérea Colombiana, the Colombian Air Force.

Beyond this, partly visible behind the plane, sat the ILB helicopter.

Red flags went up in the back of my brain.

I could not detect anyone in it or around it. No one watching us from upstream or down. This little air field, I warned myself, could be the battle ground between fresh armed troops of ILB and a ragtag, harried band of travelers.

Comandante Alfredo Gutierrez, a heavy-set, dark-haired man in olive fatigue dress, met us at the dock.

"Bienvenidos, amigos! You look tired and hungry. And wet! How did you get so wet? We have no rain today."

Joe blurted: "Those goddamned sons-of-bitches in that helicopter—."

I cut him off. "We'll tell you all about it later, Captain."

"Bueno. Go now to your quarters in the barracks, then we have lunch set out beside the pool. *Comemos!* Let's eat!"

"The pool?" asked Joe. "You have a swimming pool here?"

The canoe never emptied faster. Within minutes the tired travelers had found their rooms in the barracks, stowed their gear, changed clothes and plunged into the green waters. Joe wondered in mid dive whether water would harm the jaguar teeth in his necklace. The others surrounded Dana, showing her the basic principles of swimming. Spider and Joe hurled storms of water at each other. For the moment, at least, she had forgotten about eels. Joe had forgotten Tiata. Mo splashed with the rest. When had he laughed so much?

I joined them, swam a few laps, then got out and walked over to Monty.

"You didn't get to my questions the other night."

"Yes, sir?"

"About parrots. Eels, too, for that matter. Who's shipping wildlife down here? The government?"

"No."

"Colombians?"

"Yes and no."

"Foreigners?"

"Yes and no."

"Monty, you have a great skill at answering everything and nothing. What gives?"

Monty looked out across the river. "It is a big business. Birds come in from everywhere."

"Come in to where?"

"To Leticia."

"That's miles from here. The Indians have to collect animals and transport them long distances?"

"More'n they used to. Don't matter none. They make money."

"Then what?"

"What do you mean?"

"Monty, you're trying to be vague again. I'll put it bluntly. Who's shipping all these animals out of Leticia? Lots of persons? Or one person?"

"Yes and no."

"I walked right in to that one. You got any names?"

"When we get to Leticia, you'll find what you want."

"All right," I said, "You win. I'll let it go. There's one other thing. I'll be blunt again. Do you know who killed Boris?"

Monty tried to hang his head as a sign of unwillingness to answer.

I persisted. "Do you know?"

Monty nodded imperceptibly.

"Would you care to tell me?"

Monty waited a while, as though trying to decide. Then he said: "No sir."

"Are you sure?"

"Yes, sir."

I looked out across the river. "All right, Monty. I will let you keep your secrets. I respect you for that. Some time, though, I may have to have answers."

Monty looked up, puzzled for a moment, then rose and went inside the command building.

The splashing in the water continued. Greg and Chris sat at the edge of the pool, glancing upriver A canoe would be coming along, bringing their wives. But when?

Lunch consisted of fish, chicken and baked banana strips, with beer, ale and Fanta on ice.

Joe exulted. "Our first cold drinks in nearly a week!"

Then he saw the two familiar figures beside the DC-3.

"Hey! You! Goddamned bastards! You got us all wet!"

No answer.

As near as I could tell, it was Square Jaw and Fatso. That relieved me a little. They appeared to be holding back, cautious for some reason. Otherwise, they would have wiped us out before this. Blasted the canoe on the Caquetá, and sent us to the bottom to swim with the piranhas.

Chris cautioned. "Leave them alone, Joe. We had enough of them the other night."

Dana added: "I should think they'd have guns here as they did at the village."

Greg: "The Air Force must have guns, too. Those guys are just waiting to get us alone somewhere."

Joe raised his voice and narrowed his eyes. "Okay, bastards! They talked me out of it. You're safe for now."

The figures pretended not to hear. They sat on the ground and watched the group through dark sunglasses.

"Keep your eyes on those suckers," Joe warned. "If they pull out their guns, dive for cover."

I said calmly. "I don't think they are going to do anything more for the moment than watch us. I suggest you lock the doors to your rooms in the barracks if you can. Don't stray away alone."

When the rest retired to their bunks for a siesta, Joe and I remained at the edge of the pool. I wasted no words.

"Those guys up there may want you, Joe. You are a prime suspect in Boris's murder."

Joe answered: "I know that. They know that. They're still watching me. But I've been with you most of the time these last seven days."

"Most. Not quite."

"When not?"

"On the day of the murder. Right at the crucial time. After lunch, when I was bedding down for a siesta, you said you were going to walk along the trail upstream from the pond. Did you?"

"Yes."

"How far?"

"Couldn't have been more than a mile. It was a rough trail. Why?"

"Did you intersect with the Orteguaza River?"

"No."

"Did you meet anyone?"

"No."

"Then you missed Spider and the Fishers."

"Guess so."

"Or you tied up with them, killed Boris, and brought his body to the pond."

"I see what you mean. I certainly could have, couldn't I?"

"You wanted him dead, did you not?"

"Who didn't?"

"Then why did you bring the body to the pond?"

"Sorry, Barry. I'd like to answer that, but I can't."

"Why not?"

"Because I didn't bring the body to the pond."

"If you didn't, who did?"

"If I knew, I'd tell you."

"All right, Joe. This is a crude line of questioning, but I figure you can take blunt questions. How did you feel about Boris?"

"I really tried to like the guy at the beginning. He was friendly as we left Puerto Lara. I don't drink, so I couldn't relate to him there. I don't hold that against him or anyone, or smoking either. I thought it looked as though he might turn out to be a fun guy to have along."

"When did you change?"

"We diverged on the rain forest. He didn't give a hang about it. He made that clear right off the bat. I'm a biologist. I care a lot about it, about any forest. And by forest, I sure as hell mean all the native tribes and wild animals living in it."

"And when his secret got out?"

"I began to hate the bastard. No two ways about it, Barry. Began to hate his guts. I don't do that. Nobody taught me to hate. Hell, I couldn't even hate a bronc that threw me. Maybe I've lived a sheltered life, but I like people as well as animals. Both have a right to be on this planet. I can compete and get mad on the basketball court or in the rodeo arena, but that's different."

"However, you found this easy?"

"I got blinded when the man said he'd like to take all the animals and make purses and boots out of them."

"Blind hatred?"

"Never felt like that before. Never met such a bastard."

"Pretty strong, Joe."

"Damn right!"

"Really hated him?"

"Of course."

"Enough to kill?"

"Yes! Yes! Yes! I'm not going to lie. I'm ashamed of it. It's not very damned sophisticated to want to kill a man because you don't agree with him. A smart guy would solve the problem some other way."

"What do you mean?"

"Change his ideas. I thought about that. Then the more he talked, the more I said screw him. Forget him and do something at a higher level. I felt helpless. I'd go to some office. They'd laugh and throw me out. They must love ILBRED in Bogotá. Down here, a lo-o-ng way from Bogotá, I could make a difference. Logical, huh?"

"Go on."

"I could eliminate one of their agents. Scare them so they'd never send another one. A guy's got to stand up for what he believes. I believe in protecting wildlife. He was hired to wipe it out. So, I thought if we rubbed out enough of their agents, they wouldn't send any more."

"Dreaming a little?"

Joe's shoulders sagged, and he slumped in a chair. "For a while, it sounded like a rosy scenario."

I asked: "Did it pass?"

"How'd you guess? I felt ashamed of myself for giving it up. Then I was glad it passed. I felt better. I didn't want to sacrifice my own life in jail just to rid the world of him."

"Then it came back?"

"You bastard! You've got a mind meld on me. Hell, yes, it came back. Know when? After we got acquainted with the Correguajes, I took a really good look at little Tiata, and began to think. Indian tribes have lived here thousands of years. By what goddamned right does Boris move them out?"

"Logical. So…"

"He called them savages. Poured gin down them. A change came over my otherwise sunny soul. Suddenly I felt Boris was the kind of asshole who couldn't screw up the environment in the U.S. anymore, so he came here to prey on these people. Settlers and Indians alike. Get me?"

"Then you decided to kill him?"

"Not yet. The more little Tiata took me around, the more I turned against Boris. Of course, all this was confirmed afterwards in Sonke's village."

"The jaguar necklace."

"Right. Maybe I'm childish, but that was one of the happiest moments of my life. I told myself the jaguar had to die anyway. This guy from another culture, another world, another *everything*, thought enough of me to give me a very valuable necklace."

"He wanted your piranha tee shirt."

"The necklace was one helluva lot more valuable than a lousy tee shirt."

"Not the way he looked at it."

"It was the image of this guy bringing out something that was valuable to him and giving it to me."

"Then you were glad you'd killed Boris?"

"I didn't even think of Boris. My head was spinning in admiration of Sonke. It wasn't until I got away from the village that I began to see how tender and fragile and vulnerable these tribes are down here. You can kill thousands of trees, that's one thing. This son of a bitch was going to do that and also kill thousands of native people. Wipe out the whole habitat they depend on. That got to me."

"On the trip with Manyuco to the yuca patch did you formulate a plan there?"

"I was too mad. Boris insulted Spider. Bad."

"Did you get together with Spider? The Fishers? Anyone else?"

"Of course. Everybody."

"Did you hear anyone else even remotely plotting an assassination?"

"No."

"When Dana discovered the body and screamed, I ran out of the chief's hut. You ran up from the opposite direction, from the yuca hut. I thought you went out on the trail upstream from the pond."

"I did. When I got back, I just wanted to go somewhere else. I went up to the yuca patch."

"You must have run."

"I did."

"In the heat of afternoon? In the tropics?"

"I'm always trying to see if I'm tough enough to take it."

"When you came back down the trail to the pond, did you see the body in it?"

"No."

"Did you look?"

"No. I was tempted to go dive in. I was sweating, pouring."

"You didn't see anyone around?"

"Everybody was asleep."

"Not quite. If what you say is true, then the only time someone could have brought the body to the pond was when you went to the yuca patch. How much time was that?"

"I ran. Twenty minutes at the most."

"That's the crucial twenty minutes. That's the twenty minutes we don't know about. The whole village could have been asleep."

"Except me. Therefore, I'm guilty?"

"Somebody had to lift that heavy corpse and carry it to the pond and dump it in. If not you, who else?"

Joe didn't answer. The way I asked the question led him to consider it rhetorical. Joe had already said he didn't know. He leaned back on the chair and looked up at the thugs, then at the clouds.

"I'll always think of Chief Sonke. His smile—that silly giggle. I wish we could have spent a month with him...with his people. Maybe instead of hanging me, they'll exile me to one of these villages."

He got up and left.

Chris Arden-Jones and Greg Fisher did not get up. They remained by the edge of the pool, watching the empty river upstream. Watching for a canoe with a Correguaje chief, an Indian boy, and two women.

The afternoon waned. They waited as the hours passed with excruciating slowness. Waited until the outlines of the river faded with the gold of sunset. Darkness came. They got up reluctantly and went inside.

CHAPTER 51

Horacio Delgado's guitar jumped under furious pluck-ing. The strains of *La Negra Celina*, sung by him in a high-pitched voice, filled the Comandante's dining room and drifted out on the veranda in the night air.

Joe sat enrapt. He forgot to munch on the banana chips or sip his glass of Fanta. The fast-paced melody and swing-ing beat of this Afro-Cuban folk song mesmerized him.

"La Negra Celina... Si!"

He tapped his feet, slapped his leg, tried to sing along, but uttered only gibberish. The Briggles, Spider and Joe danced and traded partners.

La Negra Celina (the Black Girl named Celina) had them in her grip. When the song ended, they filled the room and the night air with shouts and applause. Then the guitar started *Romances de Mi Destino*. As an aircraft me-chanic, Horacio Delgado made a very good folk singer.

I watched from the sidelines, dryly amused at their release from forest and village, an intermission from dan-ger. They had returned, part way at least, to their own cul-tural environment. If tomorrow one of them would be in custody for the murder of Boris Kolinski, or they would all be wiped out by ILB thugs, no one seemed to care tonight.

Except for Chris and Greg, whose wives remained somewhere out there in a gigantic wild forest, or canoeing on massive rivers in pitch blackness.

I kept an eye on the windows and doors. Square Jaw and Fatso were not here, not invited by the Comandante. I had no idea where they were. Or what they were doing. Or when they would strike.

There were no other pilots here, either. Horacio was the only mechanic. Yet this was a military installation, and as such might afford us a little protection from the ILB.

I wouldn't bet on that.

Joe and the rest lost themselves in the waltzes, *pasillos* and *pasajes* of Horacio's folk ballads. Watched his gifted phrasing on the strings. Thrilled at his powerful tenor voice and astonishing vocal range. Melted before that most patriotic of songs *A Mi Colombia*, To My Colombia.

Anyone who went to prison tomorrow could take along the echoes of tonight.

Once I thought I saw Square Jaw and Fatso at the window, looking in. Horacio changed to a foreign rhythm, a bossanova, and Dana pulled Joe to the dance corner. Around they went, forward and back, hips swaying. Joe knew absolutely nothing about dancing the bossanova, but he lacked nothing in innovation under Dana's tutelage. By the time they finished, he had become soaked with perspiration.

We went to the Comandante's table of chicken and baked bananas, filled our paper plates, and returned to listen and to contemplate. Horacio's fingers, multiple voices and incredible memory produced *Mi Vaquerita. Bodas de Plata. Solita con las Estrellas. Flor de Verano. Soberbia...*

We could have listened all night.

When the time came for Horacio to stop playing and report for sentinel duty, he offered them one last request. Joe answered before anyone could speak.

"La Negra Celina!"

We applauded in agreement. Horacio bounced again through the rhythm. The dancers swayed in unison...

With Horacio gone, the tired passengers drifted away, fatigued from the trip, the swimming, the singing and dancing.

Greg and Chris came to me. "Okay," said Chris. "You said Sonke and our wives would be here tonight. Where are they?"

I had no answer. There were no miracles. All I could say was: "Night's not over."

They looked at me in anger and left the room.

With that, all the other guests had retired.

Except one.

CHAPTER 52

Before I could ask the first question, Spider gave the first answer.

"You bet your life I wanted to kill him!"

"Did you?"

She sat back and folded her arms. "I was never so insulted in all my life. Not even by my worst enemies. That *shithead*!"

"Understandable. Did you kill him?"

"I admire your persistence in this thing, Barry. But I can't see how you can pin it on anybody."

"Why not?"

"Because you have no evidence. None at all."

"How do you know?"

"I wasn't born yesterday."

"Spider, you seem sure of yourself."

"God damn right. You don't even know whether it was a murder. You *said* so yourself. How do you feel about it now?"

I smiled. "I'm still listening. Be careful, though. Square Jaw and Fatso are no doubt outside looking in and listening."

"Who gives a damn about them?"

"ILB. They want revenge. They want to know who killed Boris."

"Don't be naïve. They want his notebook."

"They're not going to get it."

"Okay, so ask if I did it. What if I did? God knows I *wanted* to. All you found was a body in the pool. No marks or clues. No witnesses. How can you pin his death on *anyone?*"

She glared at me as though expecting instant revelation. When I answered, the words came slowly and deliberately.

"Spider, I never have to pin anything on anyone."

The response took her aback. She fished for a reaction. Then she settled for a question in order to delay proceedings—a favorite tactic when she didn't know what to say.

"You passed me by on that one. What do you mean?"

"In cases such as this, Spider, the solution is not very difficult if you observe long enough."

"Meaning?"

"That the murderer reveals himself and I don't have to do much about it."

"Oh, come on, Barry. That's smug. If you think I'm guilty, how am I going to reveal myself? What are you looking for? I know there aren't any clues. I could get out of this as easy as jumping out of a canoe. You know that, too."

"Perhaps I do. Maybe I don't know yet, or even have a faint idea, what was behind Boris's death. There is always a place to begin. That's where you come in."

She sat up straight and looked me in the eye.

"What do you mean?"

"Well, Spider, for one thing, you clearly had the strongest motive. You made the most vicious threats. Even offered to lead the posse to the lynching. You were vitriolic and showed no shame in it. That is the one fact we start with."

"Okay. Of course! But how does that help? That was true of everyone."

"Not everyone. Only one person can be at the top of the motivation list. Only one person can be the prime suspect. You knew from the start that this mantilla covered your shoulders."

"Nothing secret about that."

"Well, then, it's a short distance from there to..."

She slapped the table. "Okay! Okay! I could've killed him! I would have, given another day or two."

"Why? What's your motive?"

"You have to ask? That bastard was an enemy of all wildlife. The kind of rubbish we need to dump in the garbage. You yourself would agree to that."

I nodded. "Perhaps so. I must find the shortest distance between that feeling and the ability to kill."

"I have the shortest fuse. That's what you're saying?"

"Something like that."

"Then I'd still like to know how you're going to prove it."

"I'm sure you would. My assessment of motivation is still clouded by one problem. If you so strongly protest against zoos, that means you love life beyond the capacity of many other persons. I find it difficult to understand how anyone who loves life so much could kill a man."

She leveled a finger at me. "Let me straighten you out on that right now, Mr. Investigator. I could have killed him in the name of self-defense of the entire world. The animals he put in danger couldn't have done it themselves. They couldn't fight him. I would act for them."

"Then you must have been contemplating how?"

"Sure I was. That would be the easy part, since he was such an idiot. There were lots of possibilities. I could get the Indians to help me dart him with one of their poisons. Steal his hat so he'd broil in the sun. Get the kids to bring me a coral snake to put in his sack. I'd lace his soup with cyanide ."

"You have cyanide for this purpose?"

"No, but you asked what I was thinking of."

I changed to another tack.

"I would like your comment on one curious problem. Why was the body brought to the pond?"

She would not be drawn into the question so easily. "Why do you ask that?"

"Because I want to know."

"You mean, why was it brought to the pond instead of just dumped into the river where it would be eaten by piranhas?"

"Yes."

"That would depend on the motivation of the killer, wouldn't it?"

"Correct."

"I have no answer, since I didn't do it."

"If you had?"

"I would have wanted somebody to find it. That's the rub, isn't it? If you knew why and how the body got to the pond, you'd have the answer, wouldn't you?"

"Yes. And I associate that with one other interesting fact. If the body had to be delivered secretly to the pond, it would have to come from the upstream side. Otherwise, it would have to be carried up the main trail from the river and someone would have seen that."

"Even when the village was asleep?"

"I'd never be sure that *everybody* slept. Especially the kids."

"So what are you getting at?"

"Well, suppose I conclude that the body could only have come in from the upstream side, hidden to view from the village. Set the time when Carol Lynn and Chris were taping the chief. It would have to be done by someone who knew about that trail, right?"

"Granted."

"By someone who knew that it connected with the trail along the Orteguaza River, right?"

"Yes."

"And of the visitors, only three people knew about that connection."

"Correct. So the murderers are Greg, Beryl and me?"

I leaned back and listened to the buzzing of the insects outside and watched the distant flashes of lightning as the nightly storm clouds gathered.

"So it would seem."

She stared at me with eyelids half closed. "I thought you were looking for clues."

"Spider, the search for clues is often fruitless. I would leave that to the police. What I want is methods and motivations. You have the strongest motive and the clearest means. You and the Fishers were absent from right after lunch until we met you late in the afternoon on the main trail to the river."

"Does it matter to you that we looked for birds and other wildlife all that time?"

"Of course it does."

"And that we didn't even see Boris the whole time?"

"Yes."

"Well, then, how do you connect a desire to kill him with the actual execution of the deed?"

"I don't. You do."

"I do? Have I?"

I didn't answer. She had bounced right back on every question. She had obviously thought through this whole convoluted affair. I asked: "Did the Fishers say anything to you about some desire they might have to dispatch Kolinski?"

"Yes."

"Did you think they were on the verge of carrying it out?"

"Yes."

"Just as you were?"

"Yes."

"Thank you, Spider. The night is late. I'm going to get a drink of water. Then I'll accompany you to the barracks."

She sniffed. "That's condescending. You think I can't take care of myself?"

"I want to protect Square Jaw and Fatso."

"Why, thank you, Barry. That's the nicest thing anyone has ever said to me."

I went into the kitchen to get a drink.

Spider rose and started toward the door. At which point, the door opened to reveal a wet, dirty, bedraggled Chief Sonke standing there, with Aunamunh at his side.

CHAPTER 53

With all the excitement of the return of the Huitoto group—Carol Lynn, Beryl, Sonke, Aunamunh—no one noticed, at first, that someone was missing.

Beryl and Carol Lynn, rested, clean, hungry, waited until everyone came to the breakfast table. I had checked on the whereabouts of the ILB thugs. No sign of them, though their helicopter was still on the tarmac. They were up to something, but I had no idea what. I would watch them very carefully today.

Spider asked directly: "You found Messala?"

Carol Lynn answered. "We spent the first day walking through the forest. Aunamunh took good care of us. He made fiber bags and gathered fruit, bark, leaves and edible mosses. He was fond of a purple, plum-sized fruit with black seeds. And a yellow fruit with sour white pulp and brown seeds. Then there was a bean pod with sweet red seeds. And so on. He made our beds at night out of leaves and fibers."

"Did you happen to meet any hunters on the way?" I asked

"None. Next morning we waked to a chorus of howler monkeys. After we got started, we saw silhouettes and shadows of people in the forest all around us, and began to hear drumbeats. We were getting close.

"One thing I discovered was that Aunamunh is an orphan."

"How do you know?" Dana asked in surprise.

"Sonke told me. The boy lived in Red Chief's village, three days' journey from Manyuco's village. One day he just showed up."

"Came through the woods alone? Across rivers?"

"Sonke drew a map on the ground. Traced the route. One stick figure. I couldn't believe it. I drew other stick figures as a question about companions. He erased them. I held up one finger to confirm it. He held up just one finger."

Beryl said: "He led us up on a rocky ridge then straight down to the Huitoto village. It was uncanny."

"No compass?" I asked.

Carol Lynn answered: "Heavens, no. That boy remembers every inch of this forest as though it were his own paddock."

"And the people?"

"When we got to the Huitoto *wehoopah* we didn't see any people at first, but heard some chants out in the forest, almost in a nasal tone. *Ah-hi, ah-ho, ah-ha* ... Then a couple of the Huitotos brought Katherine to us and went back into the shadows."

Beryl spoke slowly. "I didn't recognize her. I had not known her very well, true, but what we saw out there was someone I could never have recognized if we had known her a hundred years."

Dana asked: "Then she actually lived with those people?"

Chris: "She had been there the whole year?"

Beryl answered: "It seemed to me that she had always been there. I saw no remnant of the Katherine Messala that we had known in Wisconsin. She had almost completely made the conversion."

Carol Lynn spoke: "The most awesome to me was that she had difficulty with *English*."

Spider: "What are you saying?"

"So completely had she immersed herself in the Huitoto language, their customs, their environment, that she had become one of them."

Dana asked: "In only a year? That seems impossible."

Carol Lynn spread her hands in disbelief. "It astonished me. I will definitely say that. I was unaware that one could become so rusty with one's own language in so short a time. She is a remarkable woman. She devoted herself so completely to becoming someone else, to learning another and very difficult language, that she left English almost completely behind. During our conversation she stumbled over sentences, stuttered, groped for words..."

Spider: "All right, then. The final question. Is she going to stay there forever?"

Beryl answered. "I wanted to ask that the moment we met her. But the more we talked, the more we watched her, the more we saw how she had become a part of another world, I wondered if there was any bridge left."

"Did you ask?"

"I mentioned word from her family, how they wanted to know where she was. She said she had sent a message, but it must have gotten lost. And yes, she would come back."

"When?"

"All she said was...some day."

I asked: "What do you make of it?"

Beryl said: "It's beyond my ability to understand. Living conditions seemed to me so primitive. But how can I know? I never lived there. I didn't know the people."

"From what you saw, would you want to?"

Beryl shook her head. "This planet is filled with so many things other than tropical forests. All I can say is that Katherine is a breed apart."

I asked Carol Lynn: "And your language studies?"

"We didn't stay long enough. The people were secretive, not very communicative. But I got a few words. Enough, I think, for our colleague in Oxford to make comparisons."

"Did either of you see any indication about the capture and sale of birds?"

Carol Lynn: "We saw parrots flying overhead."

"Any in captivity? Any in cages?"

"None."

"Nothing else in captivity? Monkeys, for example?"

"Nothing. I began to think that it was not in them to keep animals captive."

Beryl added: "I didn't feel that they had much contact with the outside."

"All right," I said. "I want you all to relax today. We leave tomorrow for Leticia. And when we get there, I will report my findings to the Captain of Police."

Spider: "You have some findings?"

"Yes."

"You want to confide in us? Let us in on them?"

"After the captain, you will be the first to know."

Joe said: "That sounds ominous."

The door opened and Monty entered.

"Any of you seen Palkuh?"

CHAPTER 54

We leaped up from the table and raced outside.

Spreading out, we search the barracks, pool area, shops, hangars, everywhere. Joe and I ran along the bank of the Caquetá. No luck. Coming back up we peered into the helicopter.

Nothing. No sign of Square Jaw or Fatso either.

Which answered our question. Without proof, without even a clue, we all concluded that the thugs had abducted him. That was why they had come. To capture him for torture, ransom or elimination.

Or... My brain chilled at the other possibility. They would try to trade him for Boris's notebook.

I talked with the Comandante, asking where they might have taken the chief

"*Solamente una posibilidad,*" he said. Only one possibility, only one village near here.

"Palkuh's village?"

"*Si, señor.*"

"*Pero,*" I said, alarmed, "*ahorita hay todos mineros allí.*"
He nodded. The village had been taken over by miners. Palkuh was a prisoner in his own village.

I couldn't believe it. I asked the Comandante: "*Seguro?*"
He nodded. "*Creo que sí.*"

I had no choice but to go after him.

I had not finished with all the possibilities in Boris's murder. Palkuh could be a key witness in solving it. He may have made observations to clinch my conclusions.

"*Cuantos soldados tiene?*"

"*Hay tres aquí, señor.*"

"*Necesito ayuda.*"

The comandante pondered. He could not let all three of his soldiers go with me and leave the airbase virtually unprotected. After a few moments of contemplation, he agreed to let me take two.

Two soldiers and me against a village filled with armed miners.

This didn't seem right. In the first place, neither the soldiers nor I knew how to get to the village. In the second place, we hadn't the slightest idea of the layout of the village once we got there. Whether to open a flank attack, or roar in on a frontal charge with guns blazing.

In daylight? No way. At night? Worse yet.

I felt sick. I had to act, but I couldn't. None of these Rambo plans would work. There was a valuable prisoner in that village, maybe a key to my murder case. The miners were no doubt on alert. Any fast action on my part could trigger Palkuh's premature assassination.

You sure got stuck this time, my inner voice taunted. *You have an uncanny knack for getting caught in the middle of a disaster. You're hundreds of miles from help. You have little or no ammo. The miners are doubtless fortified like an Apache stronghold. Square Jaw and Fatso with 'em, too. Be sure of that. You haven't even got guns enough. Not a chance. Back off!*

I wouldn't. I'd go after Palkuh if I had to go in alone.

Wait... My brain froze.

Why *not* go in at night? Why not sneak in alone?

This sounded crazy, but I had an ace in the hole. A little guy whose home that village was and who undoubtedly knew every inch of the ground from here to there.

I would go with Aunamunh.

Gathering the group together in the dining room, I divulged my hastily conceived plan. What I hadn't planned on was their reaction.

Any ordinary human beings would have been content to let me go into that hostile territory and do this whole dirty job myself. That's where I was wrong.

Joe Muck interrupted me before I could finish describing the whole plan.

"Mister Ross," he said in a commanding, imperious tone. "If you think for one minute that I am going to let you go up there alone—."

I stopped him. "You haven't any choice in the matter. This is my job, not yours. Period."

Joe came back loud and clear. "Bullshit! Palkuh was a friend of mine. You see what I'm wearing?" He pointed to his jaguar necklace. "I'm one of the tribe, and you'd better goddam believe it. Wherever there's a brother Correguaje in trouble, there I go. And you just try and stop me!"

I felt a tinge of anger at such powerful insubordination. "I am the one here with authority."

"Where's your police?" he responded. "You can't dial 911. Authority, my ass! If you can't back it up, you ain't *got* no authority. Not over me."

Before the echoes of that pronouncement faded, Spider stood up. "Nor me either!"

Like the ricocheting spatter of machine-gun fire, all the others in the group stood up and began to speak at once, demanding to go.

It was the last thing I expected. It was also very ignorant, and I told them so. "I am trained in this kind of warfare and you are not! You can try to be brave all you want, and the net result is that you'll get killed. Is that what you want?"

Babble of voices again.

Dana's eyes flashed with fury. She stood up. "I've heard that kind of crap before and been insulted by it. Barry, I

know that you would not knowingly insult anyone. Your
heart is in the right place. You want to protect us. But I'm
going to help save that little chief and that's that."

"Not quite—," I began.

Spider overwhelmed me. "Barry, we are all pretty mad
already at what has happened on this trip. All those tales of
mercury, arsenic, eels. You can do the fighting, but if you
ever need any backup, that's where we come in."

Joe added: "I have medals for sharpshooting and you
know it."

I stopped them. "We may as well stop talking about
it! I know what you're trying to do and I honor you for it. I
will not change my mind."

Dana: "Well, if you think you're going to leave me
behind, you'd better restructure!"

Beryl, Greg, Chris, Carol Lynn, all of them burst forth
with similar sentiments.

I clapped my hands for silence. "This is mutiny."

Joe: "All right, if you're going to play Captain Bligh,
we'll tie you to a canoe and set it off on the Caquetá."

"I've told you that this is a dangerous mission."

Dana: "Doesn't matter. If one of *us* had been kidnaped,
the Red Chief would demand to go. And you'd never stop
him."

Beryl agreed. "You think that women can't handle
danger? Have I told you about my rock climbing? How
many times have you rappelled down a hundred-foot cliff?"

Dana: "If it's dangerous that is exactly why we should
all be going. You know I can give first aid, and now I'm
going along to use it."

I spread my hands in despair. "Ladies, we are going
up the Río Ramón at night. Paddling, I might add, in pitch
black—."

"I can paddle," Beryl interrupted.

Dana: "So can I."

"We are going to be carrying guns."

"I can shoot."

"So can I."

"I can't exaggerate how vicious these people can be in remote locations like this. These men are killers. They have started a gold mining operation in that village. Nothing will stop them. They won't care whether you can climb or paddle or shoot. They are going to shoot you first."

Beryl responded sharply: "Not if I shoot *them* first!"

I gave up. "You won't have any guns. I will try to find some other place for you to be brave. I just won't allow you to be put in danger. And that's that. I won't let you go."

Silence. Then muttering. Then anger.

Dana bristled. "Just how will you stop us? Pick us up? Carry us to the barracks and lock the door? If Mo goes, I go. If *anyone* goes, I go."

Joe burst out: "Now wait a minute! God damn it! Barry's right. This is a dangerous mission."

Dana asked simply: "So?"

Joe went on: "So bullets, that's what. Those little round things that come out of the muzzles of guns—."

Dana tired of the conversation. "Joe, we love you for this, but the matter is settled. I'm going to get my first aid kit."

She walked away. Beryl asked: "I still don't see why you are so sure that Square Jaw and Fatso took Palkuh to his own village."

Joe shrugged. "They aren't. The Comandante says that's the only place they could have gone. It's the nearest ILB outpost. Aunamunh agrees."

Greg asked: "Aunamunh? He's just a boy. Have you got his permission?"

All eyes turned to Monty, who bent for a whispered discussion with Aunamunh. When he stood up, he said: "Kid couldn't be happier."

Beryl said: "You don't know him. Carol Lynn and I've just been with him for three days, remember? He's a very grown-up boy. It's his village. He's an orphan. He grew up in Palkuh Mamha-uh's village. The Red Chief is his uncle."

Greg: "The boy's going to guide us into the village?"

Joe interrupted: "Not all of us. Just me. Barry and me."

"You?"

"I get to carry Palkuh back, dead or alive."

Beryl gasped. "Joe, don't talk that way."

"Sorry."

Greg: "So we're going to attack the miners?"

"We're not going to attack anybody—."

"Then why do you and Barry have guns?"

"Self defense. Only when attacked. All we're trying to do is get Palkuh out of there. Not start a revolution."

"No assault weapons?"

"No. But the miners will have them. Searchlights, too, probably. Bloodhounds, for all I know. Grenades. Rockets. Explosives. We have to prepare for a quick getaway."

Beryl: "In canoes? You're kidding."

Joe sighed. "It's all we got."

"I take it they don't like visitors."

"Beryl, you're an expert at understatement."

The conversation faded. They all looked at me. I began to think that fighting the miners would be easier than fighting this bunch. I did not have time to argue any more. Time was of the essence. Whatever was to be done must be done without delay.

I felt like my head was caught and being crushed in a vice of granite. How could I take along a platoon of sheer amateurs like this to rescue someone from the clutches of professional killers? This would endanger Palkuh, not save him.

In the end, I let my shoulders slump. There is a time to fight and a time to retreat. I was supposed to be the smart guy who knows the difference. But battlegrounds change. Combatants change.

They stood hushed and expectant, waiting for my reply. I had never seen such determined eyes.

I said softly: "Let's go."

They roared at the tops of their lungs and dashed out the door like a football squad racing for the field of battle.

CHAPTER 55

As sundown approached, Horacio and the Comandante's men loaded guns, ammunition, medical supplies, water, flares, food and flashlights into two canoes at the edge of the Caquetá. Everything went under canvas, in case of a downpour.

When the rescue team had been assembled—the Fishers, Briggles, Arden-Joneses, Spider, Joe, Monty, Eduardo, Aunamunh and two soldiers—I briefed them, first in English, then in Spanish.

"Aunamunh will sit up front in the lead canoe. He's been up the Río Ramón many times. So we have a competent guide. He will keep us away from snags and thickets. It will be very dark. No one will talk. No one will make any more noise than necessary. Not even whispers.

"Aunamunh says it will take about three hours to get there. When we do, you will remain with the canoes on the river bank, hidden in the trees. Aunamunh will lead Joe and me to the village, which I gather is several hundred yards from the river. The way will be through dense forest. Aunamunh knows a side trail. He will sneak into the village. He knows which hut belongs to whom. And where a captive might be held.

"He will rouse Palkuh and lead the chief to the edge of the village—if he can walk. I will go in and get him if he can't. Joe will carry him to the river.

"I cannot tell you how much we need to avoid noise. And especially lights. These men are renegades anyway. They're edgy. Trigger happy. Expect them to fire at noises. It's a sport, if not self defense. They get jaguars that way. Or maybe they'll get you. Any questions?"

Chris: "What about rain?"

"We get wet."

Joe added: "Skin is waterproof."

Carol Lynn: "We're going to get cold, too. I know that quite for sure. Everyone should have a jacket."

Greg: "What if we have to sneeze?"

Dana answered. "Sneeze *into* something. A handkerchief. Whatever. Muffle it."

Mo said: "Now, if we are not to talk while en route, I want to get everything straight before we leave. First of all, why not talk? Or at least whisper?"

I responded: "We could meet some of the miners on the way up. Right out there in the middle of the river. They may be guarding the entrance to the village."

"All right. What do the rest of us do when we get there?"

"You and the canoes will go a hundred yards or so *beyond* the landing point. The Comandante tells me they have a speed boat there. You will all get out, move into the woods, and hide. Eduardo will tie up the canoes. One soldier will stay by you and the canoes. The other will stay by the speed boat, watching for us. When we return, he will be rear guard while you load aboard the canoes."

Chris asked: "And if you don't return?"

"Then it gets hairy. The soldiers come in after us. And I mean the soldiers *only*. That understood?"

"Roger. How long are you giving yourselves to get Palkuh out?"

"That's up to Aunamunh. He has to find the chief."

"So you don't know?"

"No."

"You're right. That's hairy. What if the chief's not there?"

"We come back empty-handed."

"Sorry I asked."

Carol Lynn: "And what if we do succeed in retrieving him?"

"We get into the canoes as silently as we can. Then we paddle like hell. Silently!"

Beryl asked: "One miscellaneous question. Why is Joe the only one with a rifle?"

I answered. "He's a sharpshooter."

"Thank you."

Mo had another question. "Pardon my persistence, but why are we going after the Red Chief?"

I gave him three quick answers. "The man is in grave danger, if he hasn't already been wiped out. The police are a hundred miles away. And Palkuh could be a material witness to the murder of Boris Kolinski."

This last left them nearly in unison asking: "WHAT!"

I looked at Mo. "Does that answer your question?"

Mo: "My God, it certainly does. But it raises an even bigger one. What the hell is all this about Palkuh? Material witness to what?"

A chorus of voices rose. I raised my hand. "I realize that you would like to have some fast answers, and I only wanted to indicate to you how important it is to get this man out of that village alive. Time is critical and we must not delay any longer. I will ask one last time. Does anyone want to stay back?"

No response.

"I warned you all. You're up against professional killers. You already knew that. My advice is to give it up. Joe and I can go in with the soldiers."

No response.

"Okay. One other thing. The Comandante got word from Leticia. The Police Captain there wants to see us as soon as we arrive. All of us. He has some news."

Joe said: "Like the gallows are ready?"

"Uh huh."

"And if we don't come back from Red Chief's village?"

"The Captain will miss us."

Without another word they took their assigned positions: Aunamunh, Joe, Spider, Monty, Eduardo, a soldier and me in the first canoe. The Fishers, Briggles, Arden-Joneses, José and a soldier in the second.

With engines on we went down along the right bank of the Caquetá River until we reached the mouth of the Río Ramón. There we silenced the motors, detached them from the canoes and left them on shore. The passengers picked up paddles.

With that, the rescue mission headed upstream toward Palkuh Mamha-uh's village.

The setting sun cast a rich red glow across the sky and into the trees. A few minutes later the black clouds coalesced and rain began.

CHAPTER 56

Rain poured heavily as darkness closed in around the canoes. Sheets of falling water impeded passage up the narrow, winding river. Wind blew in gusts. The passengers rowed diligently, but moved with excruciating slowness. Red Chief could be alive, dead, injured, or under torture by his kidnappers. And these well-intentioned rescuers could make no faster progress than this.

Flashes of lightning blinded us. The massive bursts of electric energy came fast, almost continuously, lighting our way.

Thunderclaps shook the forest, reverberated, echoed. Scarcely had one tympanic chorus diminished than another began with an explosive crash.

Then the storm ended abruptly. Lightning flashed less frequently. Thunder died away. The rain stopped. But not the dripping. Leaves overhead shed droplets of water, obedient to every puff of breeze that followed the storm. The breezes died. A calm settled over the forest.

Sounds of water, stirred by the paddles, filled the dense woods. Air saturated with moisture, clammy and almost suffocating, seemed to muffle the little noises we made. We strained to hear some *alien* sound. Like that of an approaching canoe. Or a speed boat filled with grenades and machine guns.

Only the faintest star glow lighted our way, giving shape to the darkest shadows. When clouds passed over, no light shone at all. One had to sense instead of see.

How Aunamunh, the nearly a teenager, steered the canoes past snags and hanging vines amazed me.

The Río Ramón, to my relief, had fewer obstacles than those we had encountered up the Micalla. It also had a less powerful current. As a result, we made fair headway. I imagined that some of the arms, necks and shoulders ached from the unusual exertion. That with each painful stroke came a silent plea for Aunamunh to signal a stop.

I cursed myself for having let the Red Chief slip from sight. Square Jaw and Fatso must have been waiting for him to rise early and go down to the bank of the Caquetá. Easy to sneak up on him...

It would be quite a coup to eliminate him entirely without any witnesses. Remove the last opposition to their plans. Here, far out in the wilderness, International Land Buyers could administer its own justice. Cinch control of the village. Keep this out of the courts. Avoid the press. Colombian reporters, I'd been told in Bogotá, had become pretty nosy about ILB's work anyway. Article writers too supportive of wildlife.

My only hope was that if they intended to use Red Chief as a hostage, he might still be alive.

I wanted only that everybody in the village be asleep. Off guard. Not playing cards. Not drinking late. Just sleeping.

And Aunamunh? I crossed my fingers. He had volunteered. Obviously no one could do the job better. No one knew every contour of tree and trail around that village like he did. If he hugged the ground, he might be mistaken for a paca. No. That wouldn't work. Gold miners shoot pacas for sport. Shadowy, almost indefinable shapes went past. We could see overhanging limbs silhouetted faintly against the stars. Logs reached toward us from the river's edge. Snags clutched outward but never quite touched the canoes.

I wished we could use flashlights to spot wild animals along the shore, drinking at the river's edge. Slithering down tree trunks, hanging from limbs, flying among the trees. Or coming through the water alongside the canoe —like maybe an anaconda.

My imagination played tricks as I pulled the oar. Sometimes the faint glow from distant lightning raised the level of illumination and I fancied seeing a jaguar at the water's edge. I squinted and concentrated—it did no good. We could scarcely see each other, much less life along the river bank. By design, we wore dark shirts and jackets.

Inevitably, one paddler's oar whacked another. The sound, so sudden, so magnified in the silence, startled us. Granted, sound could not travel very far in the dense, damp Amazon forest. Any hidden sentinel, though, could hear it and fire at the noise.

I glanced at my watch. Ten o'clock. We should be getting there soon.

I watched the amorphous shapes at the oars. Everyone seemed to be holding up.

Aunamunh gave the signal to stop. Each paddler passed it along. The canoes slowed.

By prearrangement, only Joe and I paddled in the lead canoe as we approached the shore, Greg and Mo in the second canoe. The others held their oars up out of the way.

The white hull of a speedboat, anchored at the shore, came dimly into view. A sleek model. A fast model. Probably two hundred horsepower. Machine gun mounted on the front. And no doubt, I thought, ammo, grenades and explosives inside.

We were in luck. No lights. No sounds. No sentinels.

Quietly the little canoes moved upstream, then nudged the soft bank. The occupants stowed their oars. Each person slid out into the water, crawled onto the muddy embankment and slipped into the forest. Eduardo, the boat-man, tied the canoes to a tree. A soldier took up position near the speedboat.

The rest knew what to do. Be absolutely quiet. Re-main where they were. Drop to the forest floor if anyone approached. Move into action only if called.

The silence became almost absolute. Not even water dripped from the storm. A faint, repetitive croaking voice could be heard from a distance through the forest. A soft splashing sound issued from the river. Nothing more.

It was now nearly eleven. I hoped that was not too early. If so, then some of the miners might be awake, per-haps playing cards by gasoline lantern. That light in their eyes would make it difficult for them to see us outside in the darkness.

So, we'll find out. Aunamunh, Joe and I set out on the trail into the village.

CHAPTER 57

We followed the Correguaje boy, sneaking along, creeping along, scarcely moving, placing each step with supreme caution. I thanked the rain for rendering the footpath soft, the leaves and sticks limp, pliable—and quiet.

For Joe it was a nightmare. His big feet snagged exposed roots. He glanced off the unexpected buttresses of giant trees. Finding a stick, he held it up as defense against overhanging limbs. He waved the stick from side to side to brush away dense cobwebs and ward off the giant spiders that lived in them.

Aunamunh paused and listened.

Still no lights. No voices. I felt relieved. Not yet midnight. I guessed that Square Jaw, Fatso and the miners might actually *be* asleep. No fires, I hoped. Or drinking parties. Maybe they had to get to bed early so they could get up at dawn and start mining along the river bank. And what about sentinels? Did the miners need guards posted this far out in the Amazon wilderness?

Perhaps drinking parties had been curtailed while they had a captive in their midst. Or maybe the miners merely waited with submachine guns. Expecting a rescue attempt. Luring the rescuers into a trap.

We went on again. Joe almost tripped, grabbed the wrong tree trunk, and cut the side of his hand on vicious thorns. He suppressed an angry curse.

Aunamunh stopped. He motioned us to be very still. Nothing could be discerned beyond the boy. No huts. No moving human silhouettes. He knew exactly where he was.

Next thing we knew, Aunamunh had gone. Vanished completely in the gloom.

With that began the most nerve-wracking wait I had ever experienced. To keep his mind alert, I saw Joe fingering his rifle.

With my body frozen in position, I projected what could happen. Aunamunh finds Palkuh. Touches him lightly. Startles the chief, who cries out. Miners come running, shouting, shooting...

Or a poker game inside a hut. A miner picks up a light and comes outside. Sees the boy. A quick shot...

Or a dog sniffs out the boy and barks, rousing the village. Lights come on, men pour out the door with guns blazing...

Or a macaw screeches. That starts a monkey chattering. The boy meets a prowling jaguar...

I tried to shake these wild images out of my head. Ordered myself to calm down and cool off. Yet still I fancied figures coming toward us in this sea of darkness...only to disappear like ghosts in liquid shrouds.

Crouched almost as a *tigre*, ready to spring, I kept my eyes focused intently into the black hole ahead. At the first sign of trouble we would pounce. If we failed by stealth, we would take back the chief by force.

A powerful temptation to creep forward overwhelmed me. I *must*! But I didn't. We had to trust a twelve-year-old to carry out the most crucial and hazardous part of this mission.

I did trust the boy. Only—how long dare we wait for his return? That slowly began to torment me. If the miners caught Aunamunh, they could use the boy to capture the whole lot of the intruders. Drop them into the river. Every last molecule would be consumed, recycled in the natural ecosystem.

I heard footsteps.

Everything wet and soft—another deception? Yet I knew the faintest sound of footsteps when I heard them. And after that I *sensed* the presence of something in front of us.

Joe and I eased back behind the nearest tree trunk.

Joe gripped his rifle.

Two figures, one medium height, one small, approached in the pitch blackness to within arm's length. Aunamunh led the Red Chief to us. The Chief limped. He had been hurt. He threw his arms around Joe, then me—. Not a word passed among us. Not a sound.

Joe handed his rifle to me and bent down so that the old chief could grasp his shoulders and climb up on his back. Then, holding a slender tree trunk for leverage, he pulled himself and his burden up.

Without a moment's delay, we started our slow, silent trek back toward the river.

As slowly and as maddeningly as we had come from it. Palkuh, Joe doubtless thought, grew heavier with each step. His arms and legs must be straining under this almost tai ji pace—slow movement, arms outstretched, legs extended, torso twisted.

Joe swayed under the heavy load and uncertain footing, trying to avoid the spiny tree trunks. I followed inches behind, ready to seize the chief if Joe should falter.

No sound came from behind. No light either. So far, so good. The miners in the village were still asleep, guns at their sides.

After what seemed an interminable torture, we reached the miners' speed boat at the edge of the river. Joe set Palkuh down. I took the chief's arm and we walked upstream to join the others.

Every member of the group expressed jubilation in near silence. Joe carried the chief to one of the canoes and set him in it. We all got aboard as quietly as we could and picked up the oars.

Suddenly a sound of gunfire came through the forest. Light beams from powerful flashlights jabbed among the trees.

I shouted: "They found us! Get out of here!"

We plunged the paddles into the water, caution gone.

"Pull, everybody!" Joe shouted with the full force of his lungs. "We don't have much time!"

We didn't need urging. Each paddler pulled for his life. We could barely see the wall of trees on the other side of the Rio Ramón, and headed there, straining to get as far away from the dock as we could before the miners arrived.

The lights became brighter, the sounds closer. More guns went off.

Shouts rang out, muffled by the mists, absorbed in the dense tropical forest.

We moved with excruciating slowness, out beyond the speedboat, headed downstream.

Miners burst out of the trees and ran down the embankment to the edge of the water. Their lights found the intruders. Their guns took aim.

"Stay down!" I shouted, knowing they couldn't row and stay down at the same time. "Keep as low as you can!"

Guns fired. Bullets zinged across the water, whacked into the canoes and severed twigs overhead.

Greg Fisher lurched against the side of the canoe. Beryl cried out.

"I'm okay," he said, "top of the shoulder."

Beams of light converged on us as we paddled in desperation. Lights blinded us after so long in the darkness. Bullets struck the water, whined past, pinged above our heads.

Then, ominously, the miners began to clamber into the speedboat. Moments later we swerved around the bend, out of sight of the miners.

The guns still fired, though blindly now. The captive had been taken from the miners, and their rage knew no bounds.

I got out my 9mm Parabellum pistol and laid it beside me. "Keep paddling," I ordered. "They'll catch up to us any moment."

The shooting stopped. We could still hear rapid-fire shouts and curses, Latin style. Above the clatter of our paddles, I could hear the miners starting up. The engine burst into life with a rumble. The boatman gunned it.

I had a vivid imagination. I knew what was happening. In my mind's eye I could see the miners picking up grenades as the boat jumped out of the water and headed downstream toward us.

The others heard it, too. We pulled with all our might, but it was no use. My heart sank as I heard the loud whine of the speedboat coming closer, though still not visible.

You sure as hell got yourself and a dozen others in a pickle this time, my alter ego chided me. *How can you guys, with pissant paddles, get out of the way of a speedboat with armed miners coming at you mad as hell? Answer that one, smart boy.*

I had no answer. We could break away and head into the deep forest, but there wasn't any time for that. We'd have to fight. And the miners held all the upper hands.

With a burst of lights and a deafening roar, the speedboat rounded the bend and came into view. We recoiled, blinded.

The miners instantly spotted us. Snapping their automatics to their shoulders, they took aim...

"This is it," I said to myself, raising my pistol.

Weirdly, my thoughts flew back to New York City. I almost spoke aloud, as if addressing someone far away:

"Kelly, I hope to hell you see what you got us into this time...?"

CHAPTER 58

At nine next morning, I roused them, red-eyed and exhausted, out of their bunks. They grumbled. I grumbled back. It had been a late, late night, an intense night. Paddling up the river. Sneaking into the village with Aunamunh as a guide. Rescuing Palkuh. Coming back to the boats. Waking the miners. Shoving off. Being pursued in a power boat and shot at as we paddled desperately down the river...

"I'm as sleepy as you are!" I snarled. "Now, get up! I'm starving. Pack your bags and bring them with you to the Comandante's dining room. We may have to make a quick getaway."

"Oh, Barry," Mo Briggle responded, "you're just being dramatic. Go eat and come back for us at noon."

"Yeah, Barry," added Beryl Fisher. "Have mercy. We had a busy night."

"Okay," I answered. "Now we may have a busier day."

Joe stirred in his bunk. "Too right, buddy. We'd better get our asses out of here if we know what's good for us. Hear any helicopters yet?"

That got them up.

At breakfast, I insisted that Carol Lynn take the head of the table. A highly unusual step. Protocol doesn't let anyone replace the Captain of a military installation at the head of his table. *Anywhere!* Not even when the *General* comes. And here, among Latin machos, you furthermore never even suggest—perish the thought—that a *woman* replace the Captain. What about the natural order of things?

"Doesn't matter," I said. "This is a very different woman. We don't have any time for formalities. This woman must be honored for what she did last night."

The Comandante agreed, swallowing tradition. Carol Lynn, pearls and all, seated herself in the Captain's chair.

"All this attention!" she said. "I don't deserve it."

"You saved the lives of sixteen people," I said. "You deserve a hell of a lot more than head table status."

The others gathered their banana chips, corned beef, and coffee, tea or Coke, and sat at the table.

Spider said: "It was the least we could do for all the horrors that have been visited upon that village."

Mo: "I wouldn't call it a 'least' effort, Spider. That village was an armed fort."

I cut in. "Well, we all owe a great deal to Carol Lynn. What prompted you to do what you did?"

She smiled. "I was just mad, that's all. Those ruddy blackguards, excuse the language, had spoilt my vacation and I resented it. They were interfering. I didn't like that. I thought Boris had cheek, but the thugs were worse... kidnaping an old man like that. All I could think of was getting back at them."

Spider: "You did that!"

"I'm not one for revenge, normally, but last night that's all I could think about. So I said, disable them. Leave them stranded out here in the jungle. It would serve them right! Once they start down the river the mud in the petrol tank will stop them and we'll be long gone! I never thought, actually, that it would be so close."

Joe: "If it had been any closer... Well, don't think of that. It was a stroke of genius."

"Not really. A stroke of anger. I just kept stuffing that tank with all the mud I could possibly push in, as though I were choking the thugs with each mouthful. Isn't that scandalous? I got petrol all over me. The people in Oxford would call me barbaric!"

Joe said: "Okay, Barbaric, our mothers thank you, our fathers thank you, and we thank you!"

Never had they thrown such energy into a round of applause. When it died away, I brought them back to reality.

"We are in grave danger. I got you up early because we must leave as soon as we possibly can. ILB is not going to take this lying down. From the sound of the explosion last night, their boat and all the munitions on board must have gone up. And no telling how many miners blew up with it."

Beryl asked: "So what's the danger? We're at a military base."

"Don't kid yourself," I answered. "We're at a *remote* military base. If there were any survivors last night in the village, they no doubt got on the radio. ILB will be so mad now, they'll storm in here and shoot everybody in sight. And no one would ever know who did it."

The Comandante nodded. "They have political power."

"At the same time," I went on, "they're in a real pickle and they know it. We didn't intend it, but when word of last night's assault on them gets out, it will be regarded as a rebellion against their operations, their life blood. The press will trumpet it. Latin presses are favorable to the environment. This would be a juicy story. They'd tell it ten different ways. ILB would be devastated."

Chris said: "So they must stop it here."

Dana: "Stop *us?*"

"Right. They cannot let this get out or go unpunished. They already think one of us killed Boris. Now that we've blown up some of their men, we're all murderers...Well, I don't need to dwell on that. We get out of here right after breakfast."

Joe: "We were supposed to leave today, anyway."

The Comandante answered. "Amigos, we have problems. The jets are up north. We have only a DC-3 here, and it has a bad oil valve. Maybe the new valve will come today. Maybe *mañana*."

I said: "We're not going to depend on that."

Dana: "What can we do? Are there roads out of here?"

"No," I answered. "And we can't go down rivers, either, for obvious reasons. We'd be too vulnerable to air attack."

Spider asked: "Why the hell can't we just call in a jet? Isn't this an emergency?"

"*Sí, sí, Señora,*" the Comandante replied. "But it would take two hours. Maybe three."

Joe: "We'll be mincemeat by then."

Greg asked: "Can't we hole up in the forest somewhere?"

I brushed that aside. "They'd find out. They'd lay down a siege, starve us out. We'd have to live on pythons. Ants. Grubs."

"That's out!" Joe said.

"Or burn us out. All they have to do is set fire to the forest. Some hunters do that to drive animals like deer out so they can shoot them. They're experienced."

Joe choked. "God damn...that's crude!"

I said: "Our only choice is to leave. And my gut tells me it had better be fast."

"Well," Chris said, "if we have no options..."

I turned to the Comandante. "This oil valve. Is it still in the aircraft?"

"*Sí Señor.*"

"No way it will work?"

"Well, *posiblemente*. Our policy is to——."

"Oh, blast policy! Will it work or won't it?"

"Horacio is our mechanic. He might know."

"Joe, would you be good enough to round up Horacio and get him here?"

"Fast?"

"Real fast!"

"On my way."

CHAPTER 59

Just as Joe leaped up, the sound of a helicopter came to our ears. That ultra-low chopping, booming sound that seems to set the landscape shivering. We leaped up and rushed to the windows.

Another green and brown helicopter, with ILB insignia on the side, was approaching from up the river. As it came in low over headquarters, wind from its blades thrashed the trees.

"Away from the windows!" I cautioned.

The craft hovered for about a minute, circling slowly, then rose and left, flying in the direction of Red Chief's village.

Joe ran out the door.

I turned again to the Comandante. "Even if we get the DC-3 fixed, who can fly it? Can you?"

"*Amigo*, I am forbidden to leave the base without proper—."

"Yes," I interrupted. "I know. You say Horacio is a mechanic. Mechanics can fly. They take planes up for tests."

"Oh, yes. Perhaps around the field. He is not a pilot..."

I said abruptly: "Today he is! Let's ask him."

Joe came back with Horacio. I asked point blank if he could fly us to Leticia. The mechanic shifted his head around in surprise and gave a soft whistle.

"*Para Leticia?*"

"*Sí, Señor.*"

Horacio's eyes took on a worried expression. I asked how far to Leticia.

The Comandante answered. "*Ocho cientos kilómetros.*"

I calculated. "That's about three hours?"

"*Más o menos.*"

I turned to Horacio and asked whether the plane could be kept in the air that long.

"*Es un viejo,*" he said.

"I know it's an old one. *Pero puedes?*"

The mechanic shook his head, saying he didn't know.

Joe threw up his hands. "Nice brilliant escape last night. Today we get wiped out by a defective oil valve."

"Maybe," I returned. I asked Horacio to describe the problem with the oil valve. Clogged. But functional? Hmmm. Oil backs up and pours out on the wings. Caught fire last trip and they barely got it out after they landed. But it works? Yes, but he wouldn't want to trust it. Any other possibility?

At this, Horacio turned around and put his hands behind his back, lost in concentration. We let him think. And think.

Joe whispered. "Time's wasting…"

Horacio turned around and said that perhaps he could take the valve from the ILB helicopter still sitting out on the pad. Maybe he could make that work.

I translated, and added: "I would never in my wildest dreams believe such a thing possible. But we are in Colombia. They have a saying. *Nada funciona, pero todo sale bien.* Nothing works, but everything succeeds."

I turned to Horacio and asked how long it would take to make the transfer. Answer: two hours. Maybe three.

Mo said: "We got ten minutes before the goon squad arrives."

I put it point blank to Horacio. Will the DC-3 fly as is? Yes or no.

Answer: Yes, but...

Will it fly for three hours?

Maybe...

Can you fly it for us?

The Comandante objected: "He's only had minimal training."

I persisted, eyes directly on Horacio. "Can you?"

Reluctantly, Horacio nodded.

Can we leave in ten minutes? Horacio's hands flew up in the air and his eyes rolled. Then he turned abruptly and dashed out the door.

The rest started to rise. I stopped them. Turning to the Comandante, I asked: "In case of emergency, how many landing strips are there between here and Leticia?"

The Comandante only smiled.

"We go the whole way, once we start?"

The Comandante nodded.

Joe said: "Ai-yai-yai-ee!"

I turned to them. "You have all heard these conversations. You heard the helicopter fly over. We assume it will pick up Square Jaw and Fatso, if they're still alive, and be back within a few minutes. Nobody is forced to leave. This is going to be risky."

Joe: "You said it!"

Chris: "We have no alternative."

Joe: "What if we have to go down in the forest?"

I shrugged. "Who knows? A Mexican pilot once told me what happened to one of his fellow pilots who went down in the jungles of Yucatán."

"Well, go on. Don't stop there!"

"I will let you imagine what ants do to injured pilots, unless you want details..."

"I withdraw the question. Forget it. We have friendly ants."

Mo spoke up. "We've forgotten one thing."

"Forgotten?"

"Yeah. What about the Chief and Aunamunh? We can't leave them here. And Sonke. What about him? If the goons are mad, they could shoot every Correguaje in sight."

I thought a moment. "Chris and Carol Lynn. You are the language experts here. Will you talk to them? Tell them what we are up to. Ask if they want to fly with us to Leticia. Comandante, is that all right?"

"Yes. Yes."

"How will they get back?"

"I think the Comandante can arrange to have them and Horacio brought back up on one of the jets, if it's safe to do so. Monty said his boatmen can stay here and take them all home sometime next week. Can you convey all that?"

Chris said: "We have a notebook full of Correguaje words."

"Well, you better make it fast. Monty's at the dock. We can call him up to help if you need it."

"We'll manage." They took the Red Chief, Sonke and Aunamunh outside.

I turned to the rest. "I have made these plans pell mell without discussing them with any of you. I think we all agree that this is the only way out. It isn't. We can stay and take the consequences..."

They shook their heads

"If anyone doesn't want to go, we'll stay here and try to defend ourselves."

Spider said: "Barry, we're keeping Horacio waiting..."

They flew out of their chairs and headed for the door, grabbed their bags, and ran toward the plane.

Chris caught up with me. "That didn't take long! The boy and the chiefs are on the plane already. Aunamunh says if we go down, he'll help guide us out."

"He's one in a million. Keep him at your side until we get to Leticia."

"The Briggles are acting godfather for him."

"Roger."

We found Horacio working on the motor. *"Listamos, amigo?"*

Horacio looked up and shook his head. *"Momentito!"*

I ordered everyone aboard. "Horacio's working on the valve. He'll be another minute. Chris, will you find a place out here, maybe over there by the ILB helicopter, where you can observe to the southeast? Give a yell if you see any aircraft approaching from the direction of Red Chief's village."

"Right."

As soon as the others had boarded, Joe stuck his head back out. "Barry!"

"What is it?"

"There aren't any *seats*!"

"Are there benches running along both sides of the cabin, under the windows?"

"Yes. Those are seats? Is *that* where we sit?"

"Welcome to a military transport, Joe. That's where you sit!"

"But, great shit! There aren't any *seat belts*!"

"Joe, you're spoiled! Do you use a seat belt when you ride a bucking bronco?"

"I ought to. My ass still hurts from the last time I got thrown."

"You'll feel right at home! Look again. The belts and straps are there."

Joe disappeared inside.

Horacio hammered. Cursed. Grunted. He raced to the hangar. Boxes clattered. Tools fell to the floor. Minutes passed. Joe watched from the door of the plane, then hopped down. "This is running like a comic opera."

I answered. "There's only one difference, Joe. On this stage, the villain may win."

I glanced at Chris. All quiet. I scoured the horizon downriver. The morning sky, azure blue, supported only a few white puffs of clouds.

Horacio came back, carrying a huge wrench. Perspiration poured down his temples.

More banging. More clatter.

After another minute he banged the trapdoor shut and called to me: "*Vamos, amigo!*"

I whistled to Chris to get aboard. Horacio went on board, followed by Joe. I shook hands with the Comandante, thanked him for everything, and boarded.

As I took a place on the bench, Joe said: "Now it's Act Three. The engine won't start."

Greg responded. "Cheer up, Joe. If he's as good at running a plane as he was on the guitar the other night, we've got half a chance."

Joe laughed. "His guitar doesn't need motor oil."

The near-silence that followed almost drained the passengers' overtaxed nerves.

Horacio tried to start the port engine.

No response.

He cursed and tried again. Nothing happened. More curses.

He tried the starboard engine. No response. We heard him pounding on the instrument panel to no avail.

Rising and moving out of the cockpit, he ran through the cabin, leaping over the tangle of feet, legs, and backpacks in the aisle, muttering "*Momentito Momentito! Por favor...*"

He jumped to the ground, opened the engine door, and hammered again.

Joe said: "Can we still change our minds?"

"Take heart," I answered. "The DC-3 was one of the toughest and most reliable airplanes in history. It was the first successful commercial passenger plane. Thousands were converted to military—."

"I don't care about history," responded Joe. "I only care about the next three hours."

Beryl reminded him: "Past is prologue, Joe. Take comfort."

Bang! The engine door slammed shut. Horacio bounded into the cabin and danced his way over our feet to the cockpit.

This time the left propeller began to rotate. With a blast of blue smoke the engine roared into life. The passengers cheered.

The plane idled. Idled some more. Kept on idling.

Beryl asked: "Well, why don't we start moving?"

"I can answer that," Joe replied. "He's up there reading the manual."

Mo, looking out the window, shouted: "There's a helicopter approaching!"

CHAPTER 60

Horacio must have seen it, too.

The plane began to move. He taxied to the near end of the runway, swerved into position, and gunned the engines.

Another blast of blue smoke.

The DC-3 lurched down the runway, sputtering, popping, and coughing clouds of exhaust. It gained speed. Horacio tried to lift it too soon. It rose for a moment, yawed, banged down onto the runway.

I turned around as best I could and looked out the window behind. The helicopter, coming in at an intercept angle, had moved close enough so that I could see the familiar green and brown colors.

Belted in with our backs to the windows, we couldn't see very much unless we twisted sharply. It didn't matter much. Our fate lay in Horacio Delgado's hands now.

And in the power of an antique aircraft that had already flown how many millions of miles?

The deafening roar of the engines on both sides of us filled the cabin so loudly that we could hear nothing else. A metal box about the size of a lunch box came loose from somewhere up front and slid down the aisle. We lifted our feet to let it pass.

The whole craft vibrated. We felt ourselves swaying from side to side.

I saw the ILB helicopter coming closer, as though to fire across the bow. Then I saw the real aim: to get in front of the DC-3 and force it to abort the takeoff.

Horacio lifted the plane again, very nearly his last chance at the end of the runway. This time it stayed in the air, roaring out across a grassy expanse at the edge of the Caquetá River and then out over the water.

The helicopter pursued across the end of the runway, over the grass and above the river. For a few moments, the lumbering DC-3, trailing wisps and puffs of blue smoke, seemed to falter and slow. The helicopter closed in behind.

Horacio, in a now-or-never maneuver, took the DC-3 into a steep climb and a bank to the right. The engines strained mightily. The craft gained speed, crossed back over the bank of the big river, and rose above the tropical forest on a southeast bearing toward Leticia.

The helicopter fell farther back, but it, too, headed southeast toward Leticia.

"Hot pursuit," I thought. "We'll see who gets there first."

The engines of the DC-3 soon took on a resonant, coordinated sound, less vibrating, less deafening.

As the din diminished, Joe, the incurable movie buff, turned to me and shouted: "Whew! Just like the takeoff from Baskul in *Lost Horizon*!"

We climbed to three thousand feet and leveled off. The roar of the engines diminished, varied only as the plane encountered pockets of resistance and crosscurrents of low-level tropical air.

"Hang in there, Horacio," Greg called. "Keep up the good work!"

I unbelted and went into the cockpit. Horacio was frowning, eyes focused on the instruments.

As I approached, he looked up. The frown changed to a smile. Most heartening smile of the week, I thought.

"*Todo bien?*" I asked. Everything okay?

"*Bien! Bien!*" Horacio grinned reassuringly. I thought I would reserve judgment. I had so often heard that phrase "*Bien! Bien!*" Sometimes it really meant "well and good." From experience, I also knew that Latins on occasion meant it to mask their troubles. Oh well, Americans did that, too, with "Okay! Okay!" The Chinese have used "*Hen hao! Hen hao!*" for centuries to pronounce everything fine when it wasn't.

As nearly as I could determine, Horacio had succeeded in holding the aircraft together. We conversed for a while, after which I returned to the cabin.

"So far, so good," I told the passengers.

I said to Joe: "Horacio asked us to watch for any oil seeping out of the engine on the starboard side. Joe, would you keep an occasional eye on that engine?"

Joe nodded and started his vigil.

My gaze fell on the tropical forest a mile below. Since Tres Esquinas we had flown over a solid mass of vegetation, unbroken for miles. The expanse of dark green stretched to every horizon, somnolent under pillars of mushrooming clouds.

I watched Joe slump in his seat. He hadn't relaxed like that for what seemed like days. He began to hum the strains of *La Negra Celina*.

Looking across the aisle toward Aunamunh, I saw the boy glued to the window. Sonke, next to him, sat staring transfixed out his window. Must be their first flight, I mused... Palkuh had already fallen asleep.

A flash of blinding light caught my eye and I looked down. Nothing but black forest, no openings, no glades, no...

What was this? Another flash. A momentary reflection of something. Then I saw a snakelike line of light emitting from the woods, glowing with a powerful light, then disappearing. Now I knew.

The Amazon forest was not quite as "unbroken" as it looked. The mirror surfaces of hidden tributaries reflected solar glare, revealing streams known intimately only by Indians who lived down there. We knew from our trips to Sonke's village and up the Micalla River that travel along these streams resembled travel through a narrow canyon. Overhead, leaves and limbs nearly filtered out the sunlight.

From up here at three thousand feet, that canopy seemed continuous. No rivers showed until the sun, reflecting from their surfaces, outlined their winding, tortuous paths.

Then something else. A small opening in the mass of vegetation. Tiny foot trails crossing it. Faintly visible wisps of smoke curling into the air. A forest glade. A parcel of land cleared of trees. Nearby, another open patch—yes! A yuca field devoid of trees, its soil exhausted, the crop burned. Little more than tree stumps blackened by fire. Near that, a patch of yuca and pineapple, or so I guessed. Farther on, another village...

Another laughing, giggling Sonke with a necklace of jaguar teeth. Another collection of little Tiatas, Ahniyahs, and Ahmoomahs with stick dolls and reed flutes...

One by one, I watched the passengers fall asleep. Joe even slept at his post, dozing from moment to moment. We had been up so late last night. The fight with the miners seemed almost like a dream now, something from delirium tremens, something that happened months ago...

Joe waked with a start. I looked out the window. An almost invisible trickle of dark oil began to ooze from the starboard engine.

I watched intently. The oil crept along the wing in a winding, snakelike path.

I watched it carefully, saw it grow, meandering toward the trailing edge of the wing.

The path of the seeping oil widened. The volume of flow increased.

Joe looked up at me. "Should we wake Horacio?"

I hesitated. Horacio wanted to know as soon as we detected any oil.

The oil reached the trailing edge and began to flow off into the air in a furious sheet of black spray. With volume increasing, the black oozing had now spread out over a wider area on the wing, rippled by the high velocity wind. The fall from the trailing edge widened...

"Barry!"

Joe craned his neck. The trickle had now become a steady flow.

"Won't be long," Joe warned, "before the engine dries up."

I rose without a word and went to the cockpit. Horacio's face had become benign, nearly blank. He sat with seemingly not a care in the world.

I briefly explained the situation with the starboard engine. Described the flow of oil, the lake on the wing, the "waterfall" over the trailing edge.

Horacio shrugged and flipped his hands in a careless gesture. *"Oh, no importa. Aceite es barato en Colombia."*

I raised my head and exploded with laughter. Slapping him on the shoulder, I turned and went back into the cabin, guffawing so hard I could hardly find my way.

The passengers waked, startled.

"What's so funny?" Joe asked.

"I go to Horacio," I answered. "Tell him the oil is escaping onto the right wing. Describe how the wing is covered with oil, how it's leaking over the edge. The assumption being, of course, that the engine is about to catch fire as it did the last time they had this ship in the air. And do you know what he says?"

"No, what?"

"No importa. Aceite es barato in Colombia."

"What does that mean?"

"It means 'Don't worry. Oil is cheap in Colombia.'"

That broke them up. Joe said: "Okay. That does it!

That's the last time I'm going to worry about *anything* in Colombia!"

He put his head back against the wall of the cabin and went to sleep, the drone of the engines, for the moment, at least, music to his ears...

CHAPTER 61

I waked with a start to see the other passengers faced to the windows.

At the end of the flight came the greatest opening in the rain forest. The Amazon River, the Río Amazonas, master stem with a thousand branches, wide, gently curving, brown with sediment, in some ways a liquid land mass.

Joe whistled in disbelief. "Good gawd! Wyoming doesn't have anything like that. It's bigger'n the Sweetwater."

There it was! The great tan avenue of history, commerce, Indian canoes, houseboats, barges, frigates. My mind reeled. Dolphins, eels, anacondas and pirarucús. On the south bank, and for as far in the distance as the eye could see, lay Brazil. To the west, the infinite inscrutable black forest leading across Peru to the horizon. Directly beneath us, a narrow corridor of Colombia reaching to Leticia, on the country's southernmost shore.

The settlement, small and unimposing, spread over low hills on the north bank of the great river. A frontier outpost on what the Colombians called their Third Coast.

"Well," Joe said, "we may have an interesting reception."

"Square Jaw and Fatso here yet?" Spider asked.

"No, but the police are," he answered.

Horacio landed the DC-3—with three bounces and a swerve—and taxied to a far corner of the field. Monty said: "A truck will come git us. I will take your baggage to the tourist hotel. A friend of mine, Padre Olevida, wants to meet with you."

I inserted: "So does the law. I will go to the police office. Joe, you can come with me. The rest of you can look around town. I think we can find you if we need you. I intend to resolve the Kolinski matter as soon as possible, and I'll need your help."

Monty went on. "I think y'all be safe with the Padre. ILB don't bother the Church none. Well, I don't think."

Joe: "Delete that last phrase."

Horacio entered the cabin to an instant round of applause, handshakes and embraces.

Joe said: "Barry, tell him my only regret is that I don't have another piranha tee shirt to give to him. How do you say 'I'll always remember *La Negra Celina?*'"

Spider: "All right, let's cut the chatter. Where are the parrots?"

Monty answered: "River and turn left."

That was all Spider needed to know. Here, at last, lay the crux of her mission. She had a lot to do, she said. "Parrots, eel shipments—."

"Spider," I warned. "Stay out of trouble."

"Why?" she asked.

"You are a suspect in a murder case."

"Leave a message when you want me, Barry."

With that flippant remark, she departed the aircraft.

As near as I can tell from subsequent accounts, here's what happened next.

Spider and the Fishers walked down the steep dirt street, lined on both sides with ramshackle, shingle-faced shops topped with corrugated roofs. Huge window shutters, each dropped on chains like a drawbridge on a moat, became display tables. On these, merchants set out their oils, powders, combs, cups, pots, pans and a hundred other items. Beneath the shutters hung jackets and trousers for sale, and on the walls of the huts—dresses, hats, gourds, oars, nets—the paraphernalia of a riverside community.

To their ears came a cacophony of voices, hammers thudding, pans clanking, and from a loudspeaker the strains of the latest rock beat...

They made their way amid a constant flow of pedestrians, and an occasional motorbike. At the bottom of the street they reached a bare-earth walkway, well packed by the tread of feet, at the river's edge. Beryl Fisher suddenly felt as though thrust back in time. Back to the banks of the Mississippi as she imagined it must have been a century ago. No sidewalks. No board walks. No piers. Only huts and warehouses, set back here at the foot of main street, but elsewhere built as close to the river bank as the builder dared.

They stepped over piles of logs awaiting shipment and detoured around stacks of rough-sawn planks. They clambered over mounds of rock and sand, wound among barrels of oil, cans of gasoline, and broken boats pulled up on shore.

Vessels of every conceivable description lay at the river's edge: open canoes, house boats, fishing boats, barges, rafts and ferries. Beyond, a tall gray naval frigate, at anchor in the Amazon, towered over all the rest.

Spider uttered an oath. A young man in white shirt, black trousers, and old-style tennis shoes circulated in the crowd carrying the flattened skin of a caiman. "*Pieles!*" he shouted. "*Caimanes! Caimanes!*"

They turned left and soon reached a warehouse with a porch fronting the river.

Dried, pressed hides hung along the front wall. Huge letters had been scrawled across the top of the wall:

SE VENDE ANIMALES VIVOS

"I can translate that," Spider said with a grim smile. "'Live Animals for Sale.' Here's where we go to work."

Smaller animal hides adorned the wall on both sides of the doorway. The visitors made their way up on the porch and found, just inside the doorway, a series of necklaces hanging on pegs. Greg took down one composed of round wooden beads and the carcasses of ten song birds.

Spider closed her eyes and turned away in disgust. "We can't help those birds."

Beryl lowered her head. "I can't grasp this. Why would anyone buy these things?"

Greg answered: "Tourists, probably. Dealers. All we know is that someone wants to buy them, or else someone else wouldn't have gone out and caught the birds and made them."

They wandered through the room, past piles of hides, scattered boxes and barrels, and more necklaces. Then, out on the back porch, they spied a cage made of wood, with screen wire on front and back. Inside the cage, so jammed that they could hardly fly, about fifty small parrots and parakeets fought and fluttered in a mass effort to escape. Already, several dead birds lay at the bottom of the cage. Some clung desperately to the screen wire, others clung to other birds, biting and holding on, twisting, screeching, fighting.

Without any contemplation of the matter, Greg walked up to the cage and peered inside.

Spider said: "Wait!" and called the clerk out to the porch. She pointed to the cage and asked: "America?"

The clerk said: "*No, Señora. Europa.*"

Spider said bitterly: "*Fuck Europe!*" and turned to Greg. "Okay. Go ahead."

Greg lifted the peg that held the door closed, opened it, and let the birds loose. They roared out of the cage and flew away in a cloud toward the trees behind the building. Their screeching defied description.

The sales clerk uttered a shriek of anguish. "*Ay-y-y- Qué haces?!*"

She rushed to the cage to close the door, but arrived too late. *"Mama mia! Que pasó! Ay-y! Alberto! Alberto! Venga, venga!"*

Spider, Greg and Beryl stepped down off the porch and disappeared along a trail in the woods behind the warehouse.

The clerk turned and ran through the building and out the front door, shouting: *"Policia! Policia! Ladrones!"*

CHAPTER 62

Unaware of any of this, Joe and I walked to the bottom of the main street and turned right. For a while, we made our way among the dockside debris of logs, boxes, barrels and piles of sand and gravel to the loading platforms. Ragtag but ocean-going vessels lay at anchor, their inner maws open to the passage of workers bearing burlap sacks and crates.

A hawker went by: *"Pieles! Caimanes! Caimanes!"*

Joe asked: "Can I bring him down with a flying tackle?"

I grinned. "Behave yourself, Yankee."

I couldn't blame Joe, the biologist, for revulsion at seeing all the dead, skinned, caged, and packaged animals either for sale or ready for shipment abroad. The place struck him as an open-air processing lab and conveyor belt on which the wild produce of the Amazon went out to sea and to continents beyond.

Joe stopped. "Where are we going? What can we do about all this? What are you up to?"

I answered: "Monty wouldn't answer my question about who was shipping animals out of the Amazon. He said we'd find out when we got to Leticia. So here we are."

Joe said: "Wait a minute," and stepped over to a pile of boxes, returning moments later. "They are all stamped: 'PRODUCTOS FORESTALES, LETICIA.'"

"That's the answer, Joe. 'Forest Products.' My guess is that one company ships nearly everything. More economical that way. Let's see what's going out."

We came to a cage of screeching parakeets, and Joe instinctively made for it. I caught his shoulder and held him back. "Not now. I'm on a different track."

"What are you talking about?"

"Let's see who's getting what."

Joe held back, puzzled. I examined some boxes. A label read: *Contenido: Pieles.* "That's presumably a pile of hides."

Another read: *Cuidado—Fragil! Medicinas.* "That one says 'Careful—Fragile, Medicines.' And there's the name of the hospital it's going to. Could be some of the electrical mechanisms of eels that Spider's worried about."

I stopped, analyzing aloud. "The boxes, the boats, everything is marked with the name of the outfit, *Productos Forestales.*"

Joe looked around at all the barges, canoes, boats, freighters. "I thought they shipped most of this stuff out by air."

Barry: "So did I. Cargo planes may be already full. And, of course, it's logical to ship logs by freighter."

Joe said: "Wait a minute. Something's wrong." He walked over to the pile of logs, or more accurately, sections of logs, each cut to a length of four feet, with a diameter of six inches. As he looked them over carefully, a frown crossed his face. Coming back, he said: "Those logs are not marked."

I scanned the logs. "Uh-oh... You're right. I think you've earned your pay for the day, Joe."

Joe looked at me with a quizzical expression. "What do you mean? What is it?"

"How much do you know about timber and logging?"

"Not a whole lot. I slashed alongside roads for the Forest Service one summer in the Snowy Range."

"Use a chain saw?"

"Yep."

"Then you know what a stump looks like?"

"What are you getting at?"

I looked in both directions, upstream and down, before answering. "Take a close look at those logs. I mean, a very close look."

Joe squinted, his eyes scanning the logs from one end to the other.

"They look perfectly normal to me. Just long logs cut in sections."

"Sharpen up."

"Huh?" Joe scowled. "What do you mean? The bark has been peeled. Nothing wrong with that."

"Go on."

"I don't for the life of me see what—oops!" He squinted, peered more closely. "I think I see what you're after."

I grinned. "All right. Go up close. Verify it."

Joe sauntered like a tourist, as nonchalantly as he could, eyeing the workmen so that they might not become suspicious of his actions. They looked at his cowboy hat and laughed, establishing a certain impromptu camaderie.

"Good going, Joe," I said to myself.

He ambled over to a loading area, waving amiably at workmen carrying boxes into the hold of a freighter. Then, when they had gone into the hold, he took a quick peek at the butt ends of the logs piled beside the gravel mounds. After that he thrust his hands in his pockets and did a circle route back to me.

"You are goddam A-O on the mark," he whispered in surprise. "I'll be screwed! The ends of those logs are *painted*!"

I said in a low voice: "Let's turn around and leave slowly..."

Joe asked, incredulous: "Leave? Hell, we can create a storm there and stop that operation right now. Want me to show you how?"

I raised a cautionary hand. "We have to hurry. They are loading boxes now. Next, they will load the logs."

"Okay, so?"

In a low voice, I quickly described my plan. Then I spied Chris and Carol Lynn Arden-Jones coming down the main street. "Good," I said. "I'll go talk to them, work them into the plan. You go get the blood."

CHAPTER 63

While we were doing all that, Spider and the Fishers climbed up from the river's edge on a trail through dense woods. On a bluff above the Amazon, they came to a long white building lying beside a rutted road. A small sign tacked in front read:

Estación Biológica

"A biological station," Greg said. "Terrific. At last, maybe we can talk to a trained biologist."

As they approached, a voice came from behind them. "Hello. Are you from America?"

They turned in surprise to find a brown, black-haired man in his middle forties walking toward them.

Spider answered. "Why, yes, we are! We're wildlife biologists at the University of Texas. We are very interested in tropical biology."

The man didn't question Spider's false statements. Greg and Beryl glanced at her in surprise, but made no other outward movement, except to shake hands and introduce themselves.

"I'm Rudolfo Mateo," the man said. "May I show you around?"

Beryl: "Oh, we'd like that. And you speak English so well."

"No, not too well. I worked many years with Dr. Hochstetter up on the Orinoco. He was from your University. Do you know him?"

Spider lied. "Yes, of course. A wonderful man. Very brilliant."

"Please. Come in."

Mateo led the way inside. They went through a reception room, where two desks piled with papers flanked their way, into a second room filled with cages stacked one upon another to the ceiling. Another door opened into more rooms stacked with cages.

Greg and Beryl went immediately to one of the cages and looked in. Two small eyes peered back at them.

"What are these?" Beryl asked.

Mateo replied: "White-lipped marmosets. *Callithrix,* as you know."

"Oh, yes, of course."

The Fishers looked at the other cages. The little mammals with long tails cowered as far back into the corners as they could, fear in their eyes.

"Looks like you have a full house of them," Greg observed. "Are all the rest of them marmosets, too?"

"Yes. Very interesting animals aren't they?"

Spider said: "Well, of course they are. And rather rare, I thought. Did they all come from around here?"

"Most of them, yes. When they come in, they are very frightened. At first, they are so scared that if I were to approach the cage too closely, they would jump around trying to get out, and bang their heads against the cages, and kill themselves."

Spider responded in a professorial tone. "Yes, this is quite normal behavior for this species. Do you lose a lot of them that way?"

"A few," he replied.

She continued: "How long do you require to get them accustomed to human beings?"

Mateo: "Normally about three weeks."

Spider nodded knowingly. "Yes, that sounds about right. And now what will you do with them?"

"Well, we have a plane load due out next week."

Rockets must have exploded within the deep corners of Spider's dark eyes. He said it so matter-of-factly. The little primates had already been taken from their homes in the forest and put in "prisons," as she called animal cages, and now they would be crammed into an airplane and hoisted away to some far horizon. She fumed within, but tried to be outwardly nonchalant. "A plane load? For where?"

"It's a hospital. I'm not at liberty to reveal the destination, but, of course, you are well aware, I'm sure, of the benefits of medical research..."

Greg and Beryl could sense that Spider had begun a rapid burn.

"Tell me," Spider went on. "A research institution in my state is working on the electrical apparatus of eels. Are you involved in that?"

Mateo puffed up with pride. "Well, yes we are. We've received an order for four hundred eels and will get to that as soon as we can. We cut out the electrical mechanisms and ship them."

Spider's eyes narrowed to slits. "It looks to me as though your sign outside is not quite correct."

Mateo's face became puzzled. "Madam?"

"It says Biological Station. That's wrong. Wrong as hell!" She raised her voice. "You're a goddamned warehouse for the shipment of wildlife!"

With that, she brought her pack in a long swing right against his face and bowled him over the desk and into a corner of the room. Then she turned to the Fishers and said: "Let's go."

They started methodically down the rows of cages, opening every door. Marmosets screeched and leaped out, sailed in an arc to the floor, and headed for the door.

Mateo rose from the floor and shouted: "What are you doing?"

"Correcting your crimes," Spider shouted in the din. He rushed forward. "Get away from those cages!"

Spider caught him squarely on the side of the head again. He reeled, turned and rushed out the front door.

Marmosets leaped off in all directions, across the desks, up the walls, along the banks of cages, out the door, across the road, and into the forest. The deafening racket created by their screeching resembled nothing the Americans had ever heard.

Down the rows the three liberators went, opening cage after cage, ducking the flight of marmosets, which bounced from cage to cage on their way along each corridor and toward the exits. Spider opened the rear door to the station to facilitate escape, and the animals fled screeching into the trees behind the building.

After it was over, Beryl, Greg and Spider stopped to catch their breath—and to look at each other in triumph. But not for long.

Greg said: "Let's get out of here!"

They ran toward the front entrance, went outside and started down the road toward Leticia. Moments later, a Jeep with two police officers roared up the road from Leticia and stopped in front of them.

Behind, they could hear the fading chatter of marmosets swinging from limb to limb, disappearing into the forest.

CHAPTER 64

Down on the docks, we had no inkling that this was happening.

With Carol Lynn and Chris beside us, Joe and I strolled in a leisurely fashion, like sightseers, along the waterfront. Beside us, the Amazon rolled on its ponderous way, silent but all powerful. Scattered clouds interrupted the deep blue sky. The tropical sun burned down upon us, filtering through super-humid air. Even the slightest exertion brought rivers of perspiration.

We approached the old river freighter tied to the bank. Workers carried logs into the hold. Under my arm, I held a caiman hide purchased from a passing vendor. Joe protested, but it was part of my plan.

"*Buenas tardes,*" I called to the workers. "*Mucho trabajo, ah?*"

Just like any unthinking tourist would ask: "That's a lot of work, isn't it?"

The loaders paused for a moment. "*Sí, señor...*"

The overseer scowled, calling "*No te pongas allí!,*" indicating with vigorous arm movements that they were not to tarry or talk with passersby, but to get on with it and load those logs.

Without warning, Joe tripped and fell against a worker. Glancing off, he struck a log with his head and plunged to the ground. In so doing, he let out a wail that could be heard up and down the waterfront. "Ow, oh, woo-ooo ow!!"

He slapped his hand to his head. A river of red ran down the side of his face. He wailed again, rolled in the dust, and came to a stop.

Carol Lynn screamed. Chris leaped forward, fell to his knees and hovered over Joe, shouting: "Joe! Joe! Speak to me!"

Carol Lynn caught the worker's shoulder, directing him toward Joe and shouting: "Do something! Do something, quickly!"

Joe grasped his head with dripping red fingers and howled "Ow, oh, woo-woo!"

The workers bent over to examine Joe.

I slipped away and went behind the pile of logs not yet loaded. Grasping a log with one hand, I flipped it over a pile of sand. It rolled down the other side and came to a stop against a gravel mound and an oil can. Acting nonchalantly, and with one eye on the mêlée around Joe, I folded the caiman skin over the log—not too easy a task, given the hard and brittle nature of the hide.

I rose slowly, turned my back to the ruckus at the freighter, and sauntered toward the foot of Leticia's main street.

This bizarre apparition of a skin wrapped around a log went unnoticed in the bustle of the waterfront. Bizarre sights are commonplace at a tropical port filled with tourists, hawkers, Indians, laborers.

A few moments later, Chris and Carol Lynn waved away the workmen. "He's getting better," they said, smiles replacing horror on their faces. *"Gracias! Gracias!"*

They helped Joe to his feet and led him limping along the river bank until they could find a place to wash off the watercolors.

"Ow!" said Joe. "Some of that is real blood. I hit the log too hard."

"Well done, Joe," said Carol Lynn. "Want me to stuff some mud in the wound? I'm jolly good at stuffing mud into things, you know."

Joe drew back. "No! Let's go find Barry."

They gathered around me as we went back up the main street.

CHAPTER 65

The Jeep drew up in front of police headquarters just as we arrived.

Spider, Beryl and Greg got out.

"Now what have you done?" I asked. "Where have you been?"

Spider answered: "It's a long story."

The two policemen herded them inside. Through a front office, replete with uniformed officers gawking at them, they were prodded to an inner room. It was nearly bare, furnished with nothing more than a long table of rough wood and some matching benches. A light bulb in the center of the ceiling scarcely amplified daylight that filtered from outside through thick bars of a single window.

Beyond that window, they could look out over the waterfront as well as to a nearby terrace filled with vendors and their wares. The room was excruciatingly hot. The rivers of perspiration rolled more than ever down their temples.

The policemen turned and left, but remained on guard in the outer room.

Spider said: "Well, if there hadn't been so damned many marmosets, we would have been out of that building before the police arrived."

"Marmosets?" Joe asked.

Spider drew herself up. "Oh, Joe, all of you should have seen it. It was glorious. First, we let out a cage of parrots down on the river front. Then we liberated a roomful of marmosets headed for foreign hospitals."

I exploded. "Spider, God damnit! I told you to stay out of trouble."

She snorted. "I'm already accused of murdering Boris Kolinski. How can I get into any more trouble?"

A commotion in the outer room, and in came the Briggles, Sonke, Palkuh, and a churchman clad in long black robes and a white collar.

Spider said in surprise: "Where did you all come from?"

Dana responded: "News travels fast in Leticia. You three are public enemies number one, two and three."

"Why?" asked Beryl. "We should be heroes. We liberated a whole lot of parrots and monkeys."

"And lost a lot of people their jobs. Planes will go out empty tomorrow. No more birds to sell. Oh... let me introduce Padre Olevida. We met him on the waterfront."

We shook hands with the padre, whose short-cropped hair had touches of white.

Joe said: "Father, we are honored. Have you come to say last rites?"

"No, my friend," he said in a gentle voice and impeccable English. "I've come to bless you."

"Bless us? That's a switch. What do you mean?"

"You just did what I'd been hoping for years that someone would do."

Mo Briggle explained: "The padre is the author of a book on wildlife of Colombia. He's been all over the country."

Beryl asked: "Padre, you are a naturalist. You approve of what we did?"

"I suppose it is not my role in life to approve or disapprove."

"But you don't like to see animals in captivity?"

"I will confess that my heart hurts to see this going on."

"Couldn't you do anything about it?"

"You must understand," he said, "that I am only one person. I do not live here. Because I am an outsider, they look upon me with suspicion. Especially because I study animals"

"I'm confused," said Joe.

The Padre continued: "This is an animal export town. Many people make their living from this. They have no notion of diminishing species. They get together with the Indians, who bring the animals in from the forest. Then they prepare them for shipment by air."

Joe asked: "Prepare them? What do you mean? What's to prepare?"

Spider answered. "We'll tell you about it."

"Many things have been shipped out of Leticia. Rubber, gold, birds... It is a time for heroes on the frontier. I think your mister Kolinski was a hero to many of them."

Spider gasped. "You know about him? How?"

"The Briggles filled me in on the latest news. Our government is slowly beginning to realize that there aren't so many animals to go around any more. You can't go out killing five hundred at a time and expect to have any left.

"One day a great man from the Codazzi Institute came here and asked where were the parrots he used to see flying over Leticia. Then he went back to Bogotá and wrote an article called *Soberania*, all about how our sovereignty was being lost because of all the birds and mammals being shipped. Out here, though, people like Kolinski, and the ones at Productos Forestales, are heroes."

Joe said: "I can't believe it."

"That is because you live in a different world." The Padre looked at us with sad eyes. "There is evil in man that we cannot begin to comprehend. Your hearts and minds are so good that you cannot conceive what drives men to kill animals and Indians. But come, now, we must refresh ourselves."

So saying, he put his pack on the table. There he drew out a thermos of coffee and some small cakes.

"I cannot believe what the Briggles have told me," he said after a while, "what you have done to ILBRED. They are all very powerful. Your lives must be in great danger."

Greg: "You said it!"

"Especially," the padre added, "when you consider what's just outside."

They looked out through the bars again and saw Square Jaw and Fatso standing beside a vendor's shack looking at the police building.

CHAPTER 66

We were stunned. Any hope that they had been blown up in the speedboat now vanished.

"Oh, shit!" said Spider. "Begging your pardon, Padre. Those guys are after the Red Chief and all the rest of us."

"Yes," said the Padre, "I've been talking with Palkuh and Sonke. I have known them for many years. Palkuh told me what you did for him last night."

"Well," said Spider, "we're not leaving this office until those goons are gone. We'll call in the Navy from out there in the Amazon if we have to."

Padre Olevida glanced briefly out the window and turned to them. "I must tell you that Palkuh had a meeting with Kolinski and his superior in Bogotá. It was even before your trip started. Kolinski's company tried to get government officials to drive Palkuh out of his village. The government ruled in favor of Palkuh. That is why Kolinski joined your group. He wanted the Red Chief. The village and all its gold would be theirs, if they could just remove the chief."

Spider clapped her hands. "I *knew* it! I *knew* that son-of-a-. Pardon my language, Padre. I knew he was up to something dirty. I knew it."

"Those men outside wish to finish the task."

Spider smiled grimly. "Padre, if you have a machine gun under those robes, I would appreciate borrowing it for a few minutes."

The door opened. Monty Adams entered with the Captain of Police.

A young officer in a khaki uniform with emerald braid strode toward us. On his hip he wore a shiny leather holster containing a revolver.

"Ladies and gentlemen," I said, "this is Captain Francisco Rodriguez, who arrived this morning from Florencia."

The captain brushed his black mustache and spoke in strongly accented English. "I must apologize for the troubles you have met in my country. We like to have many tourists. We like *Americanos* and *Ingleses*. And we try to show you our very wonderful Colombia. I am told that you like the Amazon, no?"

We all tried to speak at once.

"Well, Captain," said Spider. "We love it too much. That's why my friends here and I are under arrest for letting birds and monkeys out of cages."

I interrupted. "I will recompense the vendors."

She turned to me. *"You will not!"*

"If I don't," I said, "you'll go to jail. They were in legal possession of those animals. By letting them go, you bought them."

She subsided.

I went on. "The captain informs me that Productos Forestales has been operating out of Leticia for a long time. They have, however, come under fire recently for exporting too many animals."

"That's what the Padre tells us."

"But now they have overstepped themselves. Captain, we have some news for you."

Spider's eyes open wide in astonishment. "What are you talking about?"

I went to the log lying on the table. "This is something even the captain doesn't know yet. He's been suspicious of it, but had no way to find out."

I took a hammer that I had requested for this purpose, walked over to the log and gave it a resounding whack! against the butt end. The painted covering caved in, pieces of wood splintered off, and a white powder spilled out on the table.

The captain walked over, picked up a sample, and sniffed it.

"*Coca!*"

He turned, opened the door, and issued a string of orders to the waiting policemen.

I whispered: "He's sending them out to arrest the head of Productos."

Spider plunged her fist out into the air. "That will end their operation! Three cheers for the eels! You saved them, Barry!"

When Rodriguez returned, he looked at me with a glance of profound gratitude, then embraced me and slapped me vigorously on the back. The crowd cheered.

He said, "I only come to this matter these last few days. Señor Ross has been *muy amable* and he help us very much. We look into ILB, radio Bogotá. We just find out some things. Now we don' like ILB. Now we get to them. Make them stop."

"You mean those thugs out there" Joe asked. "You got them under control?"

The captain shrugged. "Thugs?"

"They kidnaped the Red Chief."

The captain smiled and twisted the end of his mustache. "*Ah, sí, esos hombres.* I have news for you. These two men are under control."

Spider responded: "Pardon me, capitán, if I don't seem to believe it. You can see them from here." She went to the window, peered outside, and looked up astonished. "How did you do that? They're gone."

The captain smiled.

I took it from there. "The captain brought news that, since we've been gone, there's been an uproar about ILB. Much of it related to us."

Carol Lynn burst out. "Us? How can that possibly be? We've been so far away from everything..."

"Well, perhaps I should say, much of it related to the man you are all under suspicion of murdering."

Spider said, "The Padre has just informed us that Boris joined our group so that he could eliminate Palkuh and claim the village for ILB."

"Okay," I said, "that brings us to the Kolinski case. Will everybody be seated, please."

CHAPTER 67

They took positions at the table and on the floor. I sat on the table.

"Regardless of what has happened about Boris Kolinski, his death is a murder, and it must be treated as such. I have conversed with Palkuh Mamha-Uh and determined that Boris walked to the pond."

Gasps around the room.

"He was poisoned. The symptoms were quite clear: vomit, pink flesh, and fingertips cyanosed."

Joe: "Speak English, please."

"Fingertips had turned blue," I responded. "The matter has now resolved to a single question. Who administered the poison?"

The room was absolutely hushed. The only sounds were those that came from outside. Every eye was on me. Joe's mouth hung open.

I continued. "With the Captain here, I am going to make this an official legal proceeding. I am going to ask each of you whether you committed this act by administering poison, which we shall assume to be the prussic acid of the yuca plant. If you do not wish to answer, if you feel that your answer will tend to incriminate you, that is your right.

As I call your name, I ask only that you answer yes, no, or decline. Remember that you are under oath."

They looked at each other in a high state of nervous tension. They were tired from a long night, a short sleep, and the excitement of the escape from Tres Esquinas.

In a soft voice, I called their names. "Mo?"

He waited a moment to answer, then said: "No, sir."

"Dana?"

She shook her head. "No."

"Beryl?"

She looked around at the rest of the group, then at me, then at the floor. "No"

"Greg?"

His eyes met Beryl's for a long moment. Then he said to me: "No."

The room was getting hot. The afternoon sun baked the city. More perspiration seeped out on temples. I felt that maybe I should have selected a better place and a better time for this. But with everybody here, including the captain of police, I wanted to get the matter settled...now.

"Chris?"

"I assure you, no, sir."

"Carol Lynn?"

"No, Barry, not me."

I could almost sense the burning fever on their brows. With the eliminations so far, only two persons were left.

"Joe?" I asked.

He waited, as though thinking the whole thing through. Or relishing a moment of torture inflicted on everybody else. He had the floor. He had the moment of suspense.

"I must answer yes or no?" he asked.

"Yes," I responded. "Or decline."

"No other choices?"

I frowned. "Joe, you're stalling."

"Yes, sir."

"Yes that you supplied the poison?"

"No, that I'm stalling."

My patience was wearing thin. "Joe, this is a hot room and I am trying to get this over with. Would you give us your answer, please."

"Okay," he said. "My answer is no."

Sighs of relief came from the others. But then they all turned their eyes to the last person on the list.

I turned to her and said: "Spider?"

In that hushed room, I doubted if anyone had ever hung onto an answer with such a feeling of anxiety. We had arrived at the person most suspected, the person most angry at Boris, the person most outspoken in pursuit of his demise.

The captain did not understand all of our strain. He could not fathom all the stress we had been through. But I could see from the look on his face that he judged the moment one of extraordinary apprehension.

Spider sat at the table, looking down at her folded hands. Then she said, quietly: "No."

The others burst into a riot of noise and shouting. Their worries seemed to be dispelled. Guilt did not seem to settle on one of our group. They felt good about it, rejoiced, and celebrated.

Before they leaped up to dance, however, reality returned. They quieted down. It now occurred to them to wonder that if none of them was guilty, then who was?

Silence fell over them as they turned to me with quizzical expressions.

Joe said: "One of us is lying."

They all looked furtively at each other.

I slowly shook my head. I had one more name on the list.

"Monty?"

They were so surprised that they became speechless, unable even to gasp in shock.

Everyone turned to look at Monty, sitting beside the door. He lowered his head and said nothing.

I went on. "I analyzed from the beginning that he had the most to lose out of this. He had easy access to the poison. He may have spent the day with Boris instead of going to Sonke's village, as he claimed. In the heat of midafternoon, walking back up to the village with Boris, he could have administered the poison at the last minute and helped Boris over to the pool. He is usually unflappable, but he mispronounced Boris's name that afternoon. That's a little thing, but I caught it."

Monty sat stock still. So did the others, unbelieving, surprised, shocked, dismayed.

Spider shook her head. "Are you sure? It's not like him."

Chris: "I'm bloody sorry to hear this. What will happen to him?"

I made my presumptions. "He will have to be tried under Colombian law. I will see that he gets one of their best lawyers. He could have a defense of temporary insanity. There are several options. But even if he goes to prison, I will see that he gets a good job when he comes out."

"Where?" Joe asked. "In Florida?"

I answered: "If he wants. It may be that he will return to what he likes best. Taking visitors into the Amazon."

Carol Lynn said: "Bully for you, Barry."

"Now I would like to terminate these proceedings. I am asking the captain if he will remand custody of Monty to me instead of putting him in jail..."

The captain nodded.

Joe asked: "What happened to Square Jaw and Fatso?"

"The Comandante at Tres Esquinas radioed Bogotá. Told them about the kidnapping. Word went out to law enforcement authorities to get control of ILB's activities. The captain's men have just now taken away the guns and explosives the thugs had in their helicopter. They were instructed to get their asses out of this town as fast as they could or he would blow up their helicopter and dump the pieces into the Amazon. They headed for the airport a few minutes ago."

Joe jabbed his fist into the air. "All *right*! Only way to go, guys!"

Chris shouted: "We're free! The whole bloody thing is over!"

Spider yelled: "*We're* not free! We're still under arrest!"

The Captain answered: "Under the circumstances, Señorita, I think we drop all charges. But now somebody have to find jobs for people no longer hunting and sending animals away."

The Padre said: "I have some ideas about that. I have some rich friends. Let me see what I can do."

The Captain replied: "*Gracias, amigo.*"

Greg yelled: "What are we waiting for?"

Spider shouted: "Wait! The Padre has something else to say."

The commotion died down, and the soft voice began. "You cannot know how grateful some of us feel about what you have done. It is getting on toward evening. I have a very good friend who has a plantation not far up the river. Swimming pool. Many birds. Good beds to sleep in. Food *muy sabroso*. He invites you up to rest from your trip."

A roar went up from the crowd.

Spider: "Does that include Palkuh, Sonke, Aunamunh, Monty?"

"Yes. Yes, everybody."

Another outburst.

"And you?"

The padre nodded. "Of course!"

More howls of approval.

The padre said: "We will deliver your luggage to you at the plantation. Now, if you will follow me..."

We lost no time in leaving the captain's office. Grabbing backpacks, we poured out of the building.

The clouds rising in giant pillars above the river had become tinted with orange from the setting sun. The man on the waterfront, holding up a crocodile hide, called: *"Pieles! Caimanes! Caimanes!"*

A brown and green helicopter with **I L B** on the side rose above the trees. It curved in an arc over our heads, banked toward the north, and headed for Bogotá. Joe sent an obscene gesture toward it.

We made our way down the broken streets and past piles of lumber and rock, to the shining white 16-passenger speed boat at the river's edge. A loudspeaker on board blared the old Latin song, *I Wanna Be in Miami.*

Before we boarded, Spider accosted Joe. "You are not taking that necklace home?"

Joe lowered his eyes. "Spider, I've already decided. I don't want everybody to want one. That would just put pressure on the jaguar necklace trade. I can't give it back. Sonke would be crushed. What am I to do?"

The Padre, overhearing, spoke up. "It would make a wonderful contribution to the church."

"You?" Joe said.

The Padre smiled. "I can trade it for a boat to help some of our rangers."

The onlookers applauded. Joe agreed. We clambered aboard.

"Now listen," Joe said to me as we made our way to the back of the boat. "I understand that you have a hundred stories to tell about all the things you've done and places you've been..."

I said: "Get in and sit down."

He growled: "I am not going to be put off again. Do you understand?"

As we sat, I added: "Muck?"

"Yes, sir?"

"How would you like to come work for me? Be my assistant?"

Joe choked. It was the first time on the entire trip that I had found the cowboy unable to speak.

The Padre boarded last and waved to the captain.

The powerful motors sputtered, then roared. The boat moved out into the current.

Joe finally found voice. "What in the name of blue buckin' broncos did you say?"

The voice and the roar of the motor faded as the boat sent fountains of spray into the air and headed up the river.

EPILOGUE

Once upon a time, massive exports of wild animals, including parrots and white-lipped marmosets, really did leave by the planeload from Leticia, as did shipments of the electrical apparatus of eels. It was a time of heroes, of brave and intrepid men who "conquered" wild animals in the jungle and put them to use "for the benefit of mankind." You will find it written up in Américas, Sunset, Holiday, The Reader's Digest and elsewhere. That era came to an end with the discovery of cocaine shipped in lumber from Leticia to sawmills in North America.

At the same time, new heroes emerged, like Eduardo Arango and rangers in Colombian national parks and wild-life reserves, who fought to save the remaining naturaleza. It is a battle that has not ended. For even in North America, a bastion of protected natural wonders, rangers and public land managers are being bombed and shot by people greedy to utilize natural resources—everybody's natural resources—without restriction.

The episode of sugar given to the Indians has also emerged from Amazon history. I have no reason to doubt it, given the long history of explorers murdering Amazon Indians. Man's inhumanity to man will not soon leave the planet, but the legacy of it becomes, each year, more and more repulsive to thinking human beings. That lets us see perhaps a measure of hope for the wild forests, the endless rivers, and their inhabitants.

In 1996 the Brazilian government announced that, in collaboration with Venezuela, its federal police and armed forces would destroy more than twenty airfields and impound aircraft used in the illegal mining of gold on the Yanomami reservation, east of Leticia. The news report called the Yanomami the largest Stone Age tribe in the Americas. The plan was to remove more than 1,500 miners from the reservation.

As Carol Lynn would say: "Jolly good!"

And Joe, with a Wyoming twang: "Way to go!"

Ann Livesay

Colophon

The text of *Death in the Amazon* is set in 11.5 point Garamond3 on 12.5 point leading. Chapter titles are Neuland,with special pages set in the RotisSemiSerif and Post Antigua families.

The text stock is 60 lb Eureka Recycled Opaque. It is acid-free for archival durability, and it meets or exceeds all guidelines set forth by the U. S. Environmental Protection Agency for recycled content and use for post-consumer waste. The binding is Perfect Bind.

The printer is Commercial Documentation Services, Medford, Oregon 97501 (Doug Casey, Account Manager).

The cover, text and special character design and production are by Dan Schiffer, Digimedia, Jacksonville, Oregon 97530. All cover images are derived from copyrighted photographs of the author.

The book was produced on an Apple Power Macintosh 8500 using PageMaker 6.5.

Trademarks: Apple and Macintosh are registered trademarks of Apple Computer, Inc. PageMaker is a registered trademark of Adobe Systems, Inc.

The following is an excerpt from Ann Livesay's
forthcoming

THE MADMAN OF MOUNT EVEREST
A Barry Ross International Mystery

*October 10. Tengboche Monastery, Sagarmatha National Park, Nepal.
7:33 p.m.*

Not many people knew Ellie Stratton. She always came
across as such an independent person. More devoted to
classes than camaraderie. More a scholar than a gadabout.
Those who did know her admired her. Even respected her.
A graduate geology student at Oregon State University, she
had thrilled at the chance to come to Mount Everest with
Lane Ostermiller, one of the best professors she'd ever had,
and with six other students, for a closeup look at the
Himalayas.

As dusk approached, they sat on the meadow beside
the monastery and softly sang folk songs.

That bored her. She wandered away. She hadn't come
here to sing. She'd came to learn. On their only night this
close to Everest she wanted to see sunset come to the greatest mountain on earth.

Ellie drifted away alone across the meadow, and descended the vale lined with birch trees. She would walk
down among the rocks for a little way, despite the stories of
yetis and abominable snowmen...

Sagarmatha, the Sherpas called Mount Everest. Mother
of the Universe. At this moment in the glow of sunset, the
vast massif seemed all of that. At 29,000 feet, no peak on
earth rose higher.

Yet the fading day did not belong to Sagarmatha, up
there to the north, its pyramidal summit seen only in sil-
houette. The dusk belonged to Ama Dablam, east of the
monastery, a needle of ice and rock on which the sun poured
every ounce of its waning gold.

Ellie stopped for a moment to watch the glistening tower, its loftiest ramparts rising to nearly 23,000 feet against the somber gray sky.

It took her breath away. Rocky crags and jagged sheets of vertical ice seemed to represent time itself. In her geology classes at Corvallis, the deposition of those rocks in a Jurassic sea had no reality. As she stood before this monumental tower, and meditated on its antiquity, she felt reality in a rush of awe. Nature was so *old*.

As she stood there, merely a speck on the landscape, she thought of all humankind as so small. So young. So... *insignificant*... That was treasonous thinking. She conceded it. But she was serious...

"Ellie!"

Bea Stoelk, clad in a parka that almost obscured her face, came up behind Ellie. "What are you doing out here?"

In the soft light, Ellie's face had become touched with the glow from Ama Dablam. "I'm impressed, Bea. I wanted to walk down this way. Watch the sun fade on the ridges up there. Would you like to come along?"

Bea said: "It's getting dark and cold."

"Please?"

"All right, I'll walk a little way."

They made their descent in silence, down a slope, past a frame building and a copse of small birch trees. As they walked and watched, shadows crept up the side of Ama Dablam, turning the cliffs from gold to orange to purple.

"We'd better get back," Bea warned. "There might be a yeti out here."

"Yetis?" Ellie laughed. "Come on, Bea. You don't really believe in abominable snowmen?"

"Of course. I believe in everything."

"Even monsters up there in all that ice?"

"They come down at sunset looking for females. They have long claws. They're seven feet tall, and covered with long hair."

"Bea, you're making that up."

"Am I? Some people have lived up here for years, looking for yetis."

"Found any?"

"Footprints. That's enough for me."

"That's not proof."

"Well, after searching up here, those people say they are convinced that yetis exist."

"But no proof?"

"You remember what Lhakpa said when I asked whether yetis really exist."

"Sure. I heard him. So?"

"He said 'Keep an open mind.' When a Sherpa says that, I believe in abominable snow men. Why not? Don't you?"

"Oh, Bea. Will you ever stop being so gullible?"

Bea stopped and turned around. "You're self-reliant, Ellie. You'd *like* to tangle with a yeti. You'd relish the chance. Take the beast's measurements for science. Try to communicate with it. Well, I leave the mountains and their monsters to you. It's getting dark. I'm going back. You coming?"

Ellie almost didn't hear. She was looking again at the mountains. "I'll go on a little farther. It's so wonderful..."

"Keep an eye out. At this altitude, you never know what's real and what isn't."

Bea walked back and disappeared in the gloom.

Ellie threaded her way among the rocks and walked on. She stopped and looked up. Even the summit of Ama Dablam now lay in the murk of dusk. Only the gold outline on Everest remained, and in a few moments that would be gone.

Among the rocks, she could hardly see in the shadows. She should be going back. Without a flashlight, she could have trouble finding her way.

Well...in a moment. You only come upon an experience like this once in a lifetime...

The enormity and silence of this amphitheater enveloped her, held her. The deep blue ice, the soaring cliffs, all gray and fading now in the—.

A sound came from behind her.

No much of a sound. A scraping of rocks, perhaps.

She turned her head a quarter turn, her eyes moving sharply to the left. It sounded like a footstep. Probably Bea coming back to get her. Bea was persistent.

"Bea? Is that you?"

Her own voice frightened her, invading as it did this eerie silence.

She turned her head fully around. The shadows had become so black she could see very little except the outlines of rocks and the gray summit of Kang Taiga to the south.

No one answered. She wished Bea had not mentioned the yeti. Ellie did not dare to get caught up in the mythology of this place. Not yet. They had come to study the geology of the Khumbu Valley. That was enough for any brain at such a dizzying altitude.

She listened. Stood stock still. Heard only the nearly imperceptible, incomprehensible hum of silence. If there was a hum, she chided herself, there could be no silence. It didn't make any sense. What was there up here to make sounds? She had experienced this before, in the vastness of the Cascade Range. Here in the Khumbu, she was in an amphitheater so vast it could never be silent. She thought she could hear the echo of rivers roaring far below. Or was it yetis calling to one another?

Another small sound pierced her semi-consciousness. Another scraping of rocks.

Maybe the scarcity of oxygen at 14,000 feet was getting to her. Making her hear things. She remembered what the Sherpas said about altitude sickness. "Be very ca'ful, Miss Ellie. Go very slow. People die."

The doctor from Kunde had discussed cerebral edema. It could do strange things to human beings. Nausea, headache, heart palpitations, hallucinations...

Was she having a hallucination? Ellie felt fine, elated. Why think of herself at a time like this? With such grandeur all about, such eternity. Why think of mythical beasts? She *had* an open mind. She was self-reliant. You had to be in this age. She would know how to handle an encounter with—.

The sound came again. A footstep in the darkness. A scuffle of rocks.

"Bea?"

Her voice seemed plaintive. Less hopeful. If it were Bea, back there in the darkness, there would have been a response by now.

Ellie strained in the gloom to discern a familiar shape, some member of the group come to fetch her. Dr. Ostermiller, or Bart, Dwight, Dave... It couldn't be any of them because they would be lighting their way with a flashlight.

Only the images of abominable snowmen came to her. Hairy beasts with long claws, sharp fangs, powerful arms...

Suddenly she wanted to rush back along the path, reach the first building below the monastery, hammer on the door. She looked in vain for the beacon of a flashlight, somebody come to find out why she had not returned to camp. Only blackness. She wanted to cry out for help, a feeling she had not experienced since childhood.

Even if she did scream, who could respond? Her voice would echo all the way up to the summits, and no more.

Who was close enough to hear? She had gone farther from the monastery than she intended. Who would care? A fearful thought struck her. She had always paraded herself as independent and resourceful. Her friends thought Ellie Stratton could get out of anything that came her way: she wouldn't *want* any help. She'd consider it demeaning, insulting...

She hesitated. Without a doubt now, she knew that someone, or something—a mountain man or beast—waited behind that rock to capture her as she rushed by.

Her heart began to pound, the pumping surges welling up into her ears, damping her ability to hear, making her breathe rapidly. Her lungs, starved of oxygen, burned with heavy breathing, cold and thin air rushing in and out.

She felt a presence near. Felt it in the air. Sensed it in her weakening brain.

"Hello?" she said, more to console herself than to seek a reply.

No answer. She fought to fill her lungs with enough oxygen to keep from passing out. The Khumbu had turned from an amphitheater of beauty to a vale of terror.

The sound came again. A shadow moved behind her. A form materialized.

She drew back, almost unable to speak except in the weakest tones.

"Who are you?" she asked.

No response.

The shadow moved closer.

"Who are you?"

© Ann Livesay Sutton

About the Author

Ann Livesay is that rare combination of geologist, author, and scientific researcher who takes readers where few other writers have gone—deep into dangerous places worldwide. She has worked in these places, photographed them, and written about them in 22 nonfiction books coauthored with her husband, Myron Sutton. In the Barry Ross International Mysteries, she brings her skills directly to readers, with authenticity of locale guaranteed. She takes you in, with bold and daring suspense, and knows how to get you back out... Maybe.

To order more copies of *Death in the Amazon*, send check or money order for $US12.95 per copy, postpaid, or send Visa or Mastercard number with Expiration Date, to Silver River, Inc., 1619 Meadowview Drive, Medford, OR 97504. Or visit our Web site at http://www.silverriver.com. If you would like to be notified when more volumes in the Barry Ross International Mysteries appear, please write to Silver River and you will be put on the mailing list.